P9-DTL-185

LORD RADCLIFFE'S SEASON

Jo Ann Ferguson

Zebra Books
Kensington Publishing Corp.

http://www.zebrabooks.com

For Mary Kruger,
who inspired me and helped me get started
as a Regency author.
A very belated thanks!

ZEBRA BOOKS are published by

Kensington Publishing Corp.
850 Third Avenue
New York, NY 10022

First Printing: August, 1999
10 9 8 7 6 5 4 3 2 1

Printed in the United States of America

One

Starlight pricked through the fog twisting itself into impossible shapes along the quiet street. A distant church bell pealed twice through the night. A cat yowled before the baying of a dog silenced it. By the doorway of a townhouse on Cavendish Square, a footman stood with a lantern held high. His eyes scanned for what he could not see. Only the rattle of wheels on the street warned him that the carriage approached.

The closed carriage rolled to a stop directly in front of him, and he hurried to open its door. Stepping back, he stood without speaking as a man emerged. Not even his lips twitched as the man nearly tripped over his own feet.

The man regained his balance and turned to hand down a woman whose blond hair glowed in the dim light of the lantern. When he offered his arm, she disdained it and walked toward the townhouse. He followed, the flapping tails of his stylish coat over his rotund form making him look like a duckling trailing its far more elegant mother. Behind them, the footman smothered a laugh. Lady Lisabeth's obvious vexation was no less than he had expected and no more than Mr. Smythe deserved after his high-handed greeting to Lady Lisabeth earlier in the evening.

By the door edged with Palladian columns, Lisabeth Montague extended her hand stiffly in a motion more meant to keep Mr. Smythe at bay than bidding him a polite *adieu.* "Thank you for an unusual evening, Mr. Smythe."

"Now, Lisabeth, that is a most unwelcome way to treat an old friend."

She resettled her Kashmir shawl on her shoulders, wavering between the temptation to offer some demure hit that would strike that irritating smile from Mr. Cyril Smythe's lips or simply to have the door slammed in his face. *Old friend,* indeed! Mr. Smythe was a dreadful bore—and he presumed to call her by her given name as if they were closest of bosom-bows!

With a silent sigh, she reminded herself he apparently had no idea that his every word filled everyone within earshot with ennui. Mr. Smythe was a gentle soul, not like. . . . An icy shiver curled up her shoulders, but she suppressed it. The past was dead and buried with Frederick. Tonight had been the beginning of her new life without her late husband, and she did not want to look back.

"Good evening, Mr. Smythe," she said quietly. She dared not be too gracious, for he would see that as an invitation to press his company upon her even more. Neither could she be indecorous. He was trying to be kind. *Or just trying,* she thought, silencing her chuckle. "As I told you before, it has been an evening of rare entertainment. I daresay I shall speak with you at an upcoming rout."

"Not at the Park tomorrow?"

Lisabeth tensed. How could this tedious man threaten to send her up to the boughs with a single innocuous question? Mayhap it was because he had plagued her with dozens over the mortally long evening.

"I shall not be riding in Hyde Park tomorrow," she answered, struggling to offer him a polite smile. She feared her face would freeze in this insipid expression which she had worn since he called to take her to the *soirée* in Bloomsbury this evening. "I have other obligations."

"I trust I may call tomorrow. You will be at home?"

"No." When his round face drooped, reminding her of a chastised puppy, she relented. "I am sorry, Mr. Smythe." She held up her gloved hands in a pose of dismay she did not have to feign. "I would enjoy a ride, but I shall be engaged throughout the day in the tedious chores that have required my attention since Frederick's passing. I am sure you understand."

He bowed, accepting her dismissal with more aplomb than she had anticipated. Although he gave her hand a fervent squeeze before he took himself down the steps, Lisabeth could find nothing else to complain about in his behavior. Certainly it was more respectable than hers, for her excuses had been out-and-outers.

Lisabeth surrendered to the shivers coursing up her back, for the dampness which accompanied the fog had sunk within her. Yet a deeper chill resurrected memories she wanted to erase from her mind. Being false had become a habit she must put aside. Telling lies had been necessary before, but she was now a widow who could live her life as she wished and without the fear of what waited within the respectable walls of this house.

Rubbing her hands together, she stepped into the foyer. It was bright with light from the brass chandelier set in the curve of the long staircase leading to the upper floors. Home. In the past year, while she lived in seclusion as befit Lord Montague's widow, this house had become home as she had doubted it ever would.

She smiled when the footman followed her in and took her shawl, then stepped aside for the butler. Doherty's long face was as bony as the rest of his spare frame. Thin hair on his high forehead bounced as he nodded a greeting. He always was waiting when she returned, and she wondered when he ever slept.

"Lady Montague asked me to convey her plea for your forbearance that she retired before you arrived home, Lady Lisabeth." His voice resounded through the foyer, which was quiet, save for the clank of the pendulum in the tall-case clock set beside the arched door to the parlor on the floor above.

Peeling off her evening gloves, Lisabeth smiled. Others had been disturbed by what they saw as her servants' familiarity, but she and her household had reached this compromise upon the death of her husband, for two widowed Ladies Montague now lived within the house on Cavendish Square. Allowing her mother-in-law, Lady Edwina Montague, to retain the title of the Dowager Lady Montague seemed simpler, and Lisabeth had come to prefer simplicity.

"What a sweet goose Lady Edwina is!" said Lisabeth with a laugh as she drew off her white satin turban and ran her fingers along its single feather. "No doubt, at breakfast, she will be eager to hear all about my evening, so I would be wise to retire as well. I do not want to keep her in suspense."

As she put her hand on the black walnut banister, the butler said, "My lady, this arrived shortly after your departure."

"Thank you, Doherty." Lisabeth took the folded page. Her forehead ruffled when she recognized the scribbled handwriting on it, and she sighed. She had thought her horrible day had ended with Mr. Smythe's good night, but she had been wrong. She would read this letter now, for anxiety over what flummery Norton Radcliffe had penned might keep her awake.

She listened to the butler's soft footfalls fading into the back of the house. Dear Doherty! She wondered what she would have done if he were not about to help her deal with overly ardent callers such as Mr. Smythe and the problems Lady Edwina seemed to attract. Doherty was able to subdue the *crises de nerfs* that Lady Edwina suffered.

Thank goodness, her mother-in-law did not possess the same vicious temper as her stepson. . . . Lisabeth berated herself. To think of the dead that way was uncommonly coarse—even though she had not thought kindly of her husband while he was living. She shuddered anew at the remembrance of the two years of what had not been wedded bliss.

And she truly loved her mother-in-law. Lady Edwina might be eccentric, but her heart was generous. If her stepson Frederick had been half as kind, Lisabeth might recall him with sorrow instead of relief. Yet he was dead, and her long year of obligatory mourning was over.

Lisabeth climbed the stairs and went into the parlor where the dim light of a single lamp glittered off the striped wallpaper and the rose satin settee. She sat on her favorite chair, which overlooked the small garden at the back of the house. In the morning, the colors of the flowering bushes would lure her out into the sunshine to gather blossoms for the dining room.

She smiled. She was hosting a small dinner party a week from tomorrow. It would be the first time she had entertained since Frederick's death. No more than a score of people had been invited, for she wanted to keep the party small to suit her recent emergence from mourning. Yet, she was as giddy as a child at the thought of welcoming her friends into the house. Mayhap their bright conversation would banish the remnants of the memories haunting her.

One of which was her last conversation with Norton Radcliffe. The man had proven to be as intractable and almost as impossible as Frederick. No doubt, he had not changed.

She opened the single sheet that was covered with such tiny scribbling she had to hold it closer to her eyes to read it. She was not surprised that Norton Radcliffe had squeezed his words onto one page, for it would be unlike his nip-cheese ways to waste a second sheet on the wife of his distant cousin. She leaned back, propping her feet on a petit-point stool, and began to read.

My dearest Lisabeth,

I trust you are suffused with good health. It is my misfortune that I cannot say the same. If I had been half as wise as Frederick (dear, departed Frederick), I would have purchased a townhouse in London years ago. Instead I continue to suffer here at Norton Hall.

Lisabeth laughed softly. Norton Radcliffe had not changed. He never let an opportunity pass when he might complain. This cousin of Frederick's—at least three times removed—was both an intolerable boor and a deadly bore.

Norton took a peculiar pride in the fact that he had never spent a full Season in Town. Instead he preferred to molder away in his country home of Norton Hall and grumble about the fate that had left him a bachelor for his forty plus years. Lisabeth's hint that he must journey to London if he wished to find himself a bride had instigated a wigging that went on, nonstop, for an hour. She had hoped, with the passing of her husband, that Norton and his whining ways would be out of her life. Her hopes had been futile.

I burden you with my troubles, when I wish to beg a favor. My cousin, Tristan Radcliffe, who bears the title of the Marquess of Radcliffe, needs to be taught the ways of the ton. *He cannot learn them as long as he remains with me here or if he returns to his home of Cliffs' End. I know no one more accomplished in the skills of the Polite World than you, Cousin Lisabeth. That is why I am sending him to you for tuition.*

If the roads are not bad, you may expect he will be arriving Tuesday next. For whatever you can do to help him find a proper miss to wed and gain himself an heir for the family's title, I am most grateful.

I remain,

Your servant,
Norton Radcliffe, Esq.

"Esquire?" Lisabeth laughed.

Norton's affectations were tiresome, but she could be amused when he was far from Town and clearly intended to stay there. That was a relief, although he planned to send his young cousin without awaiting the courtesy of a reply. She hoped the lad was more open to learning manners than his cousin had ever proved to be. She would learn when he arrived on Tuesday next. That would be. . . . She looked at the top of the page.

Horror raced through her. The letter had been written more than a week ago. The Tuesday that Norton was referring to had arrived two hours before when the clock at the countess's house had rung midnight. Lord Radcliffe would be reaching London today.

Blast Norton! He should have taken into account the slowness of the mail between his isolated country house and Town. Today! The marquess was arriving today. Nothing was ready for him.

Taking a deep breath, Lisabeth rose to stand by the window where starlight was filtered by the fog. Her hands clenched in front of her. Her plans for the Season were certain to be ruined by Norton's assumption that she would be glad to spend her first weeks out of mourning tutoring his young cousin in the niceties of the *élite*.

What did she know of launching a lad into the Season? Her own first and only Season had been short, for Frederick had been quite mad for her from the moment he met her at her coming-out. Or that was what he had told her while he wooed her with court-promises that had been as worthless as his professions of faithfulness. Now she must sacrifice her first Season as a dowager to play watchdog for a youngster who might have no interest in a bride.

Norton had, with his usual lack of detail, failed to mention his cousin's age. No lad about to enjoy his first Season would be interested in buckling himself to a wife when there was a bachelor's fare available before him. Flirtations and gambling and drinking and racing . . . Oh, my! She hoped the marquess would bring his own horses and carriages, for she did not wish hers to be ruined when he rode hell-for-leather through the Park to impress the young misses who would be vying for the attention of any man with such a grand title.

What a jumble! Mayhap Lady Edwina would be of help. After all, she had raised her husband's son. Again a shiver climbed Lisabeth's back. She hoped this cousin of Norton's was not as beastly as Frederick had been. Asking the young man to leave, if his manners proved appalling beyond repair, would cause too much talk.

Lisabeth reached for the bellpull. As always, Doherty came before the sound could have faded in the kitchen. Not a hint of fatigue darkened his eyes.

Without preamble, she said, "We shall have a guest on the morrow—or to own the truth, later today. Please have Mrs. Outhwaite prepare a guest room for Lord Radcliffe and the appropriate space for any servants the marquess may have traveling with him."

"Lord Radcliffe?" Doherty's voice rose in astonishment. "And for his wife, my lady?"

"Procuring a bride is the marquess's purpose in coming to Town."

Doherty stood straighter, a sure sign that he was troubled, and asked, "Do you wish me to inform Lady Montague?"

Lisabeth understood his dismay. Two women should not be inviting a man—lad though he might be—into their home when neither of them had a husband. She smiled, pleased at Doherty's concern, although it was misplaced. Propriety would be maintained. After all, to learn what was expected in a gracious London home was why Norton was sending the lad here.

"There is no need to disturb her sleep. I shall let Lady

Montague know in the morning that we are about to be visited by the cousin of Lord Montague's cousin." When the butler relaxed at the familial connection that would give countenance to the arrangement, she continued, "I leave the arrangements for their arrival in your capable hands, Doherty. After breakfast, I will wish to speak with you and Mrs. Outhwaite about other preparations. I fear, not knowing the young man, that I am quite at a loss to suggest how we can make him feel he might run tame through the house." She laughed, but the sound was tainted with exhaustion. "As he is coming for the Season, I suspect we shall find he shall be dining out most evenings. If that is the case, he will prove to be a most compliant houseguest."

"Yes, Lady Lisabeth."

Hearing Doherty's doubt, which mirrored her misgivings that she was trying to ignore, she told him good night and went up the stairs to the next floor. Here a pair of lamps glowed on the round tables beneath the dreary paintings of Montague ancestors. She paid the dour faces no mind as she went to the door farthest from the square. She opened it to find a lone candle burning on the dressing table and her abigail Wilson slumped, asleep, in a chair by the window.

Lisabeth loved this bedchamber. She had selected it upon deciding she would never again use, after his death, the suite of rooms she had shared with Frederick. Those rooms were dark and grim, and she would be happy if the door were left closed forever. This chamber was just the opposite. In the sunlight, the walls would be a shade paler than a cloudless summer sky. Unlike the heavy furniture in the suite overlooking the square, she had had her room decorated with white pieces swathed in flowered chintz.

She tiptoed across the Persian rug and gently shook her abigail awake. Wilson's nightcap was askew on her thick, brown hair which was as straight as her thin form.

"My lady!" She jumped to her feet. "My lady, I did not hear you come in. I should have—"

Lisabeth waved aside Wilson's apologies. "Fiddle! You were wise to sleep. It shall take both of us some time to reaccustom ourselves to this schedule of fêtes and routs." A yawn interrupted her. "Now it is time for both of us to get some sleep."

With Wilson's help, she readied herself for bed. She did remember to mumble something about having her white cambric gown ready. It would serve for overseeing the preparations for their guest on the morrow.

Sleep arrived nearly the moment her head touched the pillow, surprising Lisabeth when she woke the next morning. Although she had not slept her fill, she hurriedly dressed in the tea gown with its vandyked hem. Her hair was concealed beneath a simple cap as she went down to eat a hasty breakfast.

She looked around, startled, when she discovered the breakfast-parlor was empty. Freshly cooked food was arranged on the broad oak sideboard. Footsteps came from behind her, and she turned to see a raw-boned woman in the simple gray that all the upper servants wore. "Good morning, Mrs. Outhwaite."

The housekeeper's smile was tentative. "Good morning, my lady."

"Is Lady Montague still abed?"

"She left for a ride with Mrs. Castleman."

"At this hour?"

Mrs. Outhwaite shrugged, but the motion seemed as strained as if her shoulders were bearing the burden of the sideboard. "Lady Montague was determined to go."

Lisabeth chuckled. "You were wise not to stand in her way." After spooning a serving of eggs onto a plate, she sat at the round table. She paused. "Oh, dear, I suppose she does not know Lord Radcliffe will be arriving."

"No, my lady."

She had not needed the housekeeper's answer. If Lady Edwina had known they were expecting a guest, she would not have gone out for the air. Lady Edwina seldom noticed things while busy with her own concerns, so she might have missed the hubbub.

"I am having a girl air the yellow guest room," continued the housekeeper as a maid brought fresh muffins. Frowning at the girl who had been so unmindful as to put the basket too far from Lisabeth's hand, Mrs. Outhwaite's smile turned weak as Lisabeth reached for the butter. "I have set aside three rooms in the attics and one in the stables for the marquess's servants. Do you think that will be enough?"

"We shall have to hope so. Mr. Radcliffe included nothing in his short missive about Lord Radcliffe's entourage . . . or anything else of him." Lisabeth took a sip of cocoa, then smiled. "Lord Montague's cousin has put us quite at sixes and sevens, Mrs. Outhwaite, with his request."

"I assure you we shall be ready to house the marquess and his servants, even if I must put two more girls in the back attic."

"I trust that shall not be necessary, for I recall you telling me they are crowded already."

"You are kind to think of them, my lady, but they spend little time there." She wrung her hands in her apron. "I hope this will do."

"I am sure you will manage all the arrangements beautifully, Mrs. Outhwaite. You always do."

The housekeeper's smile broadened for a moment, then disappeared again as she excused herself to oversee the myriad details of preparing for a guest.

Lisabeth picked up the newspaper which Lady Edwina had left in a mess, as the dowager customarily did. She set it back on the table. Refolding it and reading the news and the gossip were luxuries she could not savor this morning. Instead she hurried through her breakfast before returning upstairs to be sure everything was set.

"Lady Lisabeth?"

She turned to see Wilson coming toward her. From the strain on the old woman's face, Lisabeth knew her abigail was unduly flustered by the upcoming visit. "Yes?"

"The only dressing room large enough to provide for a marquess and his man is . . ."

"Lord Montague's chambers?" She frowned. "Mrs. Outhwaite told me she was airing the yellow guest room."

"I know."

Lisabeth understood what Wilson was hesitant to say. The housekeeper had tried not to put Lord Radcliffe in the grandest room on this floor, wanting to avoid causing distress for Lisabeth. Appreciating Mrs. Outhwaite's kindness, Lisabeth hoped this was not a sign of more trouble to come.

She looked at the only closed door along the hall. Shutting her eyes, she took a deep breath. Slowly releasing it, she knew she could not lock her memories within those rooms. They stalked her during every quiet moment. She saw sympathy in her abigail's eyes, but she said only, "Let Mrs. Outhwaite know we must be the best possible hosts to Lord Radcliffe. Have her air Lord Montague's rooms."

Wilson nodded and hurried away.

Lisabeth went into her room. She stared at the dressing room door. That small room was all that stood between her chambers and Frederick's rooms. She might soon despair of getting a good night's sleep if Lord Radcliffe chose to take up a bachelor's habit of coming home just before dawn from his revelry. A noisy lad would scarcely think of anyone else if he were drunk as a piper.

All of the house might be in an uproar by day's end. What Lady Edwina would think of having a young man and his soon-to-be friends in the house was something Lisabeth could not guess. One thing was she sure of. Their year of quiet mourning was over.

Footfalls rushed toward her room. When a hasty knock sounded on her door, in amazement, she looked back to see Doherty coming into the room at a remarkable pace. He halted, looking uncomfortable. "My lady, Lord Radcliffe is here."

Lisabeth gasped. What was Lord Radcliffe doing here at such an early hour? "Have him wait in the parlor."

"Yes, my lady."

When she did not hear the door close, Lisabeth looked up and noted the butler's strained expression. She never had seen Doherty so all on end. "What is amiss?"

"If I may be so bold, I must own Lord Radcliffe is not what I expected, my lady."

Lisabeth's curiosity was piqued by Doherty's unusual behavior, but she only nodded. To speak of the marquess like this was inappropriate. He backed out and shut the door.

Frowning at her appearance in her glass, Lisabeth wished she had had a few more hours to prepare. She had not guessed the marquess would arrive before midday. Clearly he was as untutored in the niceties of town life as Norton had intimated.

"This is too much for you, my lady," said Wilson with rare passion as she came into the room.

Lisabeth saw surprise in her blue eyes before she turned to her abigail. "Would you have me shirk my duty to my late husband's cousin, Wilson?"

"No, no, my lady. I know I am brazen, but I speak of my concern for you."

"Say what you will. You know I value your opinion."

Wilson folded her arms in front of her and frowned. " 'Tis my opinion that it is unseemly that Mr. Radcliffe should pass off his obligations on you."

"Mr. Radcliffe disdains Town and the Season. On the

subject of the Polite World, he would be an unfit tutor. Mayhap he hopes a woman's guidance will make the bitter medicine of such lessons a bit easier for a young blade to swallow." She patted her abigail's arm. "Dear Wilson, please do not fret. I vow to you that I shall waste no time finding this lad a match to brighten his heart. Then he shall be gone from beneath our roof posthaste."

When Wilson smiled again, Lisabeth wished she could feel as assured as her words. She went to the stairs. As she descended, she saw the disquiet remained on Doherty's long face. She took a deep breath. The lad, who held the title of Lord Radcliffe, must be more unruly than she had guessed, but she would bring the young scamp to heel before the Season was over.

"Please have a light nuncheon sent in," she ordered quietly, resisting the urge to glance toward the parlor. It would not do to have her guest get his first look at her as she peeked around the corner at him like a naughty chit. "I fear it is too early for anything else. I recall, from my own cousins, that lads are endlessly ravenous."

Doherty hesitated. "My lady?"

"Yes?"

He started to speak, then nodded. "I shall have the nuncheon brought."

Lisabeth brushed her cold hands against the white fabric of her simple gown. It was far from her best dress, but it would have to do for this meeting. The bodice was stylishly high, and the short sleeves were edged with white lace. Reminding herself that the lad would most likely consider her aged beyond belief, she squared her shoulders and walked toward the parlor.

"Good morning, my lord. I—" She regarded the two men sitting in front of the hearth. Neither was a lad, for both must be older than her two-and-twenty years. Yet Doherty had told her Lord Radcliffe waited in the parlor.

A red-haired man, who had retained his puppy fat into his middle years, jumped to his feet and bowed his head.

She stared at the other man. The elegant cut of his clothes labeled him as the marquess, for they were stylish and of the finest material. She wondered if the man, whose hair was as black as a cooling ember, had not heard her approach, for he did not stand.

"Good morning?" she repeated, unable to keep from making it sound like a question.

When Lord Radcliffe turned to look over his shoulder at her, she could not pull her gaze from his. Ebony fires burned in his eyes that were as hard as the lines ground into his well-drawn face. Lines of fatigue, she guessed. He shifted and winced. As his long fingers gripped the arms of her favorite chair, she wondered if he intended to drive his fingers through the upholstery.

Her lips tightened when he did not come to his feet. Even a bird-wit like Norton Radcliffe should have made sure his cousin was taught the most basic manners. Yet she could not place all the blame on Norton. Lord Radcliffe was invading her house on the slimmest of familial relationships.

"You need not stare like a stuck pig," he said, as if she were the unwelcome guest. "Come closer and gawk to your heart's desire, my lady, if Lady Montague you be. I doubt you are a serving lass, for a serving lass would have better manners."

Lisabeth bit her lip. She would not let him send her up to the boughs with his very first words. Even Frederick had been polite when they met. This would be far worse than she had dreaded, for this arrogant man should not be degrading her conduct when he had failed to offer her the courtesy of coming to his feet.

"Yes, I am Lisabeth Montague," she said more coldly than she had spoken to Mr. Smythe last night. "I shall not dispute your appraisal of my deportment, my lord, while I welcome you to my home."

He leaned back in the chair as she walked toward him. "And I am Tristan Radcliffe." He nodded toward her. "At your service, my lady."

"Thank you." She was not sure what else to say when he remained sitting.

An icy smile did not lessen the strain on his face. "You appear quite discomposed by my failure to acknowledge your arrival. Let me assure you, Lady Montague, the arrival of a beguiling blonde is something I would find quite impossible to ignore. To greet a lady a lovely as you, I would gladly come to my feet." He patted his legs, which were hidden, she noticed for the first time, beneath a thick blanket. "However, that is quite impossible."

Two

Lisabeth was sure there must be something she could say to lessen the strain left by Lord Radcliffe's comment, but she had no idea what it might be. Nor did he ease the situation. He sat without speaking, his hands folded in his lap, his silent companion a shadowy accusation.

"Th-thank you for b-b-being—" She closed her lips when the marquess's twitched. If he had any gentility at all, he would have informed her of his infirmity in a far more gracious manner. Sitting in a chair facing him, she clasped her hands. "Thank you for being so honest with me, my lord. I trust your journey was not intolerable."

"Less intolerable than the arrival, I would say."

Lisabeth sat straighter. Did he intend to hurl demure hits at her with every breath? Even the most uncouth lad would act with more restraint at a first meeting such as this. "I hope your arrival proves not to be a harbinger of the rest of your stay."

His dark brow arched, and, although his expression remained stern, she had the niggling suspicion he was trying not to laugh.

Mrs. Outhwaite's arrival with the nuncheon tray allowed Lisabeth a chance to draw her gaze away from Lord Radcliffe's compelling eyes. She must regain her tattered composure. This was her home, and she was being generous to open it to the cousin of her late husband's distant cousin. She must not let Lord Radcliffe make her uncomfortable again within these familiar walls.

She watched the housekeeper place the tea tray and the plates of sandwiches and cakes on a table between Lord Radcliffe and the settee. Mrs. Outhwaite glanced at her, questions filling her strained face. Lisabeth would have liked to ease her housekeeper's disquiet, but, even if she had answers to give Mrs. Outhwaite, she could not speak them in front of her guest. Lord Radcliffe's rag-mannered ways did not grant her license to be as rude.

"Do you wish anything else, my lady?" Mrs. Outhwaite asked, her eyes constantly shifting toward Lord Radcliffe and the silent man.

"Nothing right now," she said, although she wished she could devise an excuse for Mrs. Outhwaite to stay. There was none, and the housekeeper left the room.

"If you are pouring, Lady Montague, I wish only sugar for my tea," Lord Radcliffe said.

Lisabeth stiffened as his stilted words pointed out her failure as a hostess. Blast! It was vexing to have her single shortcoming lambasted when Lord Radcliffe had been discourteous from the first. She had been rainbow chasing to think there was any chance this visit could be a pleasant experience.

"Bond prefers a touch of cream," he continued as she reached for the pot.

Bond must be the other man. The temptation to remind the marquess that his manservant was welcome to enjoy his tea in the kitchen went unsaid when she saw Lord Radcliffe's cool smile. Teaching this strong-willed man the ways of the *élite* would not be simple.

"Of course," she said quietly as she prepared the cups. She offered one to Lord Radcliffe.

His fingers, as they brushed hers, were surprisingly smooth. She would have guessed such a rabshackle lord who resided in grassville would lead a rough life of riding and hunting.

Her surprise must have been displayed on her face, for he said, "My recently sedentary life has left me not myself. I hope this trip to Town will help rectify that."

"You may be assured that my household shall do all we can to make you and the rest of your party welcome, my lord," she answered, hoping such trite words would ease the tension.

"Rest of my party?" He laughed, but without mirth. "My dear Lady Montague, you must think me completely unmannered." He chuckled again, and she knew the heat climbing her cheeks had been visible to betray her. "No matter what your first impression of me may be, and I assume it has been less than favorable, you may be assured I would not impose overly on your generous hospitality. You shall be inflicted only with Bond and me."

Lisabeth was unsure which comment to respond to first. How would she convince this man to keep his tongue between his teeth long enough not to insult everyone he met? As soon as eager mothers, who had eligible daughters to marry, learned a marquess was seeking a wife, Lord Radcliffe would be inundated with invitations. But what could he attend if he was unable to stand? She wondered if Norton was laughing even now. If this was his idea of a jest, she must put him to rights at the first opportunity.

In the meanwhile. . . . She handed Bond his cup. When he gave her a curt nod, she hurried to serve herself before her trembling fingers could reveal more of her disquiet.

She kept her eyes on her task as she asked, "Will you require a room on the ground floor, my lord?"

"Let me put your mind to rest." He took a sip of tea, grimaced, and reached past her to add more sugar to his cup. "I am capable, under normal conditions which do not include three days of riding in that dashed carriage, to do more than sit like a lump of coal. Although walking any distance is a skill that has eluded me of late, you need not think that I plan to billet myself and Bond in your foyer."

Lisabeth lowered her eyes again. That telltale flame on her cheeks must be glowing red. Everything she said was wrong, but she had no idea what would be correct. Mayhap if she let him know the error of his forthrightness, he would alter his ways. Slowly she raised her eyes. The sable thickness of his hair dropped onto his collar which reached only as high as his jaw. On the cut of his clothes, she could be relieved. She had little use for the pretenses of the dandy set.

Foolishly she raised her gaze higher, and she was caught anew by his dark eyes. She could not look away. Nor did she want to, for her heart was touched by the pain she saw etched in the skin around his eyes. Mayhap his words were nothing more than a shield to prevent anyone from coming close enough to see what he suffered.

"I have disconcerted you," Lord Radcliffe said, his low voice like the rumble of wind at the eaves, "and, for that, I apologize."

"There is no need to apologize."

"Do not be less than honest with me."

She could not keep from smiling. "From this point forward, I shall not."

His chuckle gained warmth. "Our mutual cousin, Norton Radcliffe, was correct when he told me that my manners were better suited to an army mess than a parlor. When he suggested I come to Town to refine them, he gave me no hint that his dear cousin Lisabeth would be so lovely."

"Your compliments are wasted upon me," she answered, hoping no high color would contradict her assertion. "You would be wise to save such *bon mots* for when you are dallying with one of the young misses you shall meet soon."

He laughed, this time with a heartiness belying his fatigue. "Egad, what a horrible thought! You make it sound as if I am to be the prey in a fox hunt."

" 'Tis you who, I believe, shall be the hunter."

"True, and Norton said you would assist me with every facet of this hunt for a marchioness, which he insists cannot be delayed, and which I have agreed to in hopes of being done with his whining. It was for that reason that I assumed you would allow me to practice the fascinating skill of nothing-sayings with you."

"You assumed unwisely." Lisabeth took a sip of tea to escape from the amusement brightening his eyes. It warned that he would enjoy hoaxing her on every turn. Was this ill-mannered pose nothing but a jest? She was sure of nothing when he smiled so warmly. "Norton requested that I *teach* you, not suffer want-witted funnings. I would appreciate you granting me the respect you have given any teacher."

"A request you would come to regret if I were to agree. The retelling of my relationships with my tutors is not for your delicate ears." Lord Radcliffe reached to select a sandwich, but, with a wry smile, motioned for her to choose one first. "See, my lady, you inspire graciousness in me already."

"I would expect no less."

"Then, you may be disappointed." Not giving her a chance to answer, he gestured to Bond. "Take one for yourself, and find yourself a seat, so Lady Montague does not think you lurk about me like a raven waiting for death."

Bond glanced at her, flushed, then took a sandwich. "Thank you, my lady."

Lord Radcliffe selected one for himself. His smile vanished as he tried to balance the sandwich and the cup. "Dash it!" The cup wobbled.

"Let me help!" Lisabeth jumped to her feet. What a moonling she was! Lord Radcliffe must be far weaker than he wished her to think. Catching his cup before it could teeter off its saucer, she gasped as hot tea splashed onto her hand. She winced and bit her lip to silence her cry of pain. Quickly she dabbed at her hand with a napkin.

"My lady?" asked Lord Radcliffe and Bond at the same time. The two men glanced at each other before looking back at her.

"It is nothing," she assured them.

"Damn," growled Lord Radcliffe under his breath. Glowering at Lisabeth, he added, "I suppose I need to apologize for being so unthinking as to speak such a curse and for being so accursedly feeble. Mayhap I shall after you apologize to me."

"To you?" She frowned. "For what?"

"For breaking so quickly your pledge to be honest to me."

"I—"

"Do not hedge. You do not look fine. You look as if you are sorely hurt, and I should reprimand you for being so opaque as to scorch yourself rather than letting that tea splatter on my coat."

" 'Tis nothing of import," she said, although tears burned in her eyes nearly as hotly as the tea had on her skin. "I have been a poor hostess to allow you to linger here in conversation when it is obvious you wish to rest. I ask you to forgive *me*, my lord."

He leaned back in the chair and regarded her over crossed arms, which threatened the shoulder seams of his coat. "Bother! We could spend the rest of the day pleading each other's forgiveness. Why not call a halt to this?"

Yes! Let us put an end to all of this. She resisted the temptation to voice her thoughts. "You are correct, my lord. Forgive—"

"Egad!" His shout reverberated up against the ceiling and brought a chuckle from Bond. "I shall forgive you for your overwhelming kindness only if you will stop acting as if I am a leper." Reaching out, he caught her hand between his.

She pressed her other hand over her violently thudding heart as the warmth in his eyes soared through his skin to hers. When he brought her fingers to his lips, she feared her breath was trapped within her. He brushed the lightest caress on them without letting her flee his gaze.

"You need not look so frightened when I wish only to show you that I am not totally lacking in manners," he murmured. "My infirmities are not contagious."

Lisabeth flushed anew. She could not recall the last time she had blushed so often during a single conversation. Drawing her hand away, she clasped her fingers in front of her. Curse their trembling and her own cheeks which were afire! She did not want him touching her, just as she had not wanted Mr. Smythe's touch—as she wanted no man's touch which began so sweetly and led. . . .

Squaring her shoulders, she silenced the memories which assaulted her whenever she did not submerge them. Her voice was brittle when she replied, "I did not mean to suggest anything about your infirmity, Lord Radcliffe."

"But you are curious."

That he did not make his comment a question warned her that he had had this conversation many times before. That he was being forced to endure it again added to the rage tightening his lips. Dampening her own, she said, "I asked my questions only because I wish to know how to make you comfortable."

His explosion of laughter was icy cold. "Instead of answering your question, which I am certain a gracious lady like you had no intention of making so enticing, I shall satisfy your curiosity. How did I come to be like this? The answer is simple. The war, of course."

"I understand." She sat and reached for her cup. Mayhap a sip of tea would lessen the chill abruptly filling the room.

"May I say that you show uncommon insight? Few of the *ton*, who danced obliviously through the war with Boney, can guess what it is like to march into hell and have to be carried back near death."

Again Lisabeth faltered. How could she reply to such a comment? She chose the truth. "The war with France is over. I have no wish to fight another battle in my parlor. If you can tell me what you need to make you comfortable, I shall arrange with my housekeeper, Mrs. Outhwaite, to be certain it is waiting in your room."

"Anything?"

"Within reason."

He turned to his companion. "She learns very quickly, Bond."

"One must in your company," Bond replied before finishing the last bite of his sandwich.

Lord Radcliffe looked back at her, and she noticed his face was etched with exhaustion. His voice gave no hint of fatigue, for it remained rich with mockery. "I am depending on you to tell me what I need, Lady Montague. Our mutual cousin has placed my welfare and my future completely in your charming hands."

"Norton is insistent that you must find a marchioness." Reacting to his cynical words might be what he wanted. She would not give him that satisfaction, for she had been honest. She did not want a battle of words to disrupt her reemergence into the *ton*.

"My cousin is obsessed with the fear the title shall end with me."

"That sounds much like Norton. He was very concerned, when Frederick died, to determine exactly who should receive my late husband's title." She held out a plate of brightly frosted cakes and smiled as Lord Radcliffe took one with care. Hesitating, she stretched past him to offer the plate to Bond.

When the round man, who reminded her of an elf, picked up one, he said, "Thank you, my lady."

"As you can see," Lord Radcliffe said with another chuckle, "Bond needs no tuition in the gracious ways of the Polite World."

Again Lisabeth was unsure how to answer. How could this man discountenance her with so few words? Setting the plate back on the table, she said, "Your cousin has his mind set on this. I daresay you would be wise to find a young miss to marry with all haste. That would satisfy Mr. Radcliffe when he has taken your well-being to heart."

Any hint of a smile vanished from his face. "You jest."

"I meant nothing humorous, my lord."

"Then, I can only assume you do not know my cousin well. He has never been known to be altruistic."

"He is concerned enough about you to send you to Town."

"True." Lord Radcliffe pointed to the teapot, and she watched in amazement as Bond came forward to refill a cup. Not for Lord Radcliffe, but for himself. Although Lord Radcliffe did not look at her, he must have sensed her reaction. Or, it might be that he had seen its match before, for he said, "Do not look askance at me at such informality."

"It is not the way of Town."

"Some things you may find impossible to change about me, Lady Montague. Maxwell Bond served me during my sojourn on the Continent where we found it often wise to forget the canons of propriety. It is my good fortune that he continues to be willing to serve me in a manner we both find comfortable."

"Yes," she replied, rather faintly. "You are, of course, welcome to make yourself at home here, Bond."

"Thank you, my lady," he said in his amazingly resonant voice.

"My lord, the first thing we must do is—" Her voice

faded as she heard a sharp question from the foyer below. Taking a deep breath, she pulled her gaze from Lord Radcliffe's captivating eyes and looked over her shoulder as a woman appeared in the arched doorway.

Lady Edwina Montague was a wisp of a woman, appearing as if she were made of delicate porcelain. The array of exquisite jewelry she wore seemed too large. As always, her gown was a vivid—in Lisabeth's opinion, garish—green. Lisabeth had never seen her gray-haired mother-in-law wear any other color.

Lady Edwina's long nose wrinkled as she looked around the room. "From what Doherty blathered to me in the foyer, I assume one of these gentlemen is Lord Radcliffe."

"Lord Radcliffe and his man Bond, Lady Edwina," Lisabeth said. Setting herself on her feet, she went to stand beside her mother-in-law. "How fortunate that you have returned from your ride with Mrs. Castleman—I assume she is well, and you had a pleasant morning driving through the Park—in time to join us for nuncheon!" Her words tumbled, one atop the next. "Allow me to introduce you to our guest, Lord Radcliffe. However, we must not keep Lord Radcliffe long with our conversation. I fear his journey has been wearying."

Lady Edwina walked past Lisabeth without replying. Going to where Lord Radcliffe watched with a hint of a smile, she frowned. "You are no lad."

"I was once a lad, my lady, but that was years ago."

"I was told this morning, before I went out, expecting to return before anyone with a hint of decency would call, that Frederick's odious cousin Norton was fobbing a lad off upon Lisabeth. As if dear Lisabeth would know what to do with a fledgling! She was raised in a gentle household where she need not be bothered by a boisterous boy."

"Lady Edwina," interjected Lisabeth, wondering which of the servants had hurried to her mother-in-law with the tidings, "I am sure Lord Radcliffe has little interest in our foolish assumptions."

"Smash!" Lady Edwina continued to look down her nose at Lord Radcliffe. "See how sweet she is? She fears I shall injure you with plain speech when I suspect coarse words are your customary diet. Trust Norton to send you here when Lisabeth has better things to do than polish a rough diamond."

"Lady Edwina, please!" Lisabeth gasped. "Lord Radcliffe is our guest."

Again the older woman disregarded her. "That is yet to be seen."

Lisabeth was about to apologize when she saw Lord Radcliffe and his man were smiling. Her fingers closed into fists at her sides. Blast all of them! This was difficult enough without Lord Radcliffe and Lady Edwina coming to cuffs. Knowing the best course right now might be putting an end to this conversation, Lisabeth slipped her arm around her mother-in-law's shoulders. "Lady Edwina, Lord Radcliffe must rest. We shall have many weeks to talk."

"I would say 'tis quite the opposite." Lady Edwina shook off Lisabeth's arm, surprising her, for Lady Edwina was usually warm-hearted. "My lord, we offer you our hospitality tonight, but I think you would be wise to seek other lodgings, which should prove more suitable for your needs than my widowed daughter-in-law's house."

Lisabeth took Lady Edwina's withered hand. "This discussion can wait, for Lord Radcliffe and his companion must be exhausted after traveling across England." She took a deep breath to steady herself before she looked at the handsome man. Finding such a good-looking marquess a match should prove easy, once he learned to curb his tongue and regain his feet. "If you will excuse us, my lord, I shall see that your rooms are ready for whenever you fancy to use them."

"Thank you." The twinkle returned to his eyes. "I look forward to our first lesson."

A rush of heat surged over her as if he had touched her again. No, she would not be lured into believing the sweet promise in a man's smile again. She had been an airdreamer once, and there had been perdition to pay.

When Lady Edwina tugged on her arm, Lisabeth excused herself gratefully. She guessed Lady Edwina would explain her peculiar behavior once they were out of earshot of the startling marquess, but Lady Edwina remained silent, save to ask Lisabeth to join her in the older woman's private chambers.

Lisabeth sighed. She was unsettled enough without entering the room which was decorated in a rather odious shade of green which reflected off the cherry furniture in a queasy incandescence.

Choosing a chair, which was covered in emerald satin, Lady Edwina said, "Do sit, Lisabeth. I find straining my neck to look up at you almost as bothersome as the situation in the parlor." Instantly she added, "Forgive me, child."

"I understand your disquiet, for I share it." Lisabeth sat on a low bench in front of the window overlooking the square. Ignoring the rattle of carriage wheels from the street, she said, "I trust that in short order we shall acclimate ourselves to Lord Radcliffe's presence."

"Are you queer in the attic?"

Lisabeth was quite tempted to own that she must be, but was halted by the arrival of Lady Edwina's *femme de chambre*. As Cassandra set out another light meal, Lisabeth sighed. Not once, in the more than three years she had known Lady Edwina, had she ever seen her mother-in-law so agitated.

While Lady Edwina poured, Lisabeth said, "I cannot refuse a favor to Frederick's cousin."

"Of course not. Doing a good turn for Norton is generous of you, and you are showing an exemplary sense of duty to our family by accepting this obligation; but you cannot give up your life to tend to that husk."

Lisabeth could not halt her laugh. When Lady Edwina's disapproval straightened her full lips, Lisabeth struggled to control herself. Lord Radcliffe was so much more than a husk. He might be fatigued from his long journey, but the life gleaming from his eyes had not been dimmed. Even during the few words Lady Edwina had exchanged with the marquess, she must have noted that his sense of authority was not diminished by his injuries.

"My dear child," said Lady Edwina in her gentlest tone, "I trust you will endeavor to restrain such outbursts during the rest of our discussion, which is, after all, focused on your well-being."

"I shall try." She folded her hands in her lap as she had in the parlor below. She subdued a heated shiver that slid along her skin as she recalled Lord Radcliffe's courteous kiss on her hand. Mayhap she *was* queer in the attic. She had no wish to entangle her life with any man's, especially someone who was related to Frederick's cousin.

"I suggest," said Lady Edwina, "you make arrangements for Lord Radcliffe to be returned to his cousin posthaste. Let Norton deal his own tragedies instead of foisting them on you." She patted Lisabeth's hand. "I do not mean to chide your heart, Lisabeth, but your lack of sense."

Quietly, she replied, "I agreed to help."

"From what Wilson told me, Norton gave you no chance to reply."

Lisabeth's curiosity was satisfied, but vexation filled her voice. "Wilson should not be carrying tales."

"Your abigail is concerned, as I am, with your welfare. If you cannot see past your kind heart to the potential problems, then it behooves Wilson to come to me."

"I see no problem other than finding the proper woman for Lord Radcliffe to marry. The first thing I intend to do is learn what virtues he wishes in his marchioness. Then I shall seek a woman of gentle birth who matches them."

Lady Edwina shook her head in dismay. "How can you be so naive? What woman would wish to marry *him?*"

"I can name several who would marry the old gentleman in black himself if he had a title."

"You are refusing to acknowledge the truth because you pity him, Lisabeth."

"Pity him? How could I pity him?" Her assertion amazed her as much as it did Lady Edwina.

"How can you fail to pity him?" She held her hand to her bosom. "Dear child, the marquess is a most pitiful creature."

Lisabeth rose. "Lord Radcliffe is not a pitiful creature. He is a soldier who has been injured in the defense of his country. How can we turn our back on such a man?"

"He *is* a man, which is the primary reason he should leave. How shall it be perceived to have him living with you?"

"And with you." Kneeling by Lady Edwina's chair, Lisabeth put her hand on the old woman's thin arm. "I would gladly ask him to leave, but how can I now that we have welcomed him beneath our roof? He is family."

"Very loosely."

"Yes, but he *is* family."

Lady Edwina put her hand over Lisabeth's. "You deserve more than this. I want to see you happy."

She blinked back tears. Lady Edwina never once had mentioned anything about the months when Lisabeth had been married to her stepson, so Lisabeth had assumed that the old woman was unaware of what Lisabeth had endured. Mayhap Lady Edwina had sensed more than Lisabeth had guessed.

Rising, Lisabeth whispered, "If you will excuse me, I wish to be sure that everything is set for our guests' comfort."

"Where have you put them?"

"I assumed Bond would wish to be near the marquess—"

"Where?"

"—so I needed chambers large enough for both of them."

"Lisabeth, you are avoiding the question." Lady Edwina set herself on her feet. "Where have you put them?"

"Frederick's rooms."

"Oh, my." She dropped back onto her chair again.

"If you wish me to change those arrangements—"

"No, no." The old woman's face was nearly as gray as her hair. "Go and do what you must, child. I need to be alone to think about all of this."

As Lisabeth eased out of the room, she wished she could erase Lady Edwina's shattered expression from her mind. She did not like having a brangle with her mother-in-law, but there would be talk throughout the *ton* if Lord Radcliffe was expelled from the house on Cavendish Square.

She was astounded to see Bond in the hallway. When the ginger-hackled man turned, he lost his rigid pose. She struggled not to smile, for she did not want to embarrass him by revealing her amusement at his apparent guarding of Lord Radcliffe's door.

"Do you need something, Bond?" she asked.

"I believe all is well. Mrs. Outhwaite told us this suite of rooms would be for our use. I trust it shall be no problem if I put a pallet in the major's—I mean, my lord's dressing room."

"Lord Radcliffe should consider this his home during his stay. If there is anything—"

"If I may be so bold, my lady, Lord Radcliffe should rest. The trip was more draining for him than he wishes to own. I suspect he will need rest for several days. Please excuse him from joining you and the elder Lady Montague for dinner."

"Of course." She glanced at the door she had hoped

would never be reopened. When she noted Bond regarding her in confusion, she added, "Then, I shall leave you to tend him."

He nodded. "You are being generous."

"Lord Radcliffe is my guest."

"May I ask for how long?"

Lisabeth had not thought she could be more surprised by either man's outspokenness, but her voice came out in a squeak. "As long as necessary to do what Norton Radcliffe requested."

"Or to fail," Bond said with a sad glance at the door behind him.

Three

"That is a frightful expression, if I may so say."

Tristan Radcliffe continued glowering at the walls of the rooms he had been given for his use. Bond was being unusually cheerful today, which meant he was as unsettled by the whole of this as Radcliffe was. "I believe a dungeon in one of the grand *châteaux* along the Loire would be no darker than this chamber."

" 'Tis rather dismal."

"Rather?" Radcliffe chuckled tautly. "I may have misjudged our hostess. I had thought her honest in her welcome—"

"I believe she is."

He focused his scowl on Bond, although it gained him nothing. Bond was impervious to the scowls that had daunted his cousin Norton for years. "Egad, man, how can you say that? Look at this horrible room she has consigned us to. The walls are the darkest walnut I have ever seen, and I daresay the carpet is nearly black."

"Dark blue, sir."

"One and the same." He was in no mood to be soothed. Dash it! After that endless ride here from Norton's abysmally damp country house, he had hoped to find himself in more pleasant surroundings. He had been pleased to see the subdued warmth of Lisabeth's parlor and the corridor leading to these chambers. Then Bond had opened the door to this dark den which better suited a hibernating bear than a man about to make his way into the Polite World.

His hands clenched on the chair. When had he become a growling, fusty old wigsby? He nearly had died in France, but he was not dead yet. Too many years still should await him, years he should enjoy rather than complaining about the things around him.

He rubbed his forehead. If this accursed headache would ebb, he might be able to regain his customary nature which had once matched Bond's merry-as-a-cricket outlook.

"Sir?"

"I am fine," he answered. With a sigh, he added, "By the by, I suspect Lady Lisabeth would be quite as put out as my cousin Norton to hear you address me as anything other than my lord."

"I will endeavor to remember that." Bond's eyes twinkled with that blasted merriment as he walked through a door on the far side of the massive bed. "This pup is getting too old to change his ways."

"What is within, Bond?" he asked when Bond returned to the bedchamber.

"A dressing room of some size."

"And?" He might have missed the hesitation if he did not know Bond so well.

"A door."

Radcliffe sat straighter in his chair. "Now, that is something of interest. Where does this door open to?"

"I don't know." Bond emerged from the dressing room with Radcliffe's coat. "It is locked."

"Is it, now?" He chuckled. "I suspect it opens into our hostess's chambers."

Bond frowned. "My lord, Lady Lisabeth expects us to be on our best manners in her home."

"Do you honestly think that I intend to break down the

lady's door and proceed into her room with all haste to ravage her?" His smile faltered. "Even if I were able?"

"I have eyes, my lord."

"As I do."

"And I saw how you admired the lady."

He relaxed against the chair as Bond handed him the light gray coat. "Bond, rest assured that despite my obvious admiration of my cousin's cousin's widow, I know my place."

"I know that look."

"Look?"

Bond chuckled. "That 'I've got some scheme on my mind that I intend to enact' look." As he went to get Radcliffe's shoes, he added, "I'm glad to see it back, although I would be remiss not to warn our hostess of impending trouble."

"I have no idea what you are speaking about." Radcliffe smiled at his man's back. He knew exactly what Bond meant, and he was not surprised that Bond was startled to see that expression that had been missing from his face since the day death had almost claimed him. Who would have guessed that Norton's advice to come to Town would prove such a boon to his spirits?

This sojourn in Town might not be so horrible, after all. For him, at any rate.

"It is so pleasant having this time just to ourselves," Lady Edwina said as she selected a muffin from the basket on the table in the breakfast-parlor. This morning, her gown was a shade darker than the light green walls. "We should do this more often, Lisabeth."

"We usually have breakfast together," Lisabeth replied.

"A practice I believe we should continue. This quiet time *en famille* is most important."

"Oh."

"What does that mean?" Lady Edwina frowned.

Lisabeth silenced her sigh. If she had slept more soundly last night instead of tossing in her bed as she wondered how she was going to fire-off Lord Radcliffe into the *ton*, she might have understood what her mother-in-law hinted at with her peculiar comments.

"It means," she said with a smile, "that I am distressed that you continue to be unsettled by our guest's arrival."

"As you should be." Pointing with her knife, Lady Edwina added, "Do be a dear and pass me the butter."

Lisabeth handed the butter dish to Lady Edwina just as Doherty came to the breakfast-parlor. The sun glinted off his balding pate, but dismay dimmed his eyes. She took a deep breath, for she guessed he was about to announce Lord Radcliffe's arrival. That was guaranteed to raise Lady Edwina's ire again.

Instead, he held out a folded page. "Lady Lisabeth, this was just delivered for you."

When she took the page, thanking Doherty, Lisabeth noticed her hand was shaking. Dash it! She was letting Lady Edwina's vexation add to her own uneasy thoughts. Other guests. . . . With a pulse of astonishment, she realized she could not recall any other guests beneath this roof. Frederick had claimed many friends, but he had granted them no welcome here beyond a few hands of cards or an evening emptying a few bottles of wine.

She clenched the page in her lap. Those nights had been the worst. If she spoke to Frederick's friends, he accused her of flirting with them. If she did not, he was furious that she had slighted his tie-mates.

"Are you expecting bad tidings, Lisabeth?" Lady Edwina asked quietly.

"I don't believe so. Why do you ask?"

"You are crushing that piece of paper."

Lisabeth smiled with the ease of three years' practice.

"I shall never know if it is good or bad, shall I, if I crumple it up before reading it."

She did not glance toward Doherty, but saw Lady Edwina do so. Why was she creating down-pinned spirits for herself? She was enjoying her breakfast with Lady Edwina, and she should be grateful that Lord Radcliffe had chosen not to rise early after his arduous journey from northwest England.

Her disquiet blossomed into annoyance as she read the note.

> *My dearest Lisabeth,*
>
> *Our parting two nights ago left me dismayed. I know your warmest of hearts will welcome me when I call to escort you to the theatre tonight. I have taken a loge so we might have the opportunity to reconcile our differences. I am most desirous of winning your smile. Please say that you will allow me to spend this evening in your glorious company.*
>
> *I remain,*
>
> > *Your humble cum-dumble,*
> > *Cyril Smythe*

Lisabeth lowered the letter and shook her head. She did not need Mr. Smythe panting after her in the throes of calf love. Even if she were interested in acquiring another husband, it would not be Mr. Smythe. He must not realize that if he was so want-witted as to send her this unwanted profession of devotion.

Looking up, she saw Doherty by the door. "Who waits for an answer?" she asked.

"Mr. Smythe's man."

"Please bring him in. I wish to speak with him."

Doherty's eyes began to twinkle, but his lips remained straight. "As you wish, my lady."

Lady Edwina reached for the note on the table, but Lisabeth kept her fingers on it as a young man in lackluster livery appeared. He bowed so low that his nose almost brushed the tablecloth.

"Please inform Mr. Smythe," Lisabeth said, holding out the wrinkled page, "that I forgive him for sending this note. No doubt, he shall be pleased when you return it."

The footman flushed, but took the page. "I shall acquaint him with his mistake, my lady."

"You may tell him as well that there is no need for him to call here to apologize. I am sure we shall chance to meet at some rout, which shall provide Mr. Smythe the opportunity to express his distress. You may add that he would be wise to address his correspondence before he goes into dinner."

The young man nodded and bowed before leaving the room.

"Shame!" chided Lady Edwina as she motioned for more hot chocolate. "Mr. Smythe is quite besotted with you. He has no need to be fortified by port to find the courage to write to you."

"I have no interest in him dangling after me. He is nearly as boring as . . ." Lisabeth hoped the heat climbing her cheeks was not visible. "He wishes to speak only of his investments and whom he has supped with."

When Lady Edwina changed the subject to the dinner party they would be hosting next week, Lisabeth kept her gaze on her plate. She must watch her tongue. Insulting Frederick to his stepmother was unthinkable. On that one subject alone, they were unceasingly dishonest.

But it was not the only one, Lisabeth realized, as before she could take a bite of the eggs congealing on her plate, the butler returned to say, "Lord Radcliffe requests your company at your earliest convenience, my lady."

She put down her fork, no longer having any appetite. Did Lady Edwina suspect how false Lisabeth's words had been when she had asserted that finding the marquess a wife would be a task she could handle with ease? She disliked dissembling, especially with her mother-in-law.

She need not have worried about Lady Edwina noting her anxiety. Sniffing with outrage, her mother-in-law asked, "He orders us about as if he is the master of the house? This is too much, even for him."

"Nonsense," returned Lisabeth, placing her napkin on the table. "Lord Radcliffe cannot get about on his own, so, as his hostess, I understand that it behooves me to attend him when he wishes."

"And I understand it quite differently." Lady Edwina, it appeared, was not willing to be less than honest about her opinions of Lord Radcliffe. "He treats you too familiarly."

" 'Tis quite the opposite."

"I trust it will stay that way."

"He wishes only to find a wife as he promised Norton."

"Let him seek one beyond this household."

Lisabeth's eyes widened. "If you think that I would consider—"

"I have no idea what to think." Lady Edwina came to her feet when Lisabeth did. The determined angle of her chin suggested that she was ready to do battle.

Wanting to soothe her ruffled feathers, Lisabeth remained silent. She would have to find a way to tell her mother-in-law, without disparaging Frederick's memory, that she had no interest in remarrying. She intended to enjoy her life as a dowager, free to gather her friends when she wished and to speak to whomever she chose.

Sunshine swept the hallway as Lisabeth led the way to the sitting room. Bond stood by the door and gave her an uneasy smile when she looked in his direction. If something was making him uneasy. . . . She did not allow that thought to form. Of course, he was not yet comfortable in her home.

Amazement made her falter when she saw Lord Radcliffe paging through a novel she had left on a table. She had not guessed Lord Radcliffe would be interested in such tame fare; then she reminded herself that she had no idea what he might like.

She ignored the irritation pinching her when she realized he again sat in her favorite chair. He was a guest in this house and should be welcome to whichever chair he wanted. Wanting to rub her aching forehead, she warned herself not to let her lack of sleep make her a poor hostess.

Lord Radcliffe wore a somber gray frock coat atop his pale breeches. Over an embroidered waistcoat, an elegantly tied cravat closed his unfashionably low collar. She must speak with him about obtaining a wardrobe suitable for the Season. Even though, she had to own, he looked quite dashing, he would be wise to hide that strong line of his jaw from prospective brides. It warned of a stubborn nature, something she had already discovered.

"Good morning," Lisabeth began, but her mother-in-law pushed past her in an emerald whirl.

Lady Edwina placed herself directly in front of Lord Radcliffe's chair and scowled. "I find it unconscionable that you demand our presence upon your bidding, my lord."

"My message must have been misdelivered." His smooth voice was as devoid of emotion as his face. "I wished only for your daughter-in-law to know that I am willing to start my lessons at her convenience."

"Lessons? What does a rogue like you wish with lessons from a gentle lady? Can it be that you have plans of your own for the course of the classes? A course that will have grave consequences for dear Lisabeth's immaculate reputation?"

"Lady Edwina!" gasped Lisabeth, pressing her hand to her bodice as her breath caught over her heart. "Please recall that Lord Radcliffe is our guest."

"Do cut line, Lisabeth! This is between his lordship and me. I trust I have made my opinions on his visit clear."

Lord Radcliffe smiled. "Lady Montague, think a moment, if you would. Don't you find it highly amusing that I might be contemplating seducing your daughter-in-law when I consider standing a formidable task?"

"One does not need two sturdy legs to set his mind on a wayward course."

"That is true, and it is also true that if that is the sole satisfaction I can obtain from this situation, you would be uncivil to deny me that."

Lady Edwina's eyes grew wide, and Lisabeth gasped as the meaning of his convoluted words came clear.

"Good morning, my lord," Lady Edwina snapped with another of her favorite sniffs as she left, firing a parting glare at Bond as if he were an accessory to the marquess's words.

"Does she always garb herself in a bilious shade?" Lord Radcliffe chuckled. "She resembles a pea pod seared on the vine."

"I had no idea that you were an expert on ladies' fashions!" retorted Lisabeth, furious with both Lady Edwina and the marquess for coming to cuffs over ridiculous matters. And with herself for revealing her shock. She had seen Lord Radcliffe's eyes twinkling when she reacted.

He smiled. "Enlighten me, my lady, if I am mistaken. Do you wear lace and fripperies for your own gratification?"

"Of course."

"You never give a thought to the men who glance at you, admiring your golden hair and the silk which flatters you?"

"I cannot speak for Lady Edwina, but can put your mind at ease on my account. I have no wish to attract attention." That, finally, was the truth.

"Unfortunate," he said, "for I daresay the dowager Lady

Montague garners attention wherever she goes, for no man could fail to take note of her."

Lisabeth retorted, "Lady Edwina—"

"I was not speaking of *that* dowager Lady Montague, my lady, but of you."

She would have fired back an answer if she had had one. His abrupt compliment, if it were a compliment, flustered her. Sitting, she raised her eyes to meet the amusement in Lord Radcliffe's.

As if this were the most ordinary of conversations, she said, "I trust you and Bond enjoyed breakfast."

"Your cook should be commended. It was an excellent repast, brought to us by your Mrs. Outhwaite. On your orders?"

"What do you mean?"

He folded his arms across his chest, leaving her no choice but to note its breadth. It was so easy to envision him commanding his men on the battlefield or the ladies' attention in a ballroom.

"I thought," he said, bringing her gaze back to meet his, "you might have arranged with your housekeeper to provide us with food this morning so that you could confer with your mother-in-law about what to do with your unexpected guests."

"You thought wrong. I gave no such order." *But Lady Edwina probably did.* She must not voice her suspicions. She rested her hand on the carved mahogany of the chair's arm. "I am pleased that you find our home to your liking. Mayhap, then, you will consider joining us for a gathering we are holding next week."

"A gathering? A rout?"

She shook her head. "A dinner party."

"A dinner party?" Lord Radcliffe's dark eyes narrowed. "I was under the impression that you were in mourning."

"Frederick's death was more than a year ago, my lord." When she saw his astonishment at her cool answer, she did not give him a chance to ask any questions. "Lady Edwina and I have invited a few friends to join us for a simple repast, and, of course, you are welcome."

"And give you an uneven number at your table? That would be ungentlemanly of me."

"This will offer you an opportunity to meet some of the people sharing your Season."

"So you believe you may have a potential marchioness among your guests?"

"That is for you to decide, my lord."

Lord Radcliffe smiled. "On that one thing, I am pleased that you and Norton are in agreement with me, although I must own that even upon our short acquaintance, I would trust your opinions on this subject far more than our mutual cousin's. Very well, I shall be delighted to attend your fête." With a grimace, he slapped his knee. "I fear you may have taken on another obligation with your invitation."

"No more than I anticipated. The first thing is to help you cross the room on your own." Lisabeth smiled.

"You expect me to manage that in a mere week?"

"My expectations are not what you need to concern yourself with, but with your own expectations, my lord."

He rested his chin on his arm that was propped on the chair. "That answer is not what I expected."

"Norton has given you into my care."

"The best decision he ever made." A smile uncurled along his lips as he regarded her with a bold gaze. "If I may say so, you are not what I expected either."

Although she was curious what he meant, she ignored both his provocative comments and the brazen stare that seemed to seek to uncover every thought in her head. She doubted if he would be successful, for *she* could not sort out the jumble bouncing about her brain.

Quietly she said, as if the conversation had not wandered into this bothersome direction, "I would be less than needle-witted to suggest that you shall escort one of my guests into dinner in, as you aptly put it, a mere week."

"I am pleased that you are being realistic."

"Yes, but are you?"

His hands tightened on his chair. She noted again how long his fingers were. He possessed the hands of an artist, not of a soldier. "I fail to understand what you mean," he said in as hushed a tone as hers, but she could sense the tension underlying each word.

"I meant no more than the words suggest. You have been confined for months. Aren't you eager to regain your freedom?"

"That is an absurd question worthy of our mutual cousin Norton, not you."

"Then, why don't you answer it?" When he glowered, Lisabeth said, "My lord, you must understand one thing about *Le Beau Monde*. Presentation is everything. How you are perceived by others will define how they treat you. If they see you bound to that chair, I fear you shall be treated in a manner you may find offensive."

He laughed, and she frowned, baffled. His many moods were as changeable as the weather.

"So much a part of your world you are!" he said. "Perfectly groomed to be sponsoring a wayward marquess in his search for a bride! No wonder that cabbage-head Norton chose you."

"If you have no wish for my assistance—"

"No, no," he said with another laugh. "I put my future and myself completely in your hands. It is not a bad place to be, you must own."

"My lord, if you wish to continue in this manner—"

Again he interrupted her, warning her that he disdained the ways of the Polite World. "Manner? But are manners not what you are to teach me? You shall be my tutor in the ways of the *ton*. Say what you wish me to do, and I shall endeavor to comply."

"All right. First . . ." Lisabeth stood and motioned to Bond, who was struggling not to smile. "Bond, help Lord Radcliffe to his feet. If he is to regain his strength, there is no time like now to begin."

The red-haired man cleared his throat before looking at Lord Radcliffe. When Lisabeth repeated her order, Bond took a single step into the room. "My lord?" he asked, an anxious expression stealing all hint of a smile.

"You heard the lady, Bond," Lord Radcliffe said.

When Lisabeth started to smile, the marquess fired a furious scowl in her direction. She almost recoiled. Should she excuse herself? For the first time, she realized he might be embarrassed by his weakness. She turned to take her leave, but halted when the marquess called her name.

"Yes?" she asked, turning.

"Where are you off to, my lady? Are you afraid to face the challenge ahead of you?"

She did not answer as Bond assisted the marquess to his feet. Lord Radcliffe leaned heavily on Bond, and she noted how his left leg refused to straighten to support him. She had not guessed he was so hobbled or that he was so tall. She tried to mask her astonishment, but she suspected he saw it as he turned awkwardly with Bond's help to face her. His lips tightened into a straight line, whether with pain or vexation at her sympathy she could not guess. His gaze captured her with the power of an ebony flame. Wanting to look away, she could not as a single thought filled her otherwise emptied head. What did he hope to gain by imprisoning her with this gaze?

"I am glad," she said, struggling to keep her voice more steady than he was, "that a night's rest has enabled you to regain your ability to come to your feet. You must do so when a lady enters the room."

"Or risk shocking the clocks right off her stockings?"

She was amazed that he could jest with her when his jaw worked with the effort to remain standing. He gripped the back of the chair and motioned Bond to step aside. A grim look on his face, Bond nodded and moved back, his hands ready to catch the marquess if necessary.

"Presentation, as I said," Lisabeth whispered, unsure if she should speak more loudly when she feared a single breath would topple him, "is everything, my lord."

"I suspect you will repeat that often to me during our lessons."

She dampened her lips. "Can you walk, my lord?"

"That is a good question. Shall we see?"

Bond gasped, "Sir—my lord! You should make haste slowly."

"Egad!" Lord Radcliffe grumbled. "You have listened too long to the absurd lectures I have suffered from my cousin Norton."

Lisabeth was astonished when Bond rushed to her. "My lady, please make him listen to good sense. He should remember his regimen, which calls for rest and the medicine prescribed by Mr. Radcliffe's physician."

"Do not waste her time." Lord Radcliffe chuckled. "I have heeded the mewlings of that quacksalver and suffered his odious powders for too long. What good have they done me? They have not eased the pain in my skull or brought me back to health."

"But if you are to get well," Lisabeth began.

"You, my lady, are the medicine I need now." He pushed himself to stand straighter, even as his face became a more sickly shade of gray. "You dare me to prove what I have put off proving for too long. I trust you will refrain from laughing if I tumble onto my nose."

Lisabeth clasped her hands and heard Bond mutter as Lord Radcliffe reached for the next closest chair. She held her breath when he dragged his useless leg toward the chair, nearly toppling the chair over. When Bond edged toward it, the marquess growled something she suspected she was better off not understanding.

His shoulders heaved, and his jaw was clenched. When Lisabeth was about to congratulate him, he stretched to grasp the next chair. Beads of sweat speckled his brow when he was able to stand beside it.

How wrong Lady Edwina had been! There was nothing pitiful about this strong man who was fighting to regain control of his wounded body.

The only sounds were Lord Radcliffe's strained breath and the pulse of her rapid heartbeat pounding in her ears. When he reached the hearth, he faced her. He drew out a handkerchief to wipe his face, but his eyes glittered with triumph.

Bond took a step forward, but was waved away. He looked imploringly toward Lisabeth.

"My lord, that is enough for today," Lisabeth said firmly.

"Now, see here," Lord Radcliffe argued.

"No, you shall see that haste must—"

"Be made slowly." He grumbled, but allowed Bond to help him to sit in the closest chair.

Lisabeth rang for Doherty. "Burgundy," she said when the butler arrived with his usual speed. "Three glasses."

Doherty glanced at the two men and, for the first time in Lisabeth's memory, hesitated. She repeated her request. With a guilty expression, he hurried away.

"Bond?"

When Lisabeth heard how breathless the marquess's voice was, she again contemplated excusing herself. Then, telling herself not to be caper-witted, she watched Bond hovering over his lord.

"There," Lord Radcliffe said in response to Bond's earnest question, pointing to his left knee. As Bond knelt and kneaded it gently, the marquess leaned back in the chair. "Damn leg. I fear it shall never be stronger than a babe's."

"Do you wish me to get a powder for the pain?" she asked.

He looked at her, and she nearly recoiled when she saw

the agony in his eyes. "I shall be fine," he said in a clipped tone.

"My lord—"

"Bond, I said I shall be fine!"

Bond's face flushed to the tint of his hair, but he nodded.

Doherty's return with a tray allowed Lisabeth the excuse she needed to escape Lord Radcliffe's gaze. When the butler placed the tray on a table, he backed away with a troubled expression.

Lisabeth poured a glass and took it to Lord Radcliffe. His hands settled over hers as he raised it and took a deep drink. She tried to ignore her astonishment at the warmth flowing from his fingers to hers. Under other circumstances, she would not have allowed such intimacy, but she was unsure if he could hold the glass by himself when his hands shook. Or were her hands the ones shaking?

"How do you fare, my lord?" she asked.

"You worry too much." He sipped again, then lowered the goblet. His eyebrows rose as he smiled and looked down at her fingers beneath his.

Lisabeth drew her hands from the glass's stem. Blast this man! He was hoaxing her even when she was trying to help him. She should have guessed that anyone related, even so distantly, to Frederick would be unbearable. Taking a glass of wine from Bond, she urged him to fill the third goblet.

"Lord Radcliffe is learning his rôle from you, my lady." Bond's eyes twinkled. "Doherty has been kind enough to inform me how Lord Radcliffe's valet should act. I realize now it does not include sharing your wine in your parlor, my lady. If you will excuse me . . ."

Staring after him, Lisabeth was astounded to hear a laugh behind her. She turned to Lord Radcliffe.

"You inspire all of us, my lady, to assume the cloak of respectability that you wear with such elegance." As she sat, he continued, "Your insistence on doing what is proper is having a decidedly civilizing effect on two old soldiers."

"Nonsense! You were raised to this life. You simply scorn its rules."

"True." He reached for the wine and refilled her glass before pouring more into his own. "I find convention as onerous as walking."

Lisabeth smiled. "I collect you shall approach both with the same amount of attention and resolve."

"I have few doubts on that. Your mother-in-law will allow nothing to halt your success. Not only shall she insist that this weak husk, as she delighted in calling me when she thought I could not hear, stand on his feet, but she shall soon have a dozen nubile maidens dangling after him."

"Really, my lord, I find your crude words the greatest challenge to bringing you into Society."

Lord Radcliffe winced as he rubbed his left knee, but the humor did not leave his voice. "Polite conversation is a skill I fear I shall never master."

"Because you have no wish to do so."

"Quite correct again. I find common language more to the purpose than polite words which can be both complimenting and an insult." He laughed. "I vow not to put you to the blush when you entertain your bosom-bows. While I struggle to regain my feet for more than a moment's time, I shall try to learn the pretty talk that will not offend your sweet ears."

"I wish you success in both undertakings."

"I am sure you do." He lifted his glass in her direction. "For, as soon as I succeed, so do you, my lady, and our lives will be separate once more."

Four

The shouts rang through Lisabeth's head. She should have been accustomed to them by now and should have let the hurt slide away. Even though she told herself that in the wake of every episode, each more horrible than the one before, she could not.

"You are no better than a cyprian."

"Frederick—"

He ignored her. He always did when he vented his spleen, and she should have learned to remain silent. It was worse when she tried to countermand him.

As he paced before her, she tried to recall his kind smiles that she had not seen in private since they spoke their vows before a minister. In public, nothing had changed. Here, everything had, taking her dreams of happiness with it. Where was the man who had vowed that he had fallen in love with her the moment he saw her? He looked the same. Soft, blond curls twisted across his head, and his blue eyes could appear as innocuous as a child's. But not now when they burned with fury.

"A common harlot who lets out her forerooms. That is what you are," he snarled. "Why did I ever believe you were a lady worthy of my name?"

His fingers bit into her arms as he jerked her to her feet so fast she stumbled and trod on his toe. His face contorted as he looked daggers at her. She wanted to apologize. She wanted to tell him that stepping on his foot had not been intentional. No words rose from her cramping stomach as his fingers dug even more deeply into her arms. She must not cry out. She must not. The one time she had and Lady Edwina had come asking what was amiss, Frederick had taught her not to be so want-witted again.

"You clumsy, pudding-headed—"

Lisabeth sat up in bed even as her cry of "No!" rang through her head . . . and through the room. Light flooded into the chamber as Wilson rushed to the bed, her cap askew.

"My lady, 'tis all right," she murmured, setting the candle on the table.

Lisabeth lowered her arms from over her head and nodded. "I know 'tis all right." Taking her abigail's hand in hers, she smiled weakly. "Forgive me for waking you."

"You cannot help it, my lady. And you need not concern yourself about waking me." She glanced toward the dressing room door.

Lisabeth drew her knees up to her chest and wrapped her arms around them. If her shout had reached through the thick doors to Lord Radcliffe, surely he would have sent Bond to investigate by now. Mayhap—

At a knock on the door, Wilson rushed to it. She opened the door only wide enough to say, "My lady is fine. Only a nightmare."

"Who was that?" Lisabeth asked as Wilson shut the door.

"The new lass hired last week."

With a sigh, Lisabeth leaned back against her pillows. Thank goodness, it had not been Bond. But had her cries reached through the dressing room to Lord Radcliffe's ears? She hoped not, for there would be perdition to pay on the morrow if her nightmare had wakened the marquess.

* * *

"My lady?"

Lisabeth struggled to smile when she saw Bond coming along the upper corridor. His pixie appearance was accented by his forest green coat. She found herself wondering what Lord Radcliffe might have said about his man wearing the color Lady Edwina adored, then silenced the thought. It was inappropriate.

"Good day, Bond," she said. "You look as if you are enjoying a bang-up style today."

His grin broadened. "I am, and may I say, my lady, that you look well rested?"

"Thank you."

"Your nightmare is past?"

Lisabeth fought not to frown. Had Wilson thought to ease her mind by filling her head with pap? It must have been Bond at the door last night, not a serving lass. Although she wanted to ask if Lord Radcliffe had bid Bond to check on her, she said, "I am sorry—"

He shook his head. "No need to apologize, my lady. The dreams that plague us at night are something we cannot control."

"That is nice of you to say. However, I shall be sure to apologize to Lord Radcliffe as well."

"No need. I believe he slept uninterrupted last night."

Lisabeth wanted to give Bond a hug. His kindness was like a salve on an open wound. Instead, as they walked along the upper corridor toward the stairs, she said, "You seem even more cheerful than customary today."

" 'Tis because I am so pleased to be home in London again."

"Were you born here?"

"Not in a fine neighborhood like Marylebone, my lady, but the scent of the Thames was in my first breath."

"Living at Norton Hall had you traveling far from your birthplace."

"Farther than you could know, my lady. A soldier yearns for home." His smile faltered.

"If you wish to visit someone, I am sure Lord Radcliffe would—"

"I prefer to be here when the major—when the marquess needs me."

"You called him major before. That was his rank?"

"Yes. Does that surprise you?"

"The whole idea of him serving in the army does." She found honesty easier with Bond than with the marquess. "Lord Radcliffe does not seem the type of man to accept orders easily."

"He had the opportunity to buy a higher rank." Bond locked his hands together behind him, straining the buttons on his coat. "He elected to stay where his skills could be put to the best use." His full jowls fell. "Then he was wounded. If he had taken the higher rank, he would not have been in such a precarious situation."

When Bond excused himself, Lisabeth was grateful. She preferred not to think of the horrors the men must have suffered. The war was over, she reminded herself as she had so often during the five days since Lord Radcliffe's arrival. That war and her own private one. Mayhap if she could persuade herself of that, she would not need to suffer from nightmares.

Her smile returned, albeit dimmed, when she realized that although the war with Napoleon might be at an end and she might put her nightmares aside, she still had a battle to wage with Lord Radcliffe. Hearing uneven footfalls from the sitting room, she went down the stairs to the door.

Lord Radcliffe was leaning heavily against the mantel. The deep breaths moving his coat told her that he was pushing himself harder than anyone else could.

"Only had to stop twice this time," he said, looking up.

Lisabeth was surprised, because she had not guessed he

would notice her quiet arrival as he struggled to walk. As he stood straighter, she was even more astounded that his eyes twinkled with the expression she was coming to learn heralded mischief.

"Do come and join me, my lady," he urged. "I have been trying to devise an excuse to stop. May I use the chance to practice pretty talk with you as the very excuse I need?"

Lisabeth sat as he lowered himself to a chair. "You need only stop when you become fatigued, Lord Radcliffe."

"Fatigued I am, but of having to wait upon Bond or some other pitying soul to tend to my needs. I intend to bring that to an end." He massaged his knee. "The pain in my head is decreasing, but it is offset by what this blasted knee foists upon me."

"You are pushing yourself too hard. You do not have to join us at the *soirée* if you wish to remain in your rooms."

He smiled. "Can it be that you have no wish to inflict an invalid on your guests, my lady?"

"I am more concerned about them having to suffer your uncivil wit." She flushed when she realized she was being too forthright.

"Bravo!" He clapped his hands. "So there truly is more to the sparkle in your bright eyes than a mere invitation."

"I've offered no invitation to—"

"Now, now, my lady. You need not come to points on every word I say. I meant my words as a compliment, although you would rather take them as an aspersion. Why, may I ask? Have I done anything—other than presenting myself on your doorstep and causing you as much pain as this blasted knee is causing me—to warrant such a baleful glower?"

Lisabeth had no answer. Allowing Lord Radcliffe to stay here had been a mistake. She should have owned to that from the beginning, and she could have been done with the uncomfortable arrangement in a trice.

"So quiet?" continued Lord Radcliffe. " 'Tis not like you."

"How can you know what is or is not like me, my lord?" she fired back. "You have asked me nothing to get to know me."

"I have asked you several questions."

"Impertinent ones that you knew I would not answer."

"How can I know what you may or may not answer if I do not know you?"

"Each time we have spoken, you have wasted no time trying to stir the coals, and I shall not allow that today. My household was peaceful until you decided to ride rough-shod through it."

"Bah, your household was boring." Resting his elbow on the arm of his chair, he leaned toward her. "Have you always been so pretty-behaved, Cousin Lisabeth?"

Her eyes widened. "My lord, may I remind you that you are not in an army mess? A gentleman waits for a lady to give him permission to address her so intimately."

"Intimate." He chuckled. "You have a way of turning the conversation to topics that I would guess are quite forbidden to a lady in a gentleman's company. Or, mayhap, you do not see me as a gentleman." When she did not answer, he added, "Cousin Norton warned you that I have no manners. Isn't etiquette what you are supposed to teach me?"

"Hold your jaw!"

"Now, is that what a lady should say?" Radcliffe had wondered how much hoaxing she would endure before she gave him the dressing-down he deserved. For the past five days, he had tried to discover even a hint of what Lisabeth might be like behind her cool poise.

Norton had not been reticent about his opinions of his cousin's widow. Mayhap his warnings about her temper and habits that had driven her husband to distraction and beyond had been honest. Radcliffe could not guess, for he knew little more about Lisabeth than he had when he arrived. Curious why Bond had suggested he might want to treat Lisabeth gently today, he tried to guess what his man had seen that he had not.

"How can I teach you how to behave in decent society," she asked, "when you seem determined to be intolerable? More than determined, for you appear to delight in your lack of niceties."

"But I do wish to learn." He smiled and arched his brows devilishly.

"Then, you should talk less and listen more." Her eyes snapped with blue fire, but he noticed, for the first time, a shadow of fatigue around them.

He nodded.

"Nothing to say?" she asked when he remained silent.

"You told me to say less."

When she smiled, he knew he would be a widgeon not to give her as many opportunities as possible to smile again. A softness eased her face, teasing him to find out if its skin was as delicate as her ineffable warmth.

"You must understand," she said quietly, "that a lady wishes to be addressed without intimacy unless she grants you the freedom to use her given name."

"I understand that most basic of rules. You may be assured that I shall refrain from putting you to the blush by treating your guests informally. However, we are family."

"Not quite."

"Enough so you may welcome me under your roof."

"Yes." Hearing her reluctant admission in that single word, he ignored the chuckle teasing him. Surely there was more to Lisabeth Montague than this prim creature or the harpy Norton had described. He wanted to peel away the prim layers to learn what Lisabeth truly thought. "As we are family, I shall call you Lisabeth as dear cousins should, and you shall call me—"

"My lord."

He shook his head. "Not acceptable. I doubt if I can

convince you to call me anything as potentially damaging to your canons of propriety as Tristan, so shall we compromise? You must call me Radcliffe."

"But, my—"

"No more addressing me as my lord. You are my teacher, Lisabeth, and my teachers have always called me Radcliffe, except for my governess who called me by a ridiculous pet name which I shall never repeat. How can you disagree when you see how convenient it shall be?"

"Convenience is not what I concern myself with."

"Ah, that dreadful bane of propriety is overshadowing our conversation again."

Lisabeth did not want to smile, but her lips twitched. This man exulted in his crude ways, but he was so amusing that she could not help relishing this conversation. "You choose the oddest words. I have never considered propriety a bane, Radcliffe."

"See how easy it is to use my name?" He leaned back in his chair. "Mayhap we are not so different. Be honest. Aren't there times when you wish that you could shun what is demanded of you?"

"You ask the most peculiar questions."

"Mayhap you would prefer me to answer some instead."

Laughing, she said, "That might be an inspired idea. You could tell me what attributes you seek in a wife."

"Attributes?" He pyramided his fingers. His forefingers tapped as his brow threaded with thought. "What a base word for what is supposed to be such a sublime pursuit. I had no idea that I could select my future wife's virtues before I chanced to meet any of the young women who, you assure me, will be eager to have me set my cap on them."

"I may not be able to find the paragon you might choose."

His voice became sober. "Pray do not find me a paragon, Cousin Lisabeth. Nor do I have any wish to be shackled to a bluestocking or a virago." Although his eyes began to twinkle again, Lisabeth was astounded when he added, "Shall I say I wish to pay court on a pretty blonde with a sharp tongue and a delightfully eccentric mother-in-law in tow?"

"That is a very specific request."

"You know no one of that type?"

"No one who is interested in marriage."

He laughed. "Then, I shall have to settle for my second choice."

"Which is?"

"Why don't I explain in more congenial surroundings?"

"More congenial?" She glanced around the comfortable room. "Do you find something amiss with this room?"

"It is simply a prettier prison than the ones I have known at Norton Hall. I wish to savor some of the fresh air I tasted on the journey here."

Coming to her feet, she said, "I can throw open a window."

"That will offer only a tantalizing hint when I wish a full feast." He sat straighter. "I have just the dandy, Lisabeth. We must go for a ride."

"A ride?"

"Surely you do not hide within these four walls every day. Come, cousin, and show me a bit of London. 'Tis been too many years since I have had a chance to tour this city."

"I can ring for—"

His voice was soft. "Lisabeth, I would enjoy having *you* show me the city." His laughter returned. "So many times I have heard that enjoying a ride is one of the favored hobbies of the *ton*. How can I be one of *Le Beau Monde* if I do not acquire such a habit?"

"There are arrangements to be made for the dinner party later this week—"

"Which Mrs. Outhwaite can handle. A ride shall steal but a few hours of your afternoon, and think of it! You can use the time to rehearse me in the manners I shall need for your *soirée*." He strained as he pushed himself to his feet, but offered his arm. "Come, Lisabeth. You know you cannot resist this opportunity to drill me in my lessons."

Lisabeth disdained his arm. When his eyes narrowed, she knew she had been cockle-brained. Whether he thought she had ignored him because she feared he was not strong enough or because she found the idea of his touch distasteful, this proud man would be equally insulted.

"Very well, Radcliffe. We shall go, but only on the condition that you use the time to learn what you must."

He put his hand over his heart. "I shall be the best student you have, *chère cousine*."

"You are my sole student."

With a chuckle, he said, "Exactly."

Lisabeth's expectations that the ride would be a disaster seemed to be confirmed when Radcliffe insisted on taking the reins of the gig.

"My legs may not be working well, but my arms are strong enough to steer us through London traffic," he insisted when she met him in front of the house.

She had not wanted to have a brangle on the street, so she had allowed Bond to hand her into the carriage. When he did not follow her in, but jumped back as Radcliffe snapped the reins, she gasped, "We should not be riding alone."

"Why not? We are family, and you are a dowager. As I seem to recall, that unenviable state does have one benefit. You need not have a duenna lurking about you every second."

She hated to own that he was right. His relationship as her late husband's cousin's cousin should prevent the gabblemongers from wagging their tongues. "You seem to have an amazing ability to remember Town rules when they are to your benefit."

He flashed her a smile that was more brilliant than the sunshine on this crisp day. "I had not guessed you would ever use the word amazing to describe me."

"Do not get top-lofty when it was not meant as a compliment."

"But I have taken it as one." He chuckled. "And I shall not allow you to retract it."

Lisabeth was not sure how to reply. She never could guess what he might say or if he was hoaxing her. In his time here in London, all she had learned about Radcliffe came from Bond, who had vouched for him. Mayhap Radcliffe was a man of more substance than he wished her to perceive. She wondered why he was hiding that part of himself behind his sharp words.

As they followed the road edging the north side of Hyde Park, Radcliffe was surprisingly attentive as he listened to her long explanation of how to greet guests. When he asked questions, she realized he was not simply humoring her. He seemed quite honest in his interest.

She hoped he would be as cooperative at the dinner party. Shame filled her. Although Radcliffe might tease her, she had no reason to doubt his assertion that he would not do anything to embarrass her.

When she paused, he soon had her laughing as he aped Bond's complaints about *his* lessons with Doherty. "I thought it would be simpler for Bond," he said with a chuckle. "He is used to the formality of the army."

"But you were in the army as well."

He stretched his arm across the back of the seat, but did not touch her. "It may not astound you to learn that

I was as resilient to those constraints of protocol as I am to yours."

"You have been very attentive." She tried to disregard his arm behind her, but it was no easier than ignoring the day's sunshine. And it offered the same sort of blistering heat, although not so much as when his cuff brushed her. Glad for her bonnet which hid her face, she turned the subject to what he could expect at the upcoming *soirée*.

Radcliffe listened for a moment in silence, then asked, "Who is this chap Smythe? You have mentioned his name several times in an unfavorable tone."

"Mr. Smythe is a friend of long acquaintance." Lisabeth risked a glance at Radcliffe's smile. A mistake, she discovered, when his gaze held hers. "It would be unheard of not to invite him."

"Even if you loathe him?"

"I do not loathe him." She looked back at the road, so she was not tempted to speak the truth. She had learned what loathing was, and she did not feel that for Cyril Smythe. Forcing a smile, she said, "Let's just say that I find his company something I do not wish to enjoy on a regular basis."

"As you do with mine."

Lisabeth kept her voice serene. "I am very sorry if I let you think that I find your company unwelcome. You must think me a poor hostess."

"On the contrary, when I think of you, *chère cousine*, my thoughts never center on your skills as a hostess. *Those* skills I have grown quite familiar with."

She started to smile, then realized his words were not a compliment—or rather, not a compliment a gentleman should offer to a lady. Keeping her shoulders back as she fought her fury, she gasped when they grazed his arm. How had she been bamboozled into accepting this chore? She had not *accepted* it; it had been thrust upon her. Mayhap, even now, Norton Radcliffe was enjoying his joke on her. She should have known better than to think he trusted her when she had discerned the cost of trusting anyone in his family.

"And as a gentle and generous hostess," Radcliffe was continuing as if she had not reacted to his words, "I know that you shall grant your guest a simple request."

"What?"

He laughed. "So suspicious, Lisabeth? How can that be when I wish only to prolong our pleasant drive?"

Although she wanted to retort that the ride was no longer enjoyable, she asked, "What do you suggest?"

"A short journey."

"To?"

He lowered his voice to a whisper so she had to slant toward him to hear. "To Vauxhall Gardens, *chère cousine.*"

Lisabeth gasped when she discovered how close his face was to hers. Moving back, she said, "Vauxhall Gardens is on the far side of the river."

"We are only a short distance from the Thames. Why not pay a visit when the sky is blue and I can enjoy your charming company?"

"My—Radcliffe," she corrected herself when she saw his abrupt frown, "I understand that Vauxhall Gardens is most delightful after dark when the lamps are bright and there is music for . . ."

"Dancing. You can say the word." His hand curved around her shoulder, tilting her toward him. "Do you always watch yourself so carefully? I promise you that your gentle speech will not cause me more injury."

"I know how you hate your situation."

Radcliffe smiled. "How insightful of you! I thought you were speaking polite tripe when I arrived, but you sense others' pain as you try to hide your own."

"My own?" Lisabeth regarded him with a bafflement

she hoped would appear unfeigned. "You are confusing me."

"And you are being less than honest now." He chuckled again. "Say nothing when you are about to chide me for my impertinence. See, Lisabeth? You are not the only one with intuition. I have seen how you have hoaxed everyone into thinking you are leaving your mourning behind gratefully."

"What an outrageous thing to say!"

"Is it any more outrageous than the fact that you are gratified to be done with mourning because you never had anyone you wished to mourn."

He was too insightful. She should have been forewarned when Bond spoke of how Radcliffe had chosen a lower rank so he might be most effective during his sojourn in the army. Radcliffe understood himself quite well, and now he was trying to understand her. She must be doubly cautious. No one else had suspected—or acted as if they suspected—the truth of what her marriage had been like.

"You should not say such a thing," she said, although she wanted to agree with him.

"Why not? How could you mourn your late husband? After all, he was a cousin of Norton Radcliffe."

"You also are Norton's cousin."

"Which should prove my point. We are a devilishly obstinate lot who think only of our own desires."

She stiffened her shoulders so she did not flinch. He was right again. What a beef-head she was being! She should put an end to this ride with Radcliffe and make sure there was no chance they could be alone like this again.

"And, today, I desire to see Vauxhall Gardens," he went on.

"I think we should—"

"Get started on our ride there." He smiled at her as he

turned the carriage toward the Thames. " 'Tis your only choice, Lisabeth."

"I could scream."

"But you won't. That would be behavior beneath contempt for Lady Montague, wouldn't it?"

"You are twisting etiquette to your own ends again."

He winked at her. "And I shall continue to do so."

Lisabeth said nothing as Radcliffe slowed the carriage before the high wall at the front of Vauxhall Gardens. Although she had considered continuing the argument with Radcliffe, she had acquiesced.

She waited for Radcliffe to say something. He simply stared at the entrance to the Gardens. Could he see more than she could through the doors which were being opened in preparation for the evening's entertainments? She could not see any of the colonnade or the Grand Walk, only shadows within the entrance. The scratchy sound of instruments being tuned and other preparations for the night's entertainments drifted on the breeze.

The silence became uncomfortable. Was he waiting for her to say something? But what? Taking a deep breath, she asked, "Did you want to see something within the Gardens?"

"I doubt if I could walk to where I wished to go." He did not look at her.

"Where is that?"

"One of the pavilions. The one decorated with fairies enjoying a dance in the light of the moon. Are you familiar with it?"

"I have never been within Vauxhall Gardens."

Radcliffe faced her, astonishment widening his eyes. "Never?"

"No."

He frowned. "Mayhap I misunderstood, but I am certain

I recall Norton mentioning that Frederick frequented Vauxhall Gardens."

"Frederick did."

When she added nothing else, he turned back to look at the entrance. She closed her eyes. Thank goodness, he had not quizzed her, because she was unsure what out-and-outers she might have told him. Even now, she resisted speaking the truth of how, during their marriage, Frederick had sought his entertainment elsewhere even as he accused her of doing the same.

Radcliffe spoke, and she stared at him in astonishment. "My parents were introduced here. In the pavilion with the dancing fairies." He sighed. "Mayhap the evening will come when I can visit it amid the thousands of lanterns they described." Facing her, he smiled sadly. "You appear taken aback, *chère cousine.*"

"You have not been sentimental before."

"Do not judge a man when you have known him so few days."

"I never meant—"

He put his arm on the back of the seat again, but she did not pull back. As she gazed at the honesty on his face, she knew Bond had been correct. Tristan Radcliffe was more than the jester he played so well.

She was even more sure of that when he said, "While a man is far from his homeland, memory becomes more precious, for it is his lone comfort amid the insanity of war. Every man who served with me dreamed of a return to the life he had known."

"And a hero's welcome?"

"Merely the welcome of home and hearth." He sighed. "And I have been denied both by a well-meaning family."

"Radcliffe, if you wish to return to your estate . . ."

"As Norton is fond of saying, Cliffs' End needs an able and competent master, and, at the moment, I am neither.

But I shall be, Lisabeth, even if I have to shackle myself to an efficient wife to be so."

"Is that why you agreed to this?"

His laugh was cold. "Can you think of any other reason I would submit myself to this ludicrous exercise?"

Five

Bond was pacing in the foyer when Doherty came down the stairs. The butler frowned. Bond knew better than to linger here.

"Is something amiss?" Doherty asked.

" 'Tis Lord Radcliffe. He left the house more than three hours ago."

"Alone?"

"Of course not. Lady Lisabeth—"

Doherty gasped, "They went out alone?"

"Of course not," Bond repeated. "They were in the same carriage."

"Alone?" Doherty shook his head. "That is most disturbing."

"Don't you trust Lady Lisabeth?"

Drawing himself up, Doherty said, "Without a doubt."

"Then, you must not trust Lord Radcliffe."

" 'Tis not a matter of trust. 'Tis a matter of how others will perceive this. If—"

Carriage wheels slowed in front of the house. Doherty rushed to peer out the window. Throwing open the door, he had barely enough time to jump out of the way before Bond rushed out onto the walkway.

Bond leaped down the steps. "My lord, where have you been?"

"Bond, you have arrived exactly on time—as always, I

should say," the marquess said with a smile. "Lisabeth is anxious to deal with the fripperies a lady must involve herself with in preparing her household for an upcoming dinner party."

"My lord, 'tis time for your rest."

"Bah! Napping is for babes and old women." He looked at Lisabeth. With a smile, he caught her hand in his. "Come, cousin, and help this old soldier to the ground."

Lisabeth slid her hand out of his, surprised that she could. Then she realized his powerful demeanor had overmastered her, making her forget it had regained its strength more quickly than his body. "I shall leave you to Bond's first-rate care," she said, as Bond handed her out.

She was careful not to look back as she climbed the steps to her foyer. She did not want to see how much Radcliffe depended on Bond.

Handing her bonnet to Doherty, she said, "Thank you. Is Lady Edwina—"

"Lisabeth!"

"Ah, I think I hear her." She looked at the stairs. Gathering her skirts, she hurried up. A summons in that tone was a signal to toss aside decorum.

Lady Edwina motioned for Lisabeth to follow her into her private chambers. With a flourish of her emerald green silk wrapper, the older woman sat. "Where have you been?"

"Radcliffe—"

"*That* is how you address him?"

"Yes. He wished for some fresh air, so we went for a drive." She decided it would be best to say only that. If her mother-in-law discovered where they had gone, this discussion would take on an even sterner tone.

With a sigh, Lady Edwina said, "I would suggest you say nothing of that when you next see Lieutenant Ison. He was not pleased to find you not at home when he called an hour ago."

"He called?"

"To let you know that he is eagerly anticipating your *soirée.*"

"I will be sure to express my regrets when he returns for the gathering."

"He was," Lady Edwina said, looking down at her hands, "very interested in the fact that Lord Radcliffe was your guest."

"How did he know?"

"I suppose I must have mentioned it."

Lisabeth was tempted to roll her eyes in dismay. Wasn't her life complicated enough with Radcliffe in it? She did not need Lady Edwina stirring the waters when they were already muddied enough.

"Lisabeth," Lady Edwina continued, "I wish to hear your decision about the situation with Lord Radcliffe. There have been questions from my friends, and I must be aware of your plans."

"My plans have not changed."

"So you will let him stay here?"

"I cannot ask him to remove himself. What would our friends think?"

"That you were aware that his presence might inhibit gentlemen from calling upon you." Lady Edwina pursed her lips in disapproval. "Lisabeth, you are young and as beautiful as the day Frederick brought you home as his bride. You need not waste your youth tending to Lord Radcliffe."

"I shall not."

"Why not ask Lord Radcliffe to hire himself suitable lodgings elsewhere? If he is interested in learning the ways of Society, then you could call, properly chaperoned, of course, which would be more to the purpose."

"I have promised—"

"A mistaken thing foisted upon you by that bird-wit Norton. Lisabeth, this can ruin you in other men's eyes and put you permanently on the shelf."

Rising, Lisabeth said, "I pledge to you, Lady Edwina, that Radcliffe will do nothing to destroy my chances for another marriage."

"Can you be certain of that?"

"Yes, most certain."

When her mother-in-law smiled, Lisabeth ignored the guilt taunting her. She had not been false, because Radcliffe's intrusion would not alter her plans for remarriage, for she had none . . . and she wanted none.

"How many times is that?" Radcliffe asked as he watched Lisabeth rush past the doorway of the grand parlor where this evening's guests were to gather.

"An even dozen." Bond stood with his hands clasped behind his back.

"She shall most certainly wear herself out before the first guest arrives."

"I believe she is enjoying herself."

Radcliffe smiled, but did not answer. He doubted if Lisabeth was finding the last-minute preparations entertaining. Instead, he suspected she was letting them consume her so that she need not come into this room where he sat propped like an ancient relative who must be included in the evening's festivities.

His smile became a frown. Blast it! He had intended to be able to walk about the room by the time this *soirée* was under way. Sitting like a lump was not how he had planned to spend this evening.

Pushing himself to his feet, he ignored Bond's extended hands. He did not need Bond's help to stand any longer. And he would be damned to perdition before he spent the evening being the object of unwanted pity. His hand clenched on the back of his chair as Norton's voice rang through his head, warning that Radcliffe might want to rethink his decision to go to Town *now*.

"Wait a few more months," Norton had suggested.

Radcliffe did not recall his exact response, but he doubted if he could repeat it in Lisabeth's hearing. After whining at him for more than two months to do his duty and give his title an heir, Norton had done an about-face as soon as Radcliffe elected to visit London.

"You shall tire yourself out before the guests arrive," Lisabeth said as she entered the sitting room.

"I doubt if the mere act of standing in one place will undo me." His smile returned as he admired the sight of her in pearl-colored silk. Mother-of-pearl, he realized, when the gown shimmered with each motion. Blond curls cascaded along her neck from where her hair had been swept up on her head, drawing his eyes to a single strand of pearls about her throat. His gaze did not linger there, but edged down along her curves that were wrapped so perfectly in this creamy confection. Sensations he had feared were no longer possible surged through him as he imagined unwrapping this pretty package and warming away her *sang-froid*.

His hand was on her arm, halting her from scurrying past him, before he had time to stop it. When she looked at him, her lips parted with a gasp of surprise, his fingers slid up her soft skin to cup her elbow. The temptation to taste those lips was too much to be ignored, and he watched her eyes widen as he bent toward her. He released the chair, intending to put his arm around her shoulders and gather her closer.

Her choked moan struck him viciously as she yanked herself out of his arms and cowered. Staring, for he could not believe what his own eyes were showing him, he put his hand out to still the trembling he could see.

"Lisabeth," he whispered, "if I have done anything—"

"I must return to the preparations," she answered in a brittle voice. "Excuse me."

"Lisabeth . . ." He cursed as she rushed out of the room like a frightened child.

Bond cleared his throat, reminding Radcliffe that he was still in the room. "My lord," he said quietly, "I think you overmastered her."

"I think you are developing an irritating habit of not speaking plainly." He gripped the chair and pushed himself away from it. Wanting to snarl at his left leg that refused to support him, he leaned on the molding around the door.

"My lord," Bond said, following him, "if you wish me to speak plainly, I would say that your attentions quite terrified her."

"But why? She is not a maiden who has never been admired by the gentlemen. She is a dowager, and I did not step over the boundaries of her strict submission to protocol." He shook his head. "This makes no sense. I don't understand it."

"Neither do I."

"But," Radcliffe said, fisting his hand on the molding, "I intend to."

Lisabeth stood by the door and welcomed her guests. She was certain her smile had bamblusterated all of them until Hamlin Ison arrived. The lieutenant, who wore an immaculate black coat over his waistcoat that was striped with blue, looked like a Viking with his broad shoulders and sun-bleached hair. When he smiled, the corners of his bushy mustache tilted.

After greeting her, he asked, "Is something amiss, Lady Montague? I noticed how you keep glancing toward your parlor. Is there something I might do for you?"

"Of course not." She let him bow over her hand, but

drew it back before he could kiss it. "I fear that I am as anxious as a girl being fired-off that this evening will go well."

"I am certain, with you as our gracious hostess, that it will progress smoothly."

"I hope you are right," she added under her breath as she watched him greet Lady Edwina.

She had made an utter twit of herself earlier. Reacting to Radcliffe that way was sure to create questions in his fertile mind that she did not want to answer. How could she have been so want-witted? She could not let her mind linger on that now. She must concentrate on her duties as hostess.

A more sincere smile tilted her lips. Those duties would give her the very best excuse of how to avoid Radcliffe this evening. She was supposed to be searching for a prospective wife for him.

Appraising her guests as she welcomed them, Lisabeth decided, in quick order, that Miss Delia Gibbs would be an apt dinner partner for Radcliffe. Miss Gibbs was escorted tonight by her brother, so Lisabeth could easily arrange for Miss Gibbs to sit with Radcliffe during dinner.

Miss Gibbs was enjoying her second Season, having seen her older sister married well the previous year. With hair as black as Radcliffe's, she was considered handsome. Miss Gibbs would not be tangle-tongued in his presence, for she was a renowned prattle-box.

"Of course I would be delighted to meet your marquess," Miss Gibbs gushed, clearly not noticing how Lisabeth flinched at the words *your marquess*. "All the world and its brother have been abuzz with curiosity about your guest."

"Then, why don't I have Lady Edwina introduce you to him?" She smiled at her mother-in-law.

Lady Edwina shook her head which was topped by a

bright green feather. "I see some friends arriving, so, Lisabeth, why don't you introduce Miss Gibbs to him?"

Wanting to be honest with her mother-in-law, but unable to be, for she had no idea how to explain without revealing her shameful secrets, she nodded. "This way, Miss Gibbs."

Lisabeth's anxiety was unfounded. Curiosity about him focused the conversation around where Radcliffe stood, his hand resting in a nonchalant pose on the chair, so she would be able to offer a quick introduction to Miss Gibbs and leave before his gaze caught hers. When her guests learned he was titled, well-juiced, and seeking a wife, one unmarried woman after another drifted toward him.

"Now, that is an interesting duo," said Lady Edwina as she came into the parlor.

"Who?" asked Lisabeth.

"Lord Radcliffe and Lady Prospera Fry." Lady Edwina tapped her chin with her finger, which was topped with her favorite emerald ring. "Do you think even a marquess has enough money to settle *her* gambling debts?"

Lisabeth almost chuckled at her mother-in-law's baleful tone. Lady Edwina had developed a deep dislike for the attractive widow who had bested her at too many games of cards.

Radcliffe and Prospera? No, that would not do. He needed a wife who would be his partner in running Cliffs' End, which had been too long ignored. Prospera would be loath to leave London and its whirl.

Crossing the room, Lisabeth collected Miss Gibbs and her brother from where they were talking with Mrs. Castleman. She had promised to help him find a wife, and she would not renege on her promise, even if doing so brought her back into the conversation whirling about him. As she led them to where Radcliffe was holding court, she could see no reason to complain about her charge. His waistcoat and breeches were pristine white. His navy coat had a collar that rose with stylish height along his jaw. With his black hair brushed from its typical disarray, the sharp line of his jet brows accented his response to every comment.

But, she noticed, his smile was as strained as her own. She would bring Miss Gibbs back to Radcliffe's attention and make her excuses to tend to other matters.

"And here is our hostess," he said.

Lisabeth resisted recoiling from the barely restrained fury in his eyes. He must have taken insult at her reaction before. He need not, because her instinctive motion had developed long before she had met him. Again she longed to explain. Again she could not speak of that shame.

Turning to Prospera, she said, "I am sorry I was delayed so that I could not introduce you to Lord Radcliffe."

The tall brunette patted Radcliffe's arm. "No need. His family and mine have a friendship of long standing. We were chatting about his cousin Norton."

Mayhap that explained Radcliffe's sour expression, for she had come to guess that his and his cousin's time together had not congenial. "Forgive me for intruding, but Mr. Hinkle asked if I would convey that he wishes the pleasure of your company, Prospera."

"Does he?" She ran a fingertip along her chin. "If you will excuse me . . ." She hurried away.

Miss Gibbs chuckled. "She is quite transparent, isn't she?"

"Is she?" asked Radcliffe.

Instead of explaining how Prospera and Mr. Hinkle shared a love of playing cards for high stakes, Lisabeth took Miss Gibbs's hand and drew her forward. "This is Miss Delia Gibbs, Radcliffe. Miss Gibbs, my late husband's cousin's cousin, Lord Radcliffe." She resisted urging Radcliffe to be gracious as she quickly introduced Miss Gibbs's brother.

Her anxiety was for naught, because Radcliffe's smile, as he bowed his head to Miss Gibbs, was amiable. "A pleasure to meet you, Miss Gibbs, and you, Gibbs. I trust you are enjoying the Season."

"Yes, my lord, although I found it pleasurable last year to have my sister at my side. Now that she is successfully wed, I have come to depend on my brother Galen to escort me."

"I am sure that condition shall not be long in duration." His scintillating smile brought an answering one from Miss Gibbs. "Could I importune you and your brother to sit with me and Lisabeth?"

Before either Gibbs could answer, Lisabeth said, "I fear my duties as your hostess do not allow me the luxury of enjoying your company now."

"Fiddle!" Radcliffe took her hand and seated her next to him on a low settee. Smiling at Miss Gibbs, who selected a chair, he said in a conspiratorial whisper, "Lisabeth has been quite beside herself with concern about this evening. She wishes to make my coming-out a memorable one."

"I am sure it will be so, my lord," answered Mr. Gibbs. A sallow edition of his sister, he rarely spoke louder than a mumble.

"Lady Montague," his sister added, "is having a sort of coming-out as well, for she set aside Society to mourn her husband. How wonderful that dark period of your life is over, my lady! Just last week, Miss Castleman and I were saying that we couldn't wait for your party. 'No one is as gracious as Lady Frederick Montague.' Those were my exact words. I am sure that—"

"Lisabeth is a wonderful hostess." Radcliffe's smile broadened, but she noticed his eyes had not warmed. "That is the reason our mutual cousin requested that she oversee my education and introduction to Society."

Miss Gibbs giggled. "Lady Montague is overseeing your *education*, my lord? I would have guessed you to be out of the schoolroom."

"Learning continues every day. Why, earlier this week,

Lisabeth taught me how to exchange pretty talk with ladies like you. Although I must own, Miss Gibbs, that it would be difficult to be anything but complimentary to you."

Lisabeth struggled to keep from frowning. As she listened to Radcliffe lather Miss Gibbs with flattery, she sensed his words were intended to have a double meaning. She wondered if anyone else was aware of it. Why should they be aware of the words he used like a honed sword? Each one pricked her, reminding her of the horrified expression he had worn when she rushed out of this room earlier.

She was rescued when Doherty whispered in her ear. Standing, she said, "Excuse me." She walked away with her butler before Radcliffe could ensnare her in his gaze again.

Taking a deep breath, Lisabeth held her hand out to the man entering the foyer. She girded herself not to flinch when the rotund man bowed over her fingers. "Mr. Smythe, I was beginning to fear you had decided to forego our fête." Only in her mind did she alter *beginning to fear* to *hoping*.

"Do you think that I would miss this chance to extend my apologies for sending that out-of-hand note?" He reached for her hand again, but she deftly avoided his pudgy fingers. A frown flitted across his lips. "Do I take this to mean that you are distressed, my lady? It was my intention to express my admiration, nothing else."

Lisabeth sighed. Arguing with Mr. Smythe was something she did not want to do. To own the truth, she had forgotten all about his ill-thought-out note. "I am not still distressed with you, but you must forgive me for rushing away. I must see to the needs of my guests."

"Will you join us for whist later?" When she hesitated, he hastened to add, "I spoke with Lady Montague today at the Park, and she assured me your guests would be playing. I trust I can count on you to join us."

"I shall see." She hated playing cards. Once, she had enjoyed the games and the conversation, but that had changed when she discovered how Frederick disliked losing to her or anyone else.

Arranging for Mr. Gibbs to be her escort into dinner might have only worsened any chances that Lisabeth would enjoy this evening. Mr. Gibbs followed her, seldom speaking, like a duckling after its mother.

She tried to be kind to him, for she suspected he was denied the chance to say much at home. As the evening wore on at an intolerably slow pace, she began to wonder if Miss Gibbs had become a prattle-box because she wanted—as Lisabeth did—to fill the silence left by her laconic brother.

When the clock chimed midnight, Lisabeth led the way across the hall to the dining room. Mrs. Outhwaite, with her usual skill, had the table sparkling with the best china, crystal, and silver. Fresh flowers created rainbows along the white tablecloth. The colors were accented by ribbons tied to the candelabra on the long table and the sideboard.

As her guests sought their places, Mr. Gibbs offered his arm, and she put her fingers on it. He escorted her to the head of the table. A spasm of dismay caught in her center, for Radcliffe was sitting in the chair on her right where Mr. Gibbs, as her escort, should sit. Wanting to believe he and Bond, who must have helped him, had selected the wrong chair out of ignorance, she started to turn to Mr. Gibbs to explain the situation.

She halted when Radcliffe's eyes flashed a challenge. Instantly she knew he had not chosen that chair by mistake. His skill with conversation during the evening confirmed that he knew well the parameters of Society. He knew as well that if she asked him to move, she risked making a May game of him in front of prospective brides.

Her lips tightened. He had no misgivings about putting her to the blush.

Hoping her guests had not noticed her hesitation, she wrenched her gaze from his. She smiled at Miss Gibbs, who was standing, uncertain, by the table. "Do come and sit with us. I am sure Lord Radcliffe would be pleased to hear of your sojourn to Bath with your great-uncle."

He aimed a furious glower at her, but Lisabeth ignored it as Miss Gibbs sat on his right while Mr. Gibbs seated Lisabeth, then took his chair on her left. Another pulse of dismay sliced her as she noted that Lieutenant Ison was not amid those at the table, but she nodded in understanding when Doherty handed her a note. A quick glance at it was enough. The lieutenant was making his excuses because he had to return to duty in garrison.

Wishing he could have taken her with him, Lisabeth silenced the untoward thought. She had looked forward to this evening for the past year, so she would enjoy it.

If it was possible.

Six

Lady Edwina smiled as she surveyed the dining room as Mr. Smythe seated her between him and Mr. Gibbs. Glancing along the table, she listened to the light chatter. Lisabeth's first party was a rare success, and that was not only because her daughter-in-law's friends were happy to see Lisabeth out of mourning. Mayhap Lisabeth had been wise not to ask Lord Radcliffe to leave, for he intrigued her guests.

Her eyes narrowed as she stole a surreptitious look toward Lisabeth and the marquess. Miss Gibbs was prattling, and her brother was as silent as a sealed tomb. That was to be expected. What was unexpected was how Lisabeth seemed to be enthralled with each word pouring from Miss Gibbs's lips.

Lady Edwina vowed to speak to Lisabeth at the very first opportunity she had to get her alone. No one, most especially Lord Radcliffe, who seemed to miss nothing, would fail to note how obvious Lisabeth was in her attempts to appear as if the marquess's outrageous behavior at choosing a chair next to hers did not unsettle her. Such actions on both of their parts were sure to catch the attention of the *ton*, and then Lisabeth would find her task of obtaining the proper arrangements for both her and the marquess even more formidable.

"You seem lost in thought this evening, Lady Montague," said a rumbling voice.

She turned her gaze to Mr. Smythe and nodded. "I am, and, if I may, I would like to share one of them with you."

Mr. Smythe's round face broadened with a smile. "You know I always am intrigued by your opinions, my lady."

"You may not be by this one, for I share Lisabeth's dismay that you sent that ridiculous missive to her. You should have known better than to try to coerce her in that manner."

"I know now." He worried his napkin before draping it across his lap. "However, I wished to let her know my devotion."

"Before the lieutenant could?"

Mr. Smythe colored as he lowered his voice. "Ison has been lurking about her like a beast about to leap on its prey."

"You are concerning yourself needlessly. Lisabeth is determined to test her freedom before she chooses another husband. Have patience, Mr. Smythe."

"My note to her offered only friendship."

"You should be commended, but Lisabeth needs time now to decide what she should do."

"Excellent advice, but . . ."

"Speak your mind, Mr. Smythe."

She watched his gaze edge toward Lisabeth and the others at the end of the table. "May I speak it directly?"

"I would hope you always would elect to be truthful with me."

"It was a mistaken thing to invite the marquess to stay with you."

Lady Edwina nodded, not surprised at the turn in the conversation. She had seen how Mr. Smythe had fired daggered glares at Lord Radcliffe throughout the evening, especially when Lisabeth was speaking with the marquess. "We did not *invite* him, you should understand."

"Then, why——?"

"He is of Frederick's cousin's family. You know how gentle-hearted Lisabeth is. She would not turn a leper from the door."

Mr. Smythe's mouth remained tight. "He seems determined to monopolize her time."

Chuckling, Lady Edwina said, "You are letting your jealousy blind you, Mr. Smythe, for my ears quite clearly hear Miss Gibbs filling the conversation with her bibble-babble." She patted his hand, then moved aside as the soup was served. "The evening is not yet over. Let us watch how it unwinds while we enjoy the king's books."

"Cards?" Mr. Smythe perked up like a young bird hearing its parent arriving with food. His smile returned. "I had forgotten you would offer such entertainment tonight. You are much the gamester, Lady Montague. I hope we may be partnered."

Lady Edwina smiled, knowing that she would enjoy this evening more than she had anticipated. "You are very kind to think of my pleasure when I know you would rather spend time with Lisabeth."

"That might be arranged. Mayhap your daughter-in-law will join us at the table."

"Lisabeth usually makes herself absent when cards are played."

"If I might be so bold as to venture a comment," he answered, "cards were much favored by the late Lord Montague. The association may bring her pain."

Lady Edwina looked at Lisabeth, who wore a stilted smile. Miss Gibbs must be even more long-winded tonight than usual. Lady Edwina sighed. For the past year, Lisabeth had not revealed that much emotion. She had been kind and attentive to her mother-in-law. She had spoken as kindly to her friends when they chanced to meet about Town. She had tended to the matters of this household, but she had closed herself up as completely as she had the room she once had shared with Frederick.

Watching Lisabeth's eyes soften when Lord Radcliffe turned to smile at her and say something too low to be heard along the table, Lady Edwina was not sure whether to smile or frown. Lord Radcliffe was invoking those sentiments Lady Edwina had feared Lisabeth had buried along with Frederick.

"She seems to fancy his company," Mr. Smythe muttered, warning Lady Edwina that he still was wallowing in resentment at Lord Radcliffe's conversation with Lisabeth.

"She is his hostess."

"Mayhap he would wish her to be more."

Lady Edwina motioned with her spoon. "Do eat your soup before it grows cold, Mr. Smythe, and, while you do, consider this question: Do you think I will allow my daughter-in-law to buckle herself to a man who is as lame as Cripplegate?"

He smiled. "I am glad that we are in complete agreement on this."

"So," she said, with a smile to match his, "am I."

Radcliffe smiled his thanks to the maid serving the second course. When the young woman flushed before batting her eyelashes at him, he almost laughed. The baggage must think that he was trying to initiate a liaison. She was more than mistaken. He had no more interest in her than in the young woman sitting beside him. Miss Gibbs had been punishing his ears for the past two hours with her *on dits*. He had listened, trying to sort out the myriad names filling her stories.

As he picked up his soup spoon, he wondered why Lisabeth had selected this most unsuitable dinner partner for him. He had thought, in the wake of her vow to obtain him a wife, that Lisabeth would have made every effort to select the perfect woman for him. Instead, she had chosen a lass who was trying so hard to impress him that she was making the worst possible impression.

He glanced at where Lisabeth was trying to convince Mr. Gibbs to say more than two words in a row. Across from Miss Gibbs and next to Lady Edwina, a well-dressed man, who could not have been much taller than Lisabeth, was trying to get her attention.

"Mr. Gibbs," Lisabeth said, "the gathering at Lady—"

The other man interrupted, "Yes, Mr. Gibbs, you should listen well to Lady Montague. She is welcome in the finest homes in London and beyond."

"That is kind of you to say, Mr. Smythe," Lisabeth replied.

"Kindness is easy when it is the truth." He gave her a broad smile.

Radcliffe dipped his spoon into his soup to hide his smile, but continued to watch Lisabeth as he sipped. Didn't she see how her insistence to follow the rigors of protocol were trapping her into this situation she found far more uncomfortable than his own? Miss Gibbs might babble, but she was well-intentioned. Mr. Smythe had intentions as well, and Radcliffe suspected they were all aimed at courting Lisabeth.

She must have sensed his gaze on her, because she looked toward him. Hastily she turned back to Mr. Gibbs and Mr. Smythe. Questions taunted him, but he had no time to ask them. He owed Miss Gibbs the duty of being a pleasant dinner partner.

"So you have recently returned from Bath?" he asked, hoping that she had not spoken of that trip while he had let her words drift past him unnoted.

"My uncle finds the waters most refreshing, my lord." Her eyes widened as she smiled. "It is said that the waters have healing properties. Perchance, you might try them sometime."

"I doubt the odious waters of Bath can perform the miracles of the Jordan River, Miss Gibbs." When she frowned in confusion, he struggled to keep his smile in place. Had the young woman been given no education beyond how to smile at a potential swain? "Did you sample the waters as well?"

She fluttered long, dark eyelashes. "To own the truth, I did not. I did not have the time. There is so much to do in Bath. 'Tis a glorious place. I cannot begin to tell you how many routs and hops I attended."

He said something that encouraged Miss Gibbs to continue her tales of unequaled conversations in the Pump Room, while her great-uncle drank the waters. She seemed to require no audience other than her voice. She was a charming thing, despite her nothing-sayings, and quite pleasing to the eye as well, but. . . .

The formalities of the dinner party were tiring him more than he had expected. His arms seemed to weigh as much as his barely useful legs, and a yawn tickled the back of his throat. It was not Miss Gibbs's endless gabble, for he was struggling against fatigue rather than ennui. As the meal went through its courses—each excellently and succulently prepared—he thought with anticipation of when the party would reach its end.

He could remove himself. A weary smile tilted his lips as he recalled Lisabeth's first lesson. If he had Bond help him to bed before the end of the *soirée*, everyone in the *ton* would be whispering by the morrow that Lord Radcliffe was too weak to endure the rigors of a London Season. He heard Lisabeth's voice in his head. He must present the image of a man far along on his way to recovery. He had endured his time in the army. Surely he could survive this endless evening.

At the scrape of a chair, he watched Lisabeth come to her feet. Every motion she made was as graceful as a flower swaying with the wind. Raising his eyes, he saw sympathy glowing in hers. His lips tightened. He wanted no pity. He had vowed that from the moment he had discovered he was not going to cock up his toes.

He smiled at Miss Gibbs, but his words were all for Lisabeth. "I have been hearing about the entertainments in Bath. Mayhap I shall take the Bath Road one of these days myself to investigate what you have been so kind to enlighten me about. Don't you think that is an excellent idea?"

"I would be delighted," Miss Gibbs hurried to say, "to introduce you to friends of mine there. The Hunts know all those of the Polite World who have homes in Bath."

"It sounds perfect." He looked up at Lisabeth. "Don't you agree?"

"It would be an excellent opportunity for you to meet more of the *ton*."

"It would, wouldn't it?" He propped his chin on his hand and held her gaze. Emotions flickered through her eyes, but all his efforts to tear away the mask of her serene smile were for naught. By thunder, he detested this icy façade that concealed her true feelings.

Lady Edwina set herself on her feet. "Please join us for further entertainments in the parlor." She lowered her voice as the guests stood and wandered out of the dining room. "If you wish to retire, Lord Radcliffe, we will understand."

"I would not miss a moment of Lisabeth's party," he replied.

"Do not overassert yourself." She smiled. "This is only the first of many evenings you will enjoy during this Season."

Radcliffe resisted grumbling that he had little interest in more evenings of endless conversation about people he did not know and trying to remember the names of all those he met. Complaining would play him into Lady Edwina's hand, when, to own the truth, he was far more fascinated by her daughter-in-law's slender fingers.

"I find the whole of this invigorating," he said, as the others stood. "Just as you suggested I would, Lisabeth."

Miss Gibbs giggled. "You should not underestimate yourself, my lord."

"Or my hostess?"

Again Miss Gibbs gave into giggles. "You are so amusing! I had not thought anyone who has suffered what you have could have such a wonderful sense of humor."

Lisabeth tensed as Radcliffe did. Miss Gibbs clearly saw her words as a compliment. Before an uncomfortable silence could strangle those still at the table, Lisabeth hurried to say, "I am delighted you have found the company so diverting this evening, Miss Gibbs. You will be playing whist, won't you?"

"Of course." She glanced at Radcliffe. "Will you be joining us, my lord?"

"If you will grant me a moment, I shall be joining you and the others."

"I shall find us excellent seats." She gave him a glorious smile and rushed out of the room, herding her brother ahead of her.

Lisabeth was startled as sorrow flooded her, although she could not understand why. She had listened to Miss Gibbs's light laugh during dinner and knew the young woman was delighting in Radcliffe's company. This should have been perfect, for it meant Lisabeth was doing as Norton had requested. And the sooner she could find Radcliffe a bride, the sooner he would be out of her house and out of her life.

Lady Edwina said as she hooked her arm through Mr. Smythe's, "Let us hurry. I would hate to see that prattlebox claim the very best seat amid the tables."

Lisabeth started to follow them, but paused when her name was called. She turned to Radcliffe, who was pushing himself slowly to his feet. Again she was amazed, as she was each time, how powerful he appeared when he was standing. She fought her instinct to turn and flee.

Rather, she pasted a smile on her face and wondered if her cheeks would ever ease from the stress left by this unceasing smile. How could she have guessed when she began the plans for this evening that it would turn out like this? She had seen the questions in Radcliffe's eyes all evening, but she had no idea how she would explain what had happened when she had fled from his company earlier.

"Lisabeth," he said, as he hobbled along the table, letting his fingers slide along the back of the chairs.

"You aren't leaning on the chairs!" she gasped before she could halt herself.

His smile was cool. "I have found that less medicine and more exercise increase my strength."

"That is good."

"If you think that is good, why are you backing away from me?"

"I am not—"

He stretched out his hand and clamped it over hers on the back of a chair. "But you are, Lisabeth."

"Release me," she whispered.

"Or?"

"Radcliffe, if you think you are being funny, I can assure you that I do not agree."

"Ah, there is your haughty tone again." His fingers loosened over hers, but not enough to let her slide her hand away. "Why won't you answer my question?"

"I see no reason to. Please release my hand."

"I see no reason to." Leaning toward her, he said, "I would greatly appreciate an answer to my question, Lisabeth."

She trembled. She tried to halt it, but she could not.

"Radcliffe, I have my guests who are waiting for me to join them."

"So that is why you are scurrying away from me like a frightened child?"

"Yes." And it was . . . partly. A small part, but enough to allow her to agree without the guilt of speaking a lie.

His fingers lifted away from hers. "If you wish to make my evening more diverting by trying to hoax me, you have failed on both counts."

"Radcliffe . . ."

"No more half-truths," he whispered, putting his crooked finger under her chin. "Promise me that, *chère cousine.*"

She gazed up at him and nodded. When he spoke, she watched his lips, unable to tear her eyes away from their fascinating motions.

"No," he said lowly, "don't make this an unspoken vow, Lisabeth. Tell me that you will be honest with me. Let me know that I can trust you while you teach me the proper way to ingratiate myself with the *élite* while you seek a wife for me."

"Will you be as honest with me?" Again the words burst from her before she could halt them.

"You negotiate a hard bargain." As a smile glided along his lips, his fingers slid up her jaw. "I agree, Lisabeth, if you will."

"I agree."

He chuckled, and she pulled back. Did he have a midsummer moon about him? One moment, he was as serious as a judge announcing sentence. The next, he was laughing.

"Lady Montague!" came a voice from the hall. Mr. Smythe's voice, she noted with a sigh.

She turned to see him standing in the door. Her first pulse of dismay that he might have seen her and Radcliffe standing so close vanished. Mr. Smythe was smiling. In anticipation of the cards waiting to be played, she guessed.

Her dismay refocused on herself. Why was she upset that anyone saw her and Radcliffe in discussion? She had made it clear that her only plans involving him were to find him a wife. Yet, if that were so, why did her cheek where his fingers had brushed her skin still tingle with a sweet warmth? She must be the one who had been born beneath a midsummer moon, for she had learned the cost of trusting honeyed words.

And Frederick had been unceasingly solicitous during their short courtship. Radcliffe was irritating now. How much worse would he be if she trusted him with her heart?

She *was* mad! Thinking like this was proof of her insanity.

"Do not let me delay you," Radcliffe said, the hard edge returning to his voice. "Your guests are waiting to enjoy the pleasure of your company, *chère cousine.*"

"Please refrain from calling me that," Lisabeth whispered as she fought to keep her smile for Mr. Smythe in place. "I find it most offensive, for I am not your cousin."

"In truth, no, but your late husband was—"

"I have not forgotten the complexity of the relationships which brought you under my roof, Radcliffe. If you wish me to be honest, I would find it much more comfortable to return to the titles we used upon your arrival."

He laughed. "Comfortable? Is that all you seek, Lisabeth?"

"Why are you arguing when, even amid the free-and-easy life of a soldier, you were required to conform to protocol? Bond is your friend, but have you ever called him Maxwell?"

"He would be distressed if I did."

"Yet—"

Again Radcliffe chuckled. "My *chère cousine*, you are such a hornet when roused! Then your blue eyes spark until I swear they will cut through me like a well-honed sword. Why should I spend time funning Bond when it is much more delightful to do so with you?"

Lisabeth was spared from having to answer the unanswerable by going to speak with Mr. Smythe. She let him sweep her into the parlor where Lady Edwina was anxious for Lisabeth and Mr. Smythe to join her and Mrs. Castleman at the card table.

Caught up in her obligations, Lisabeth did not need to think of Radcliffe again. But she did. As she walked about the room, seeing that her guests were entertained or to bid them a good evening as the dawn approached, she was aware of his gaze following her. It was like a hand upon her shoulder, offering a comfort, a strength . . . and a delight, but she dared not trust it.

When she lowered her guard and looked toward him, he smiled as if he were privy to her innermost thoughts. She was sure she had not betrayed them. Or had she? She was not certain if, in spite of the promise he had made her, he would be honest.

She had been a want-witted widgeon once. She never would be so skimble-skamble again. The vow she had made to Radcliffe tonight had not been her first. Keeping her mind on the one she had made to his cousin Norton would be the best way to bring a satisfactory end to this and enjoy the Season she had looked forward to through the past year. She would find Radcliffe a wife quickly. Let some other woman put up with his peculiar ways!

Seven

That was most peculiar!

Radcliffe opened his eyes and peered through the dim light oozing past the drapes. Lamplight from the square, he suspected, for the hour must be far from dawn.

The sound came again. A soft sound like a broken-hearted child weeping over a lost toy.

Pushing himself up to sit, he silenced his curse as his left leg refused to move. Blast that leg! He was well-tired of its weakness. As he was regaining his strength here in Town, his patience with it was diminishing.

He forgot the ache along his leg as the sound whispered into the room again. Curiosity gave him the strength to stand. Peering through the thick twilight, he took note of where Bond was sleeping beside the door to the hall. On guard, he thought with a smile. His smile wavered when he recalled how Bond blamed himself for Radcliffe's injury. None of them had escaped, unwounded, from that battlefield, although some of the scars were invisible.

He frowned. Someone *was* weeping. It was harder not to snarl out a curse when he realized the sound was coming from the direction of his dressing room. Had a maid hidden in there and now was too afraid of interrupting his sleep to come out?

Trying to keep his lurching silent, Radcliffe went to the

dressing room's door. "Who is in here?" he asked in a near whisper, not wanting to disturb Bond.

A worthless hope, he realized, when the answer came from behind him. "Is something wrong, sir?"

"I heard what sounded like someone weeping. I thought someone might be within. Will you check?"

"Of course, sir." Bond went into the dressing room and emerged in a trice.

"Well? Who is within?"

"No one, save me."

"Then, who is weeping?"

Even in the shadows, Radcliffe could see Bond's face tighten. "I cannot say for certain."

He recognized that indefinite tone. Bond had an opinion he did not want to air. "If you were to guess . . . ?"

"Lady Lisabeth's dressing room is on the far side of the door."

"So the sound might be coming from her maid?"

"I cannot say for certain."

Radcliffe pushed past his man and went to the door. A single touch told him it was locked securely. A faint light emerged from beneath it, and he heard the murmur of voices. Not in the dressing room, but from beyond it. This was a puzzle.

Turning back to Bond, he said, "Your expression tells me you are not unacquainted with this sound."

"No, sir."

"Is this why you have implored me on many mornings to be especially gentle with Lisabeth that day?"

"If she has been denied sleep as well—"

"Or denies us sleep, it would be easy for words to grow heated." He nodded with a grim smile. "You always show great sense, Bond."

"I try, sir."

"Show more on the morrow when you will need to ask the lady's abigail to allow you into her lady's dressing room to recover a button of mine that has unfortunately rolled under the door. If the topic of such sounds is broached in some manner or if you can determine a way to solve this enigma, it will be all to the good."

"I understand, sir."

Radcliffe nodded. "Do let me know what you discover." He glanced back at the door as the light that had been flowing under it was extinguished. The night was silent again. "I will be very, very eager to know."

Lisabeth looked up from Mrs. Outhwaite's accounts as Doherty cleared his throat in the breakfast parlor door. She wondered how long the butler had been waiting patiently while they discussed ordering food and arranging duties.

"Lady Prospera Fry is calling, my lady," he announced.

"Prospera?" She rose and gave the housekeeper a quick smile. "I believe we were close to done, Mrs. Outhwaite."

"Of course, my lady." She smiled.

Going out into the hall, Lisabeth was glad that neither Doherty nor Mrs. Outhwaite voiced the thought that must be playing through their brains as it was through hers. Lady Edwina would not be pleased to have her greatest rival at the board of green cloth in her house uninvited.

She slowed as she heard the light sound of Prospera's laughter coming from the sitting room. It could not be possible! The rumble of a deeper laugh reached her just as she entered the room to see Lady Edwina wearing a scowl. Her mother-in-law was glowering at two chairs with their backs to the door.

"Lisabeth!" called Lady Edwina with the fervor of a drowning man grasping an outstretched hand.

Lisabeth gave her mother-in-law an encouraging smile and walked to where Prospera was coming to her feet. She fought to keep her smile on her lips as Radcliffe stood, too, his hand on Prospera's chair. They were a well-matched couple, both in darkly handsome looks and in Radcliffe's plump pockets that would serve Prospera's habit of high wagers well.

"Do forgive me for calling like this," Prospera said as she took Lisabeth's hands. A light fragrance flowed out from her as ethereal as the gold silk of her gown. "I wanted to thank you for inviting me to your *soirée* and to invite you and Lady Montague and"—she flashed Radcliffe a coy smile—"Lord Radcliffe to join me for a ride in Hyde Park."

"Prospera informs me," Radcliffe said with a smile as flirtatious as hers, "that one's education in the ways of the Polite World will never be complete without a few turns about the Park."

"Do join us." Prospera squeezed Lisabeth's hands gently.

Us? Looking from Radcliffe to Prospera, Lisabeth could not curb her curiosity. They obviously had been speaking with great camaraderie before her arrival. And Lady Edwina? When had her mother-in-law joined the conversation?

"Of course Lisabeth will join you," Lady Edwina said with an intensity that warned of her dismay. "My lord, you should know that it is unseemly to be riding about alone with a lady who is not part of your family."

"But two lovely ladies by my side makes everything all right?" He chuckled. "I do believe I shall come to appreciate certain aspects of Town life."

Lady Edwina ignored him and Prospera's laugh at his words. "Lisabeth, go and get your bonnet. I shall have Doherty let Lord Radcliffe's man know to join us."

Us? her mind asked again.

Radcliffe was not so reticent. "May I assume that you are coming with us, Lady Edwina?"

"I do enjoy a ride in the Park," Lady Edwina returned.

"Lisabeth, do hurry. Let Cassandra know I wish my bonnet as well."

Oddly vexed to be treated like an obedient child while the others continued the conversation that she had not been privy to, Lisabeth hurried up the stairs. It was clear that Lady Edwina was ready to set aside her distaste for Prospera in the face of her greater distress at having Radcliffe in the house. Although such a match would be an obvious answer, Lisabeth found it disturbing.

She had no chance to wonder why as she gave Lady Edwina's messages to Doherty and Cassandra and rushed to her own room. She almost collided with Bond at her door.

"Pardon me, my lady," he mumbled, scurrying away before she could reply.

As Wilson brought Lisabeth's favorite bonnet with the row of flowers along the brim, the abigail said, "A button from Lord Radcliffe's waistcoat popped off and rolled under the connecting door into your dressing room, my lady. Bond came to retrieve it."

"Then, why was he acting like a thief skulking away?"

Wilson smiled and shrugged her shoulders. "I could see that he was quite uneasy to be intruding in your private rooms, my lady. Strange, isn't it?"

"What?" she asked as she tied the bonnet's ribbons under her chin.

"How Bond is such a gentleman, and . . ." Wilson clamped her lips shut. "Forgive me, my lady. I should not have said such a thing even in jest."

Lisabeth nodded. She could not chide Wilson for saying what she herself had thought on more than one occasion. Bond was struggling to fit in with the household while Radcliffe took delight in questioning every precept of decent society. Sharing poker-talk with her abigail would suggest she was no more well-mannered than Radcliffe, so she went out of the room with the same speed she had entered.

As she came down the stairs, she wished she had lingered a moment more in her rooms. The door was thrown open, and she could see Prospera's lovely open carriage in the street. Lady Edwina and Prospera must already be outside, for only Radcliffe and Bond remained in the foyer.

Radcliffe glanced up at her and murmured something to Bond. She could not hear what it was, but Bond nodded and bolted out the door.

Holding out his hand, Radcliffe said, "Allow me to assist you out to the carriage as a gentleman should, *chère cousine.*"

"Should you?"

"Don't you mean *can I?*" He smiled as she crossed the foyer. "Do allow me to practice on you, so I might know the proper way to escort a lady to a carriage."

"Do you expect me to believe that you do not know how to do that?" she asked, pulling on her gloves that Doherty had waiting on a table.

"I expect you to assist me as you promised, Lisabeth."

At his irritated tone, Lisabeth looked up and saw he was smiling. She was furious with herself for falling prey to his bait. "I shall when you need assistance."

"Be so kind as to enlighten this opaque man. If I need remind you, yet again, Lisabeth, you are my teacher and should be teaching me the idiosyncrasies of *Le Beau Monde.*" He laughed when her eyes widened in amazement. "I wish to experience every countenance of the life of the *ton.*"

"An outing in the Park *is* the perfect way for you to meet those we shall be seeing at Her Grace's party tomorrow."

"Do you intend for me to map out a plan to cut a swath through the hearts of the innocent virgins seeking a husband?"

Heat billowed up her cheeks. It was most doubtful that Radcliffe would change, or that she would become accustomed to his outspoken ways. " 'Tis possible you might meet some, although I daresay Prospera may wish otherwise."

"Prospera is a family friend, as you are, Lisabeth."

She was uncertain whether to take comfort or despair at that comment.

She need not have worried, because he continued, "I still need tuition in the intricacies of *cartes des visites*. This shall be an opportunity for you to illuminate me. You will help me learn what I must to find the perfect wife for me, won't you?"

"Yes," she said, her voice no louder than a whisper as he drew her hand within his arm. She was being jobbernowl, but, when he touched her this chastely, she could only think of wanting him to caress her with more fervor. For a moment, not even the knowledge of how loving gestures metamorphosed into pain could put a halt to the longing.

She must find him a wife without delay. She must, before her foolish heart betrayed her again.

Radcliffe steered smoothly through the parade of carriages and riders clogging the routes within the Park. The sensation of the reins was comfortable in his hands. This one habit of the *ton* he would be glad to have as his own.

"Your cousin Norton should come to Town as well," Prospera said when he edged the carriage around a group of people talking by the side of the road.

"My attempts to convince him to join me on this sojourn bore little fruit," he replied. "As you can see, he remains at Norton Hall while I enjoy your company."

"I thought you were at Cliffs' End before coming to London."

"It was thought that the dampness of the air at Cliffs' End would slow my recovery." He rested his elbows on his knees as he let the horse drop to a walk. "As I am not a doctor, I had to trust those who had studied medicine."

Prospera chuckled. "You do not strike me as the type of man to heed any opinions that are contrary to your own." Turning to Lisabeth, who sat with Lady Edwina behind them, she asked, "Don't you agree?"

"Without question."

Radcliffe laughed as he glanced over his shoulder. "Why do I feel as if I am about to be ambushed when I have done only what has been requested of me?"

Lisabeth arched her eyebrows, but did not reply.

That brought another peal of laughter from Prospera, who asked, "So tell me, my lord, is it true that your family's name has a most appalling source?"

"Yes, it is true. A millennium ago, those living on the cliffs at the very end of the land painted those stones red with the blood of their enemies who tried to displace them. Red cliffs evolved into a more civilized Radcliffe, although barely more civilized, I am afraid Lisabeth would say, if she was not being so polite."

By a clump of trees not far from where the Serpentine widened, Radcliffe stopped the carriage. Bond jumped out and turned to help the ladies. As Lady Edwina went to sit in the shade, Bond hefted out a basket.

"What is in that?" Radcliffe asked when Prospera took the basket and carried it to Lady Edwina, who was wearing the most garish green bird on her hat that he had ever seen.

"Lady Montague told me that she wished to take a pause for some lemonade," Bond said.

Lisabeth smiled. "She hopes to collect a circle of friends for a few hours of gossip as she does every day when she comes to the Park."

"A delightful way to spend the day," Radcliffe answered grimly, then added, "Doesn't she become bored with doing the same things every day?"

"Apparently not."

Radcliffe waved Bond aside as he was about to assist Lisabeth to the ground. "I believe it is time I played the gentleman."

"Here?" She put her fingers to her lips as the question came out in a squeak.

He smiled. "Why not? You don't think I am going to stand to one side and let another assume my duties for the rest of my life, do you?"

Bond backed away a single step. "If you need my help, my lord—"

"You may be sure that I will ask for it."

Holding out his hand, he grasped the side of the carriage. He watched as dismay and trepidation swept across Lisabeth's face. When he reached in and took her hand, her gaze locked with his. All sounds of the birds and the water and conversations and carriage wheels and horses' hoofs vanished into the cacophony of his heart beating in tempo with the pulse of craving spiraling through him. The sun's heat and the breeze against his face were eclipsed by the tender warmth of her gloved fingers in his. Not even the sunlight on the Serpentine glowed like her eyes as he drew her toward him, her lips parting with a single breath that seemed to pierce through him to his very soul. How would her lips taste? He desperately wanted to savor that forbidden delight. To perdition with Society's dictates! He had denied himself too much for too long.

He put up his hand to curve it along her cheek and bring those luscious lips to him. Edging forward a half step, he wobbled. He cursed and seized the side of the carriage before he could fall backwards into the dust.

"Radcliffe!" Lisabeth cried, jumping to the ground and grabbing his arm. "Bond, come and help!"

"I do not need his help." He would have added more, but Bond, with his accursed alacrity, was already steadying him.

"Help him!" Lisabeth gasped. "Let me get you some lemonade, Radcliffe."

"I have no need of any damned lemonade." He caught her sleeve before she could dash away. "Lisabeth—"

Her shriek startled her as much as it did him, for a flush climbed her cheeks to erase the gray that had swept over her when he halted her. He released her as he stared at the horror in her eyes. When she backed away a single step, then another, before turning away to hurry to the banks of the Serpentine, he did not give chase.

He had viewed that terror in the eyes of the men he had had to command to face death and worse on the battlefield. Once he had grown inured to it, but not now. Not when he saw it in Lisabeth's eyes.

Eight

Lisabeth tossed stones into the water. She should go back to the others, to apologize to Radcliffe and to Bond, who had gaped at her as if she were bereft of every hint of sense, to pretend as she had from the day she had first entered Frederick's house as his wife.

"I am sorry, Lisabeth."

With a gasp, she turned to discover Radcliffe behind her, resting his shoulder against a tree. "What did you say?"

"I said I was sorry." He gave her a lopsided grin. " 'Tis something I say so seldom, so do not ask me to repeat it again."

"You have no reason to apologize."

"I must, for you took off as if a pack of wolves nipped at your heels."

Looking past him, she asked, "How did you walk here?"

"Bond helped me, and I suggested he might want to get some lemonade to ease his thirst in the wake of his work." He gestured toward the ground. "Do you mind if I sit?"

"Of course not!" How thoughtless she was! Her pain was in the past. Radcliffe had to suffer his every day.

When he placed a small rug in an opening between the protruding roots of the tree, he asked, "Will you sit with

me? I shall endeavor to do nothing more to distress you."
He grinned. "I collect I shall fail."

Lisabeth smiled as she had not in longer than she could
recall. This most irritating man could also be so kind. The
temptation to pour out her heart, scouring it of pain,
teased her, but she simply sat on the edge of the rug and
watched as two young boys raced down to the Serpentine
to sail boats made of sticks and paper.

With a gasp, she cried, "Lady Edwina!"

"Prospera will keep her company."

"But Lady Edwina does not . . . she . . ."

"Do not be afraid to speak the truth to me!" He chuckled. "Lady Edwina detests Prospera, save when they have
a set of flats in their hands."

Her eyes widened. "They are playing cards here?"

"I fear I am being a bad influence on all of you rather
than you teaching me the proper ways of the *ton*." He
drew up his right leg and folded his arms on his knee.
"They are teaching Bond the finer points of some game
that requires three hands. I did get them to promise not
to hold him to any losses he incurs today."

Lisabeth was not sure if she was more shocked that Lady
Edwina and Prospera were including Bond in their card
game or that they did not intend to collect their winnings
from him. "Amazing," was all she could say.

"That leaves us to enjoy this beautiful day with our duen-
nas in close attendance."

"So I may teach you about a day at the Park."

"I understand it quite well. One comes to be seen, especially if one has a new hat." He tapped the brim of
Lisabeth's leghorn bonnet.

"I fear this is not a new hat."

"Good, for it does not flatter you, *chère cousine*. Tomorrow, I shall take you to a milliner's shop and purchase you
a prettier one."

She laughed, glad not to be at odds with him. When he

demanded to know what was amusing, she said, "I cannot imagine you in a milliner's shop with ribbons and lace surrounding you."

"No? I went with my sisters often."

"You have sisters?"

He grimaced, then laughed. "Four older sisters, Lisabeth. Enough to break any lad's spirits, but I somehow survived until my father arranged for their marriages."

"But why were you in Norton's care if you have sisters?"

This time, his smile vanished and did not return. "When they learned I intended to purchase a commission, they were outraged. Each of them vowed to disown me if I bought it."

"And they truly did?"

"Not entirely. They did come to visit me at Norton Hall, each reminding me that I should have heeded them instead of my cousin."

"Your cousin?"

He picked up a pebble and tossed it into the water as she had. "Norton often spoke of the tradition in our family of service to the Crown."

"You should have let him fulfill that tradition if it was so important to him."

"I should have." He smiled again. "You have a wonderful way of putting things in their proper perspective, Lisabeth."

"I simply know Norton well."

His hand that was draped over his knee brushed her fingers, not taking them in his, simply making a connection between them. "I have heard that he and Frederick were very close tie-mates."

"Yes."

His brows lowered when she added nothing else. "If you do not want to speak of this, you need not."

Lisabeth looked at where Lady Edwina and Prospera were laughing with Bond. Although she longed to be honest, she could not risk injuring her mother-in-law by bringing shame on their family.

Drawing her fingers away from his, she said, "It is too lovely a day to be lost in the past."

"You are right. Why should we be thinking of what happened years ago when I should be enjoying this afternoon and this special company?"

When he smiled, she did, too. She had to own that Radcliffe's company added spice to her days, even though many times his comments were far from palatable. No one could remain indifferent to him, including her.

"I believe you are trying to avoid your lessons, my dear Lord Radcliffe."

"My dear Lady Montague, I believe you are right. And why should I heed them? My sisters married well without suffering the indignities of a Season in London."

"Most people consider it an honor to be part of the Season."

"I am not like many people."

"No," she said softly, "you are not." He was nothing like she had imagined a cousin of Norton Radcliffe might be. Nor was he at all like Frederick. Or was she simply hoaxing herself? Frederick had been attentive during their courtship, so flatteringly attentive that she had not seen his feelings as the obsessive jealousy they became.

"Lisabeth?"

She raised her eyes to meet his. "Yes?"

"Where are you?" He leaned toward her. "Didn't we agree that we would forget the past for this afternoon? I—"

His voice vanished, and Lisabeth followed his gaze to where a man on a black horse was reining in and tipping his hat in her direction. Coming to her feet, she noticed Lady Edwina tossing aside her cards and rushing toward the rider. Lisabeth wanted to groan. Lady Edwina had that glitter in her eyes which Lisabeth had not seen since Lady

Edwina had introduced her stepson to Lisabeth. It could mean solely one thing. Her mother-in-law intended to do some matchmaking.

"Good afternoon, Lieutenant Ison," Lisabeth said as he dismounted. "When did you arrive back in London?"

"Lady Montague, a pleasant sight as always, but one I can enjoy so seldom," he gushed. Taking her hand, he bowed over it.

Swift fire seared her, shocking her. She never had had this sensation with Lieutenant Ison. When he straightened, she saw his eyes narrowing as he looked at Radcliffe. Only now did she realize Radcliffe was standing, and his hand was on her arm. The fire was from Radcliffe's touch, not the lieutenant's.

"You are too generous," Lisabeth said tritely, for all other words were soldered within the heat surging through her. Stepping toward Lady Edwina to draw her into the conversation, she hoped her motion looked normal rather than fleeing from Radcliffe's fingers which unsettled her with the merest brush against her sleeve.

"It's as always a pleasure beyond words to see you as well, Lady Montague," Lieutenant Ison said, lifting off his hat to tip it to Lady Edwina. The sun sparkled on his blond hair. "I called at your house, and Doherty was generous enough to tell me you were riding here. Do you think me beneath reproach to chase after you?"

"Of course not." Lady Edwina laughed lightly, another warning to Lisabeth that her mother-in-law had hopes of wedding plans for her. "You are a dear to come and seek us out." Slipping her arm through his, she added, "Lieutenant Hamlin Ison, may I introduce you to the Marquess of Radcliffe? Lord Radcliffe, this is Lieutenant Ison, who I dare to say is one of the dearest friends of our family. Isn't that true, Lisabeth?"

Lisabeth knew it was useless not to smile. Her mother-in-law only wished for her to be happily settled. Mayhap she need not worry. Both Radcliffe and the lieutenant were military men who had served during the war. Surely they would form an instant connection, so she might turn the conversation away from uncomfortable topics.

She was astounded when Radcliffe's voice was icy as he said, with the barest civility, "Lieutenant."

"Radcliffe, did you say?" Lieutenant Ison replied as coldly. "*Lord* Radcliffe? Have you put aside your commission, my lord, since the debacle at—"

"As Lisabeth has reminded me on more occasions than I wish to recall, the war is over, Lieutenant. I suggest we refrain from boring her with tales of our wartime exploits, both real and exaggerated."

The blond man fingered his mustache as his brows dipped in a scowl. "It was not my intention to cause her a moment of ennui." Turning to Lisabeth, he held out his arm. "May I show you that clump of flowers by the trees? I know how you enjoy flowers, my lady, and you must tell me all that happened during your *soirée* after my duties required me to return to my work in garrison."

Lisabeth hesitated when she saw the glint of barely restrained emotions in Radcliffe's volatile eyes. Why was he putting himself in a stew? An appalling thought refused to be ignored. Was Radcliffe more like his cousins than she wished to own, ready to explode into anger with the slightest provocation . . . or without? She could not ask in front of Lieutenant Ison and Lady Edwina. Mayhap the best thing would be to end this graciously.

"I would like looking at the flowers, Lieutenant," she said quietly. "If you will excuse us, Radcliffe, Lady Edwina."

"What a pretty couple they make," Lady Edwina murmured, flashing Radcliffe a smile.

Radcliffe scowled and did not reply. Blast it! Tapping his fingers on the tree beside him, he squinted through the sunshine to watch Lisabeth laughing as Ison said something to her. Ison! An utter shuttlehead.

But, he had to own, Lady Edwina was correct. Lisabeth seemed even more delicate when standing beside Ison. The lieutenant had the massive build that most women seemed to find appealing, although he had no idea if Lisabeth shared that opinion. He had seen no portrait of her late husband—other than one of Frederick Montague at his father's knee—so that gave him no clue. If rumor was accurate, Ison was swimming in lard. It would not be a bad match, except. . . .

"Lieutenant Ison is quite agog with Lisabeth, don't you know?" continued Lady Edwina. "It was so incredibly convenient that he was not sent to the Continent during the hostilities, so he was here to escort her, after Frederick's death, when she was required to call upon his barristers."

"How incredibly convenient for both of them!"

Lady Edwina chuckled. "Sarcasm, my lord? I thought you would be glad to see Lisabeth being squired about by someone other than Mr. Smythe to whom you seem to have developed an instantaneous antipathy."

"Do you consider Lieutenant Ison proper husband material for your daughter-in-law?"

The old woman laughed. "You must have been an amusing lad! I suspect you will overmaster the young misses at the *soirèe* tomorrow evening with that whetted sense of humor."

Again Radcliffe did not answer. Why was Lady Edwina worrying herself about his chances in making a match when she should be concerned about Ison's intentions in making a match with her daughter-in-law? Lady Edwina was revealing an unbelievable lack of perception. If Norton had sent him to *her* for tuition, Radcliffe was sure he would have returned to the country before this. Good fortune had returned to him when his irritating cousin had selected Lisabeth.

Lisabeth. . . . His brows arched when he heard Lisabeth laugh again. He cursed silently. If Ison was half the profligate he had been in years past, Lisabeth should be wary. Radcliffe did not want to see her married to that moonling, but he had no idea how, when he could barely hobble, he could halt her from walking down the aisle to take her vows with Ison or any other man.

" 'Tis a good thing that I did not have to pay my losses," Bond said as he buffed a shine into Radcliffe's boots.

"That bad?" Radcliffe kneaded his knee. By all that's blue, would it ever stop tormenting him? He had walked but a few steps today. Mayhap the pain was to remind him that his attempts to out-do Ison at his own game were doomed to failure. He should let Ison play the tin soldier, for eventually the truth would melt away his well-polished façade. That would be the wisest thing to do, save Lisabeth might get lured into believing Ison's bangers about his importance to the army.

"Worse." Bond chuckled.

"Worse than what?"

Bond stood and set the boots on the floor. "I suspect you haven't been listening to me, sir."

"I suspect you are right." Radcliffe shifted in his chair. "Sorry, Bond."

Fishing a finger beneath his waistcoat, Bond then held out his hand. "Mayhap this will ease your mind."

"This?" Radcliffe plucked a key from his man's hand. "What does this open?"

"The door that connects your dressing room to Lady Lisabeth's."

For one of the few times he could remember, Radcliffe could think of no answer. He stared at the iron key in his hand. He had seen its like dozens of times before and paid them no mind. But this was different. He did not need

Lisabeth's voice in his head reminding him that he must play the part of a gentleman. He knew no chap of the gentry would even consider keeping this key to a lady's most private chambers. Slowly, his fingers closed over the key.

"When I went to retrieve the button I had shoved under the connecting door," Bond said, as stiff as when he had given reports on the activities of the French, "Wilson was busy with some matter. She told me to get the button myself, so I took myself into Lady Lisabeth's dressing room. Seeing the key sitting in the lock, I recalled what you told your men so often. Never allow—"

"Never allow any opportunity to pass you by, for it might not come again." Radcliffe looked up at Bond, who stood at attention. "Dammit, Bond, we are not about to assault a French stronghold. We are Lisabeth's guests."

Bond's shoulders drooped from their taut stance. "But, sir, I had been sure that finding the key was what you wanted me to do in order to solve the puzzle of who was weeping in the night."

"I said nothing of taking the key from the door."

"No, but I understood you to mean that." Dismay ruffled Bond's forehead. "If I misunderstood, I will return the key posthaste."

Radcliffe tossed it into the air and caught it easily. "And how exactly do you plan to tell Lisabeth that you have purloined the key to the door that stands between her reputation and ruin?"

Sputtering, Bond shook his head.

"I should have made my wishes clearer," Radcliffe said with a sigh. "Let me ponder this, Bond, and figure out the best way to handle this without putting Lisabeth to the blush."

"And still ease your curiosity about that sound of weeping?"

"Our curiosity, it seems." Radcliffe smiled wryly. Pocketing the key, he added, "That is one problem among many."

"You shall solve each of them, sir."

"You have a great deal of faith in me."

"Some things will never change."

That was true, and he had noticed how Lisabeth shied away from any turn of the conversation that suggested she might be looking to remarry. Mayhap he was worrying needlessly about Ison. Lisabeth might see him as someone to stand between her and a more earnest suitor, such as Mr. Smythe. That would fit in with her well-ordered world, but he knew how quickly all of one's assumptions could be turned inside out.

"I hope you are right, Bond." As if it were the most precious vow, he repeated, "I hope you are right."

Nine

Lisabeth put aside the *Morning Post* and picked up the letter that Wilson had brought to her when she woke. No matter how she tried, she could not ignore it. When she had recognized Norton Radcliffe's handwriting, she had set it aside, intending to finish reading the paper first. Rather, her thoughts returned again and again to the note.

Dearest cousin Lisabeth,
   I trust by this time Tristan has arrived safely and without incident at your lovely home.

Lisabeth stared at the page, betwattled for a moment, then laughed. She had become so accustomed to calling the marquess Radcliffe that she had forgotten his given name was Tristan.

   I suspect you have your hands full with endeavoring to teach him to act in a civilized manner.
   Please keep me informed of his progress and which young woman, if any, he might become intrigued with. If you cannot find him a wife, I shall, of course, understand. I know that I have beseeched a grand favor of you, cousin, but, as I wrote before, I can think of no one more capable.
   If either you or the marquess find that launching him

*into the Polite World becomes too burdensome, do not
hesitate to arrange for Tristan to return to me.*
  With all due affection and gratitude,

                          Your cousin,
                          Norton Radcliffe, Esq.

Tossing the letter onto her bedside table, Lisabeth rose.
Norton remained oblivious to those around him. Otherwise he would know that neither Lisabeth Montague nor
anyone else would convince Lord Radcliffe to leave London until he wished to depart.

She started to ring for Wilson to help her dress, but
hesitated. Picking up the letter again, she frowned. She
did not like the idea of sending reports on Radcliffe to
Norton, although cousins they might be. Norton was showing an uncommon interest in his cousin's private business,
although she could excuse that in light of how Norton had
nursed Radcliffe back from near death.

She folded the letter and put it in a book on her table.
Later she would decide how and when to answer it.

As the distinctive sound of Radcliffe's hesitant steps interrupted the dusky sitting room's stillness, Lisabeth
looked up with a smile. Every day, more of his impressive
strength returned. Her eyes widened when she noted he
was dressed as if for calls. His dark coat was free of any
lint, and his boots shone even in the dim light. As the
tall-case clock in the foyer below chimed a single time, she
realized he must be preparing to go out. But where? She
had made no plans for the afternoon.

But she had, a nagging voice teased her. She had planned
to spend the afternoon with Radcliffe.

"Ah, here is where you are hiding," he said, as he rested
one hand against the molding of the sitting room's door.

"Hiding? I believe I have been in plain sight all day. I trust you rested well after yesterday's callers."

Radcliffe laughed. "You enjoyed watching that jaw-me-dead Miss Gibbs flirting with me, didn't you?" Sitting on a chair beside where she was curled up with her feet beneath her on the settee, he rubbed his left knee. "I have never met any person who could talk so long without pausing to take a breath. My sympathy for her brother increases each time I speak with Miss Gibbs, which seems to be every time I turn around."

"I thought you two were in first oars with each other."

Again he chuckled. "My ears are ajangle with her prattle. I endeavor to see her better attributes to discover if they match what I seek in a wife."

She put the book she had been reading on a table. "There are many ladies who might be interested in your company."

"As interested as Ison was in yours at the Park?"

Lisabeth ignored the warmth climbing her cheeks. "I believe I told you on the way back from our ride with Prospera that Lieutenant Ison is a friend."

"I suspect he would wish to be more."

"You have the right to your opinions, Radcliffe."

"Even if they are wrong?" When she did not answer, he sighed and relaxed. "You should tell me to keep my nose out of your concerns."

"Why should I bother? Telling you previously to mind your own bread-and-butter has done me no good. I had no idea that I was acquiring a doting uncle at the same time I took on the task of teaching you."

His voice was sharp with surprise. "Doting uncle? Is that how you see me?"

" 'Tis nothing more than a manner of speaking. I could have said brother, although I never have had a brother to dote on me." Folding her hands in her lap, she said, "It matters little, Radcliffe, other than to ask you to let me tend to my own life while I help you with yours."

"Which you have managed quite well so far. Far better than I anticipated, for, in a continuing effort to be honest with you, I did not expect you to welcome me."

"You have given me every opportunity to give you your *congé.*"

Radcliffe smiled. "But you have preferred to suffer."

"I have suffered your insufferable ways," Lisabeth retorted, "but it seems quite obvious that our work has achieved a modicum of success, for Prospera has been as faithful a caller as Miss Gibbs."

Grimacing, he stood. "Yes, and Miss Gibbs is anticipating my *visite* within the hour. With luck, she shall have run out of things to say before I arrive."

"Radcliffe!"

"Pray do not sound astounded, Lisabeth. If you recall, you agreed we must be honest with each other through this abominable pursuit of a wife for me."

"If you do not appreciate Miss Gibbs's company—"

"Or Prospera Fry, who has frightened Bond with her suggestion that they must play cards again. This time, for real stakes. I believe he is more scared of her and her devil's books than he ever was of the French army."

Lisabeth smiled. "I did notice him avoiding her and making the most incomprehensible mutters of excuses to leave whenever she turns the conversation to cards."

"Which she does frequently."

"If you wish, I shall speak with Mr. Tobler about his daughter Adelaide. She is a fair and sweet child."

"Does she have a brain?"

She laughed. "Are you the same man who said he had no interest in wooing a bluestocking who would bore him nigh onto death with her opinions?"

" 'Tis better to be inflicted with misapprehensions than bored by a ceaseless bagpipe."

"Radcliffe, how shall I find you a wife when you cannot curb your uncivil tongue?"

Putting his hands on the arm of the settee, he leaned forward until his nose was only inches from hers. She was sure her heart had stopped in mid-beat, for she could think only of the warmth of his breath on her face as he laughed softly. Caught by the glow in his ebony eyes, she struggled to breathe. A sensation, which was unsettling, but decidedly pleasing, coursed through her.

"Tell me, Lisabeth," he said in a hushed voice that resonated within her, setting every nerve to tingling. "Is this Miss Tobler as pretty as you?"

She swallowed roughly. "You shall be quite pleased, for she has sparkling eyes—"

"Like you."

"—and shining hair—"

"Like you."

"—and you shall find her a pleasure to talk to—"

"Like you."

Lisabeth slid along the settee and rose. Steadying her voice, she asked, "Do you intend to let me finish a single sentence?"

"I just did." He lowered himself to where she had been sitting and rubbed his leg again. "However, I would be quite the cad not to allow you to introduce me to this paragon of femininity. No doubt, she shall be at one of the *soirées* we soon will be attending."

"She has just had her coming-out, so I am sure she is anxious to enjoy as many of the fêtes as she can before she decides on an escort." Looking at the hearth that blurred in front of her eyes, she sighed.

"So sad?"

She smiled—or tried to smile—as she raised her gaze to discover he was standing beside her. When his brow threaded with bafflement, she knew her attempt had been unsuccessful. "No, not sad. Just remembering."

"Your Season?"

"Yes," she answered, no longer startled by his astuteness. "It did not last very long."

Glancing toward the foyer, which was empty, Radcliffe said, "I assume Frederick Montague found you quickly."

"At my coming-out."

"He must have been quite besotted with you."

"That was what he told me."

"And you with him?"

Lisabeth went to the window where rain was following the pattern of the glass. "My husband is dead these twelve months and more. Why speak of the past?"

"Or ill of the dead?"

"That seems to be what you are doing, Radcliffe, not me."

"Did you enjoy being married, Lisabeth?"

She could not silence her gasp of astonishment. As heat slapped her cheeks, she was sure they were as red as his waistcoat. She struggled to say, "My opinions on marriage are my own."

"I thought we were truly friends."

"We truly are."

"As well as family."

"That is almost as true."

"Then, *chère cousine* Lisabeth," he said softly, "tell me what I can expect, if you are as successful as Norton anticipates you to be, and I find myself buckled to a bride. Will it be as blissful as the courting?"

Turning away, she said, "Life is not filled with endless bliss, Radcliffe. You should know that as well as I."

He edged in front of her to keep her from leaving. "You sound dolorous. Could it be that you enjoyed neither the wooing nor the wedding?"

"Radcliffe, my marriage is over."

He locked his hands behind him as his eyebrows arched in the cynical way that usually made her laugh. When she said nothing, he murmured, "Norton was an ass to give you an added burden when you were about to make a life for yourself."

"I have a life, one that I enjoy very much."

"But it is empty, Lisabeth."

"I fear you mistake being alone with loneliness. I am neither. I have my dear mother-in-law and many friends who fill my days."

"Who is giving you a look-in today?"

Lisabeth faltered, then flushed. "No one."

"Then, whom do you call upon this afternoon?"

"I made no plans to visit anyone."

"That sounds like being alone and being lonely, Lisabeth."

Arguing with this intractable man was futile. Radcliffe twisted every word she spoke.

"If you would be so kind, *chèere cousine,*" he continued, "I would appreciate your company this afternoon."

"I thought you were calling on Miss Gibbs."

"I am. Will you come with me while I fulfill this obligation?"

"I should—"

He took her hand and folded it between his. "I promise you. I shall ask no more questions that make you uncomfortable."

"You promise *that?*"

He smiled. "You are right that that may be impossible. Better I should promise to *try* not to ask any questions that will make you uncomfortable."

In spite of herself, Lisabeth smiled at his beseeching expression. She could not stay angry with Radcliffe when he teased her with this rare gentleness. She should decline, but heard herself saying that she would be with him as soon as she collected her bonnet and pelisse to protect her dress from the rain. As she went up the stairs, she wondered when *she* would be the victor in the battle of wills between them.

Lightning seared the sky, announcing the slow rumble of thunder along the streets as Lisabeth stepped from the carriage in front of Delia Gibbs's home. She vacillated between rushing up the steps and waiting to see if Radcliffe needed assistance. When the sky became alight again, she shivered.

"Are you afraid of storms?" Radcliffe asked as he eased out of the carriage with her coachee Crandall's help.

"Of course not." Another flash of lightning made her gasp, proving that her words were out-and-outers.

"I think we should get away from this tempest to enjoy the one within."

Lisabeth laughed. "Radcliffe, you told me that you would behave yourself prettily this afternoon."

"I was most careful with my vow, which was that I would say nothing untoward to Miss Gibbs. With you, I shall own to the truth as always." With an ease he could not have enjoyed even days ago, he managed with the footman's help to climb the steps and twist the doorbell.

A dour butler escorted them to a door that was hidden by the shadows of the dual staircases leading upward in a gentle curve. Within, a small room was brightly lit against the storm. As each time Lisabeth had entered Delia Gibbs's pale pink sitting room, each piece of furniture, each painting, and each figurine was perfectly arranged to accent its beauty.

"Lord Radcliffe! How kind of you to call." From a satinwood settee, Miss Gibbs rose, a smile brightening her face. It wavered. "Lady Montague?" Miss Gibbs's amazement was evident in her choked greeting.

Radcliffe interjected, "I do trust that you will forgive me, Miss Gibbs, for taking it upon myself to invite Lisabeth.

She expressed a desire to see you, and I thought it would be diverting to spend the afternoon with London's two most charming ladies."

When Miss Gibbs twittered a delighted answer, Radcliffe glanced at Lisabeth. His eye closed in a slow wink, and she struggled not to laugh.

"Do come in," Miss Gibbs urged. "On such a grim day, I am pleased to sit with dear friends by the hearth in my favorite room."

"That would be pleasant," Lisabeth said.

Those were the last words she spoke during the call which seemed longer than an hour. If Radcliffe managed more words than she, she did not hear them. Miss Gibbs allowed no silence as she prattled about a party she had attended the evening before, describing each event in painfully minute detail.

Lisabeth breathed a sigh of relief when she was handed back into the carriage. Another round of thunder detonated overhead, and she pulled the curtains over the windows to keep out the impending storm. She heard Radcliffe urge Crandall to get them home before the next onslaught of rain.

Radcliffe heaved himself in and sat beside her. "Did you notice that Miss Gibbs's esteemed brother was nowhere to be seen? Do you suppose she invited me to call this afternoon in hopes of compromising me?"

"Compromise *you?*" She laughed. "That seems a most unlikely scenario. Mayhap she hoped you would take the opportunity to propose."

"Egad, what an appalling thought! I swear I would go deaf within the year from her bibble-babble."

"Take care, Radcliffe."

"What do you mean?" he asked, his voice as abruptly serious as hers.

"She is quite taken with you. You must be careful not

to hurt her by letting her think you wish more than friendship with her."

"That is one lesson you have failed to teach me, *chère cousine*. How does one end an *amour* without breaking a young woman's heart?"

Her eyebrows arched, imitating his most irreverent expression. "An *amour*? I was jesting."

"But I thought—"

He wore such a boyish expression of dismay that she could not keep from laughing. Putting her hand on his arm, she said, "I find it difficult to understand how you can command a company of unruly soldiers, yet you find it impossible to deal with Delia Gibbs."

"Do you suggest that I march up to her—quite an expectation when I find walking a chore—and order her to scotch her hopes? What a rapper, *chère cousine!*" He put his hand over hers.

"Telling Miss Gibbs the truth might not be out of the question."

"Such a stickler you are for truth." Humor left his eyes. "Why, then, do you hesitate to speak it to me?"

"I have been honest with you."

"Most of the time."

She smiled, straining every rigid muscle in her face. "Then, you should be grateful, Radcliffe. I am surprised you have not learned that having someone being honest with you most of the time is more than you can expect from most you meet."

"So cynical?" With a laugh, he tapped the brim of her bonnet. "I thought that was my task."

"Not prying into my life should be your task."

"Such a killjoy you can be when you become the tutor."

"I—" Her retort vanished into a gasp when she was almost bounced from the seat.

His hand tightened over hers, and she gripped the window ledge as the carriage turned sharply. It rocked, and she shrieked.

Her fingers were ripped from the window as the carriage teetered. Strong arms surrounded her, pulling her against Radcliffe's hard body. Pain erupted through her skull as they were tossed against the wall.

Shouts rang from the street as they skidded sideways. A frightened horse trumpeted as she buried her face against Radcliffe's coat. She thought she heard him say something, but his voice vanished into a crash. She stiffened, but the carriage remained upright.

Slowly she opened her eyes. The dark wool of Radcliffe's coat was rough against her cheek. She tensed as the vehicle bounced again, then realized the motion was Crandall jumping from the box. His furious shout told her that the near accident had been caused by another's recklessness.

"Lisabeth?" came a voice closer to her. "Are you hurt?"

"I am shaken, but I shall be fine," she whispered. Looking up at Radcliffe's taut face, she asked, "And you?"

His lips were so straight they barely moved as he said, "I have been worse."

"Worse? Are you hurt?"

He winced as he moved his left leg. " 'Tis just this damn leg. Do not look so despairing, cousin. I suspect it is nothing more than a cramp brought on by my attempts at heroics. I should know by this time that playing the hero is a painful game."

Instead of answering, she threw aside the curtains and peered out the window. Her eyes widened as she saw two drays in pieces, and the produce they had been carrying littered about the cobbles. She ignored the squawking chickens as she shouted to Crandall.

The wiry coachman nodded when she ordered him to take them back to Cavendish Square posthaste. "And carefully!" she called after him as he climbed into the box.

Only then did she turn back to Radcliffe. When she saw

his face was paler than it had been only moments before, she bit her lip.

"I am fine!" he snapped before she could speak.

"That is yet to be seen. I intend to send for the doctor when we—"

"No doctor!" When she regarded him with amazement, he added in the same fierce tone, "I have had enough of their poking and powders and endless bewailing about the poor major who would never walk again. Why would I want to listen to another?"

Lisabeth said quietly, "No, Radcliffe, on this you shall not bully me. I insist that we send for a doctor."

He did not answer. White puckers at the corners of his mouth warned that he was suffering intense pain.

The carriage stopped, and she jumped from it before the footman could open the door. When Crandall asked if she was all right, she nodded and urged him to help Radcliffe.

"I can walk by myself!" argued Radcliffe as he climbed awkwardly from the carriage. He waved aside the coachman, who glanced at Lisabeth uneasily. "I told you that I am fine."

"Just be careful. You—"

Lisabeth screamed as Radcliffe took a single step and collapsed to the walkway. She heard Crandall shouting for Bond as she knelt on the wet stones. Radcliffe's eyes were closed, his face contorted in agony. She pressed her hands to her mouth when she saw blood trickling along the side of his face. She did not want to think what this new injury might mean.

Ten

Lisabeth smiled as she emerged from the shop and settled her reticule on her arm. She needed this morning out to tend to errands. In the week since the carriage nearly had tipped over, the doctor had insisted that Radcliffe remain in his bed to rest his leg. Bond had been kept busy trying to persuade the marquess to rest. He had hinted that Radcliffe would appreciate a visit from her, but Lisabeth pretended to be oblivious or reminded him that a lady did not pay a visit to a gentleman in his bedchamber.

This morning, she had mentioned that she was sending a letter to Norton to let him know of the accident. Bond had not been able to hide his dismay.

"I think that would not be the wisest course, my lady."

"He is one of the marquess's closest relatives."

"But Mr. Radcliffe riled my lord so much I believe that we came to Town to escape him."

"I had no idea."

"Do not mistake my words, my lady. Mr. Radcliffe's solicitude for his cousin has been deep. He never forgot, as I haven't, how close the marquess came to death. However, I fear his concern manifested itself in vexation for my lord, because Mr. Radcliffe always insisted that the marquess regain his strength before he tested it."

"Norton and I disagree on many subjects, and I fear this is one." Lisabeth had smiled as Doherty brought her shawl. "Radcliffe was unable to discover what he could accomplish until he tried."

"So I have said on more than one occasion, but my words were not heeded by Mr. Radcliffe."

"Norton values no one's opinions as much as his own, but I'm surprised Radcliffe was as deaf to your suggestions."

Bond had assumed the taut expression his master was predisposed to using when he intended to say no more.

She allowed him to take his leave because she was just as happy to put an end to this conversation. She did not want to own to Bond that while she had been readying herself to go out, she had heard loud voices from the other side of the connecting door. Wilson had whispered that Radcliffe found himself as feeble as he had been upon his arrival at their door. The thin veneer of his patience that had cracked so often before now seemed utterly shattered. Her abigail also whispered that Bond was dismayed beyond distraction. Again, Lisabeth heard what was not said. Lisabeth should visit Radcliffe and soothe him as she had before.

She had not. Instead, she had come to Mr. Allott's gentleman's shop, not far from Mr. Lock's hat shop. Her shopping done, she could delay returning home no longer. Behind her, Wilson carried the packages they had collected during their errands. Mayhap what she had bought for Radcliffe would ease his distress that was upsetting her whole household.

Lisabeth's happy expression faded when she realized she had not visited Mr. Allott's shop since her father's death. There had been no reason to go to the tailor, for Frederick with his finicky ways never had allowed her to buy him even the most mundane piece of clothing. He had insisted they both dress in the highest style of the dandy-set, and Lisabeth wondered if that was why, for the past year, she had been unwilling to join Lady Edwina at the modiste's shop.

Hearing Wilson's puffing, Lisabeth motioned for Crandall to relieve her abigail of the packages. She let the footman hand her in while the purchases were stored in the boot. With a smile, she moved aside to give Wilson more room on the comfortable seat.

"Back home," Lisabeth told Crandall through the window. As the coachman steered the carriage into traffic, she turned to thank Wilson for her help and discovered her abigail was asleep.

She closed her own eyes. That could mean but one thing. The nightmare had come again last night, disturbing Wilson's sleep. How she wished it would vanish from her head, never to return. Nothing she had done eased its grip.

Even the weeks since Radcliffe's arrival at Cavendish Square had not banished it. Although her days were busy and filled with the challenges presented by having him as her guest, allowing her to forget the past, it pounced on her when she slept. In fact, the nightmare had called upon her more frequently, almost nightly, since he had presented himself at her door. Mayhap, and she prayed this would be so, it would leave when he made a match and bid her *adieu.*

Her teeth clenched against the pinch of consternation that had become familiar each time she thought of him marrying. Why was she being so skimble-skamble? Finding him a wife was her goal as well as regaining the quiet life of enjoying the Season as she had envisioned for the past year. The idea of succeeding should bring a trill of anticipation, not a rumble of dread.

Lisabeth, upon their arrival at Cavendish Square, took a single package from among those in the boot. She knew Wilson and Doherty would attend to the rest. Climbing the stairs, she untied her bonnet and set it on a table before going up the next flight and along the hall.

She faltered when she realized Bond was not at his usual post in the passage. Had he and Radcliffe gone out to take the air? Impossible! Mayhap he was within with Radcliffe.

Raising her hand to knock on the door, she froze. Was she witless? Until Radcliffe took up residence within, this door had been locked. She had not entered the room since the hour of Frederick's death, and she could not now.

She whirled away. Her reticule struck the door, pushing it ajar, and she gasped as she heard, "Come in."

Caught in indecision, she could not move away.

"Come in!" came the call, louder this time. "Dammit! I see you lurking out there. Come in."

She took a deep breath. To dart away like a mouse afraid of the cook's broom might cause more problems. She would go as far as the open door. No farther.

Pushing the door aside, she saw Radcliffe propped amid the pillows on the bed she once had shared with Frederick. He was tossing something that glittered into the air and catching it as he stared at the open door to the dressing room. Was he so bored? If so, Bond should be here to keep him company.

He would greatly appreciate a chance to talk with you, my lady, when I must be elsewhere. Bond's voice, which had held a tinge of a scold, rang through her head.

"Come in, come in," Radcliffe said with impatience.

Lisabeth tried to step into the room. Her foot refused to take that first step.

"Why are you dawdling . . . ?" He looked at her, his eyes widening and pushing at the bandages along his face. "Lisabeth! I had no idea it was you."

"I suspected that." Oh, how easy it was to speak these commonplaces instead of her true thoughts. Why had Bond said nothing about the extent of the damage to Radcliffe's cheek? He had spoken only of the doctor's insistence that Radcliffe rest before attempting to walk around the house again.

"You look well."

"I suffered little damage, as you know."

"So I *heard.*"

She could not help flinching at the emphasis he put on that single word. "How do you fare?"

"If you would stop loitering in the doorway and come closer so that I do not have to shout, you might be able to see for yourself."

"A lady should not—"

"Chère cousine," he said, an amused sparkle in his eyes, "come in and explain to me why you chose that color to wear today."

Looking down at her muslin gown, Lisabeth smiled. Radcliffe might be vexing beyond words, but he also could ease her fears as no one else had ever tried. The sprigged material of her gown held a hint of green. It was true that she usually avoided wearing the shade her mother-in-law fancied, but she loved this fabric.

She lifted her gaze back to meet his and wondered if her heart had become as frozen as her feet. When he held out his hand to her, she edged into the room, drawn by his incredible eyes and her own longing to savor his touch. His fingers curled around hers, not capturing them, but welcoming them as if they had been too long from the place where they were meant to be.

His face, which was shadowed by a low mat of raven beard, had lost its glow of health, even when sunshine streamed in through the window. As he shifted to face her, she wanted to cry out with the pain that tensed his mouth. He had already suffered more than any one man should.

"You are my second unexpected caller in the past two days," he said quietly. "Lady Edwina visited me yesterday before you and she went out."

"She did?" She should just make an excuse and leave

before the dark walls constricted upon her, releasing the shriek burning in her throat.

"It appears she is becoming more accepting of me living here. She sat and played cards with me for more than an hour."

Lisabeth chuckled, amazing herself. How could she laugh *here?*

"What is so amusing?" he asked.

"Do not pride yourself on being acceptable, Radcliffe, when Lady Edwina would welcome Old Nick himself into her house if the devil knew how to play a fast round of cards."

He smiled, but the expression was still strained. "I see there is no danger of me becoming self-satisfied in this household." Before she could hasten to apologize, he asked, "What is in your oddly shaped package? Bond told me that you were visiting your *couturière.*"

"Mademoiselle was busy, so I took the time to do other errands."

"Shame." Radcliffe laughed. "You know that is a falsehood."

"Falsehood?"

"I heard you telling Wilson before our call on Miss Gibbs that you had no plans to have a new dress made for Mrs. Castleman's fête."

"I did not realize my conversations had become so intriguing." She should go. Now! But he still held her hand, his warmth urging her to forget the coldness that the very thought of entering this room created within her.

"Can it be that you have mistaken yourself into believing that I do not find everything about you intriguing?"

Rather than answering, she placed the package on the bed. She turned to go, but his hand did not release hers. She could pull away. Yet, to do that might add to his injuries. Why, oh, why had she given in to the temptation promised in his eyes and come in here? How many more times was she going to be a complete chucklehead?

"What is it?" he asked.

"A surprise," she replied, trying to keep her voice light, "and, if I tell you what it is, it shall no longer be a surprise."

"I am overwhelmed, Lisabeth," he answered, "that you are bringing me a gift. I thought a lady received gifts from a gentleman, not the other way about."

"As you keep reminding me, we are family."

"And I am no gentleman." He slipped his right hand beneath the covers before reaching for the package.

"Did you lose something?" she asked.

He smiled. "No."

"But you—"

"For a lady, Lisabeth, you show an uncommon interest in a man's private concerns. Do you want me to tell you of an itch that has been plaguing me this morning?"

She knew her cheeks were alight with fire when he chuckled. When his hand relinquished its hold on hers, she started again to turn. The call of her name halted her.

"Do help me with this, *chère cousine.*" His voice dropped to a husky caress. "Do not leave so precipitously."

"Radcliffe—"

"Stay. Please."

She pressed her hand to her heart that suddenly was throbbing with sympathy that this proud man had been reduced to pleading. Wanting to tell him the truth of why she did not want to linger here, she could not.

"I shall stay to see you unwrap this package. Then I must—"

"Honesty. Be honest."

"Then, I must go." That, at least, was the truth. Every breath she took was harder than the one before it. Was she unnerved only by memory, or was it the sight of Radcliffe in his open-necked shirt that revealed how much strength he still possessed? She did not dare to think too long on that.

Radcliffe undid the brown paper. When he pulled out an ebony staff topped with a silver handle, he turned it from one side to the other, oddly without comment.

"If you do not like it," Lisabeth said into the discomfiting silence, "I can choose another at Mr. Allott's shop."

His stiff smile pulled on his lips so tightly that his voice sounded alien. "It is not that I do not like it or your kindness in thinking of me, but I vowed when I discovered that I had evaded death that I would never use a cane and become the picture of pity."

"But this is not a cane!" She took the staff. Holding the top, she struck a pose with the silver tip against the floor. " 'Tis a walking stick, and not a single gentleman, who considers himself among the Pink of the *Ton*, would be seen without his during a promenade in the Park."

"A walking stick?"

Lisabeth handed it back to him. She watched as he ran a single finger along the smooth wood. She had been a muttonhead not to speak to Bond about this before she ran off to buy such a gift. How could she have guessed that Radcliffe would be sensitive about something as unimportant as a cane? Then, she realized, with a flash of painful insight, that he wanted nothing to suggest his infirmities were permanent.

"Forgive me, Lisabeth," he said, startling her anew. "I should have told you how much I appreciate your generosity in obtaining me what every respectable male of the *élite* should possess. You are proving to be a *professeur exemplaire.*"

"I consider that a compliment."

"You should. In a short time, I shall be aping your pose, and you shall tell me that I look much the dashing *roué.*"

"You are supposed to wait for compliments, Radcliffe, not anticipate them."

"Odd, for it seems you always anticipate any kind words I might speak to you." He twirled the stick between his hands. "How can I be expected to know how to speak pretty court-promises when you have failed to provide me with edification in this vital aspect of wooing a lass?"

Again Lisabeth decided that the best choice was to avoid answering. "I must go, Radcliffe. I am glad you are pleased with your gift. I thought you would be. I—"

"You are prattling like Miss Gibbs." He grasped her hand, gathering it in between his. "You make it difficult to thank you for your kindness."

"You might find it easier if you resorted to honesty rather than flummery."

"You appreciate honesty no more than you do silliness, Lisabeth."

"I really should go." Surely he could sense how her pulse was racing like the runaway horse that had caused the carriage accident last week.

"As you do each time I try to compliment you. You discard my words as if I were hoaxing you. Did you ever consider that I might be honest when I say that you are a joy for the eyes or that I enjoy your razor-wit?"

"Did you ever consider that I might be honest when I tell you that I have no wish to hear such compliments?"

"Why?"

She clenched her fingers by her side. She had to get out of this room! Tears flooded her eyes. She blinked them aside. To surrender to weeping would bring a renewed barrage of questions from him, and she wanted his sympathy as little as he wished hers.

When his hand brushed her cheek, she gasped. Had a single tear escaped to betray her as she had been betrayed too often here? His fingers turned her face toward his, and she realized he had slid to the very edge of the high bed. His eyes were oddly even with hers. She had seen them below hers when he was sitting and above hers when he stood. Never like this.

"Lisabeth," he said softly, "pray do not take a snuff at everything I say. You are trying to help me. I wish only to return the favor."

"I have no need of help."

"No?" His fingers along her face swept down to her nape as he drew her other hand to his uninjured cheek. "Why, then, are you fleeing from the world as I did before you inspired me with your shrewish words? Believe me, *chère cousine*, when I tell you that anguish, if left alone, will fester and consume you. Let me help you."

"I thank you, Radcliffe, but there is nothing you can do to help."

"If there ever is anything I can do . . ."

"I will be certain to tell you." She gulped. "Radcliffe, I must go."

"Yes, I see that you must." He slid her hand down his cheek, grazing her hand with the rough texture of his unshaven face. He held it to his mouth, then bent to press his lips to her palm.

Her senses exploded into longing as her breath battered her chest before surging through her to weaken her knees. As he raised his head, his gaze enveloping her, he tugged gently on her arm to bring her toward him. She wanted to taste those lips with her own. She wanted to delight in the fire of his hands burnishing her skin. She wanted—

With a horrified cry, she jerked herself away. This time when he called her name, she did not slow. She had been want-witted to enter that room. To stay had been even worse. To make the same mistake she had before was unthinkable.

She raced into her room and closed the door of her bedchamber behind her. Staring at the dressing room that led back to the other room, she could not escape the truth. The passions she had vowed never to experience again were being resurrected by Radcliffe. Fighting to submerge them again, she closed her eyes and repeated the vow she had whispered every night after marrying Frederick. She had been betrayed by love once before and would never be again.

"You worthless harlot!"

The shout matched the pain racing through her skull. She tried to escape. There was no escape. Raising her hands, she knew she had made a great mistake. The blows fell upon her like a tempest until she shrank to the floor.

"Lisabeth?"

She dared not look up. That would start the torture anew.

"Lisabeth?"

Through the agony in her head, she realized it was not Frederick's voice. Another man's voice. A gentle voice that promised . . . she was not sure what it promised, but it must be better than what she knew now.

She raised her head and blinked. She was lying in her bed in the room where she now slept alone, but she was not alone. A shadow slipped across her bed, its darkness a comfort instead of fearsome.

A hand covered hers. A strong, smooth hand. Radcliffe's hand.

"Do not be frightened," he murmured. "Forget the past."

She wanted to answer, but sleep took her again. This time, for the first time since she had discovered the truth behind the lies of vows of love, honor, and cherish, her dreams were sweet, not bitter.

Eleven

If Radcliffe used the walking stick to help him in his attempts to walk, Lisabeth did not know. She could not risk going back into his private chambers again, although she found herself sitting, often for more than an hour, staring into her dressing room and listening to the mumble of voices on its far side. To go back there again chanced uncorking the tight capsule of memories. Even more dangerous were the cravings that haunted her when she recalled his feverish kiss on her hand.

Had he truly come into her room the past few nights to ease the nightmare? She could not ask him, because she was so uncertain of where the dream ended and reality emerged. Wilson had not mentioned having her sleep disturbed, so Lisabeth could not pose the question to her abigail.

It was better, she told herself, to let Bond supervise Radcliffe's recovery. After all, she had been right when she said she should not be visiting him in his bedchamber.

The uneven sound of his steps told her that he was walking, albeit slowly. She suspected he was pushing himself to the limits of his endurance . . . and beyond. Bond reported to her daily about Radcliffe's progress and always ended with an invitation to join Lady Edwina and Radcliffe for cards. Somehow, she always had devised an excuse that was true.

Lisabeth was astonished to come out into her small garden to discover Radcliffe sitting on a cast-iron bench by the door. Her amazement must have been emblazoned on her face because he said, "You need not gape at me as if I'm a beast from the jungles of India."

"I did not realize you could walk this far."

"You might have," he said, pushing himself to his feet, "if you had accepted a single one of my requests to join us for a convivial afternoon."

"I sent my regrets."

"Which sounded as if you did not have many regrets."

She wanted to smile when she saw how easily he used the walking stick as he crossed the uneven stones by the door. To lower her guard to his charm even an inch was sure to ask for renewed disaster. The bandage that had wrapped his cheek was gone, and only a small mark showed where that laceration had been.

"Radcliffe," she said in her coolest tone, "you have been in Town long enough to know how hectic the Season can be. Between callers here and the calls I must make, my afternoons are full."

"Dammit, Lisabeth!" he snapped.

"You should watch what you say."

"As you should. I tire of these thumpers you try to get me to swallow as the truth!"

She folded her arms in front of her. "If you wish to know the truth, Radcliffe, I have been making many of these calls on your behalf. I know only a few of the eligible maidens embarking on this Season. By enjoying a bit of scanmag with my friends, I can ask about those who might be of interest to you."

"How kind of you!"

"It is only what I agreed to do."

"And Lisabeth Montague never breaks her word?" He laughed sharply. "That is amusing!"

She frowned. "Why are you in such a ferocious mood

when I did no more than what you and Norton requested?"

"Because I am bored, my *chère cousine*, with endless games of cards and struggling to walk from one side of my room to the other. That is why I came out here. I swear I have crossed that room a score of times today."

"If you are bored with tame scenes," Lady Edwina said as she and Bond came out into the garden, her gown a forest green that seemed unwelcome in the spring scene, "you should try something more challenging. Mayhap a garden path?"

Radcliffe's smile grew taut. Had Lisabeth arranged for her mother-in-law to shadow her on the unlikely chance that she might encounter him? Even days ago, he would have discounted such an idea as ludicrous, but no one had been able or willing to explain why Lisabeth had fled from his side with that expression of horror on her face. He had seen it too often. Had no one else noticed it? Curiosity taunted him, demanding he satisfy it. Curiosity, however, was not the only thing bedeviling him to be satisfied. A single sample of the flavor of Lisabeth's soft skin only honed his yearning to bring her close again.

"My lord?" prodded Lady Edwina, warning that she was as impatient for his answer as he was growing to have Lisabeth in his arms.

"The garden path?" he asked. "Can you be anxious to see me go head over teacups?"

The older woman chuckled. "There is little chance of that when you confine yourself to walking in the house. But, if you are to find a wife, you must go beyond it. Mayhap you wish to avoid any chance to fail. I would wager that you cannot reach the back wall of the garden."

"Would you?" He leaned his arms on his walking stick.

"My lord," Bond cautioned, giving Lisabeth a supplicatory look, "you have come far today. It might be wise if you rested."

"Yes," seconded Lisabeth. "Do not let Lady Edwina goad you into something foolish." To her mother-in-law, she added, "Radcliffe is learning that a recovery is best when it is a slow and steady one."

Slow and steady? Did Lisabeth have any idea how her words echoed the ones Norton had thrown at him so often? She could not guess how such tepid advice riled him. He had escaped Norton's absurd coddling. If Lisabeth intended to treat him the same, mayhap he should prove to her, right now, that he would not subject himself to such silliness again.

Coolly, he said, "I must remind you once again, my *chère cousine*, that I am no longer a sprig. I know what I can do."

"You and Lady Edwina can stop creating a dust each time you speak."

"Lisabeth," her mother-in-law replied with a laugh before he could speak, "I believe Lord Radcliffe can contend with me without you plaguing him with your anxiety."

"If you continue to hazard your well-being, Radcliffe," Lisabeth argued, "you may be unable to find yourself a wife. Miss Gibbs has accepted your rebuff, but you cannot meet another young woman if you are confined to the house."

Lady Edwina laughed. "Dear Lisabeth, you are making my point exactly. I daresay 'tis time for you to test your wings, my lord. You have nested here too long with all of us clucking over you. So will you take my wager that you cannot walk to the back wall of the garden without toppling onto your nose?"

"What do you offer to sweeten this gamble?"

"You are brass-faced, my lord."

"On the contrary, for I offer only to do as a fair lady has requested. Can I be faulted for requesting a favor in return?"

Lady Edwina ignored Lisabeth's protests. "What can you request, my lord, when you have been able to run tame through our home? Is there some small thing we have failed to grant you?"

Radcliffe glanced at Lisabeth. It was so easy to admire Lisabeth in her cambric dress of a pale pink that matched her cheeks. During the time since she had become his hostess, he had seen the admiration that followed her wherever she went. Not only the men of *Le Beau Monde*, although Radcliffe understood why they were enchanted with her golden curls and enticing form, but the women, too, who were eager to share Lisabeth's company. Her gentle heart and ready smile endeared her to her friends, but she was not smiling now.

"Do not prove to us," she said, "that you are short a sheet."

"Do not pinch at me. As I said, I believe I have enough years to know what I am doing."

"You cannot deny that you still are my student, can you?"

He smiled. "No, I cannot deny that."

"Nor can you deny that you remain as rag-mannered as when you arrived."

"I would not attempt to deny that either."

"So you need more lessons to complete your entrance into the Polite World." She pointed to the bench. "If you would sit, Radcliffe, we can begin."

"In a few minutes, *chère cousine*." Radcliffe patted her shoulder, and Lisabeth gasped. He fought not to as well. Had the casual motion sent fire searing through her, as it had him, as if a bolt of lightning arced between them?

Lisabeth sat on the bench as Radcliffe continued to look at her. Why had she not gone back inside as soon as this inane conversation began? That might have put an end to this absurd wager, and she would have avoided any chance for him to touch her.

Knowing she must say something, she managed no more than a whisper. Mayhap the others would think her voice was strained through anger, which was partly true. "If you want to risk your recovery, Radcliffe, I shall not halt you."

"I know I can walk to the back of this handkerchief-size patch of greenery you call your garden." Turning to Lady Edwina, who was listening with a smile, he said, "A wager it shall be. If I fail, you may ask of me what you will, and I suspect you wish me and Bond to remove ourselves."

"My lord," Lady Edwina said, "you put words in my mouth that I cannot imagine speaking."

"Then, it is just as well that I said them for you." He grinned. "However, you must agree that when I succeed—"

"You are very sure of yourself, my lord."

"*When* I succeed, you shall agree that for a week, you and Bond will take tea together."

"*Bond* and I?" The old woman shook her head. "I find your request baffling, my lord."

"Do you?" demanded Lisabeth, her lips tight with fury. She found anger easier than examining the strange emotions swirling through her. "Think of what he wants!"

Radcliffe turned to her. "What do I want, Lisabeth?"

"If Bond and Lady Edwina take tea together . . ."

"Then, you and I shall as well." He smiled. "You label me a ramshackle fellow, but I assure you that I am suggesting this so you may be proud of me when I return to the swirl of Society."

"Proud of you?" she shot back. "For risking your recovery?"

"On one hand, you dress me down for being reluctant to attend my lessons. Now you are outraged that I would try to arrange a time when you would have my undivided attention for your lessons."

"I shall decide when the lessons shall be."

"We can discuss it at tea."

"Yes, do cut line, Lisabeth," added Lady Edwina. Stepping to one side and motioning toward the curving path, she said, "I accept your conditions, my lord."

Bond pleaded, "My lord, please listen to Lady Lisabeth."

"Fudge!" Radcliffe snapped. "If you do not believe I can do this, prepare to be surprised."

Lisabeth clutched the seat of the bench as he stepped off the uneven stones onto the narrow path. Biting her lip, she kept her warnings unspoken. The stones amid the dirt were precarious and could throw him. Seeing anticipation on her mother-in-law's face and despair on Bond's, she held her breath as Radcliffe began his journey, one that would have come easily before he had been wounded.

She ignored the greenery's perfume and the song of the birds. The sun was hot on her bare head, but she was cold inside as Radcliffe maneuvered warily. She did not want him hurt again, especially over something as idiotic as a wager. Hearing Bond's whispered prayer, she put her hand on his arm, but no comfort awaited them while Radcliffe was being headstrong.

Each step he took was a separate agony. More than once, when he wobbled, Lisabeth was tempted to run to his side. She heard his breath straining, and she glared at her mother-in-law, who refused to meet her eyes.

Radcliffe's triumphant laugh announced the moment when he reached the back wall. Bond rushed to him, the red-haired man's face wan with consternation.

Ignoring him, Radcliffe turned to Lady Edwina. "As you can see, I have successfully traversed the garden, my lady."

"I stand corrected." Lady Edwina smiled. "You *are* able to walk to the garden wall. If I had been wise, I would have wagered that you could not walk there and back."

"About that you may be right."

Bond drew his lord's arm around his shoulders. "Lord Radcliffe, let me help you."

"In a moment." To the older woman, he said, "In accordance with our wager, Lisabeth and I shall be allowed to enjoy a private tea for the next week."

"I pay my wagers." Her faded eyes twinkled. "We must

have another wager soon, my lord. I would be happy to win and give you and your man your congé."

"Until then, we remain your guests. Yours and Lisabeth's," he added as he looked to where Lisabeth remained on the bench. When he smiled, she turned and walked into the house, her back as straight as a beefeater's. She needed no words to reveal her outrage, but he was unsure if she was more furious that he had attempted crossing the garden or that he had succeeded. But he had a week to discover the truth of that and, he hoped, many other things.

Lisabeth glanced up as Wilson entered the bedroom. Her abigail tiptoed, and Lisabeth wondered if Wilson thought she would go unnoted.

"Wilson, pray do not skulk about," she said irritably, then realized she was venting her spleen on the wrong person.

As Lisabeth began to apologize, Wilson interrupted, "Think nothing of it, my lady. I know you are sorely tried by Lord Radcliffe and Lady Montague's wager in the garden."

"You do?" Lisabeth went to peer out the window. She wished the day was as dull as her spirits, but the sunshine remained glorious. That Wilson had learned of the wager warned that the story must have been spread through the house. She should not be surprised, for the servants enjoyed gossip as much as their employers, but she would rather not be the focus of the household's sympathetic glances.

"My lady, may I suggest that I speak with Bond? He seems a man of uncommon common sense."

Facing her abigail, who was wringing her hands, she said, "I doubt it will do much good. It is up to me to unravel this jumble. I must teach the Marquess of Radcliffe that he cannot come into my house and take it over." She smiled as if her next words did not rivet her with that familiar pain which followed every thought of finding Radcliffe a wife. "Tea we will have together this afternoon and every afternoon for the next week, but not alone."

"My lady?"

She smiled as she reached for her shawl. "I promised Norton that I would find his cousin a marchioness. Radcliffe has proven that he is hale, so now I shall ensure that he has a parade of eligible misses to practice his new skills upon."

Wilson chuckled. "What do you plan to do, my lady?"

"Ask Doherty to have the carriage brought around post-haste."

Lisabeth suspected that Wilson did more than pass her message to the butler, for the carriage was ready before she was. Doherty gave her an unexpected smile as she hurried out the door. If Wilson had not been able to hold her tongue about Lisabeth's scheme, she hoped word of it would not reach Bond and then Radcliffe before she had a chance to put all the pieces in place to give Radcliffe a Season he would not soon forget.

The houses on Brook Street were awash with the sunshine dancing off the bricks. A single tree edged the walkway in front of each house, but the meager shadow could not challenge the light.

Crandall, who was sitting on the box of the closed carriage, held the reins in one hand while he ran the other against his nape. He appreciated that he had not been turned off from his duties after the carriage came within ambsace of falling onto its side. Instead, Lady Lisabeth had sent a message to the stable to ask of his condition and insisted that he call a doctor if he was injured. Once he heard that both Lord Radcliffe and Lady Lisabeth would be all right, Crandall had been relieved.

Turning onto Grosvenor Square, the carriage slowed. The footman jumped to the ground and hurried to open the door. Lisabeth adjusted her silk shawl as she stepped onto the walkway. The small ache within her had become anguish, but she ignored it with the skill she had gained from ignoring the agony that had been hers during her marriage to Frederick. She had vowed to find Radcliffe a wife, and she would.

When the Castleman butler opened the door, he bowed her graciously into the narrow foyer. She grimaced. The heavy wood paneling belonged to a grander house than this one, but Mrs. Castleman delighted in what she called her miniature manor house.

Ushered into the drawing room, Lisabeth was greeted by Mrs. Castleman. The lanky woman wore every year of her life ingrained in her face. Each turn of season had torn away a bit of her flesh to leave her gaunt skin and bones, but one did not notice that when she smiled.

"My dear Lady Montague," she gushed as she placed a perfunctory kiss on Lisabeth's cheek, "I was so pleased when you sent the message that you might be calling. I do wish Emeraude was here, but she is out on her own calls. You know how young women are. Like butterflies, flitting everywhere, but landing nowhere long."

Lisabeth sat on a hard chair. "I must own to being pleased that your daughter is out, for I would show a sad want of manners to speak of my errand in her presence."

"I guessed you had a reason for calling." Mrs. Castleman reclined on a settee. "There is nothing amiss with your dear mother-in-law, is there?"

"Lady Edwina enjoys high health, as usual. She hopes to see you in the Park on the morrow."

Wafting her hands in front of her face, Mrs. Castleman chuckled. "She will, for I have the most delicious tidbit to share with her." She went on in a whisper, "I have heard Lady Prospera Fry is much in trouble again with her father.

He has cut her off, saying he will pay no more of her gambling debts until she finds a husband."

"She should have little trouble finding a man interested in gaining his son a title."

"With her debts? The man must be far up in the stirrup if he takes on her debts." Her eyes sparkled. "Can you name a man who is both rich and a bit of an addle-cove?"

Suspecting the direction of the conversation and not wanting to give Mrs. Castleman the chance to suggest Radcliffe as a match for Prospera, she said, "I came to ask your permission to invite Emeraude for tea today."

"You need not seek my permission, my dear. I do not doubt that she could learn much from your social graces."

Knowing that she should accept the victory, honesty compelled her to say, "Lord Radcliffe will be joining us. I am sure he will be delighted with the opportunity to speak with Emeraude."

"You are jesting, Lady Montague," Mrs. Castleman gasped, sitting straighter.

"Lord Radcliffe is interested in meeting a young lady who possesses intelligence and beauty. Your Emeraude has both."

"Listen to yourself." Wagging a finger, she did not lower her voice. "You should be thinking of a husband for yourself instead of a wife for that man."

"Mrs. Castleman, I—"

"Do not give me a back-answer."

"It was not my intention to bicker, but—"

"My dear Lady Montague, I cannot help but take note how *on dits* state that Mr. Smythe and Lieutenant Ison are dangling after you. Why are you involving yourself with the pursuit of a wife for a man who can offer nothing but his title?" When Lisabeth started to argue, Mrs. Castleman continued, "I wish you could see the situation without a cloud of emotion blinding you."

Paying no attention to the yearning to cheer aloud that

Emeraude would not be trying to find a place in Radcliffe's heart, she said, "I am not blinded by emotion. I am obliged to fulfill a promise to a member of my husband's family. Would you do less?"

"My answer to your invitation must be no," she intoned in repressive accents. "My daughter is of such a gentle constitution that I believe if she sat with the marquess, someone would have to be sent running for smelling salts. I will not have my Emeraude involved with a Mr. Hopkins."

Lisabeth stood, swallowing harshly as she tried to speak past the rage clogging her throat. Mrs. Castleman's lucubrations always vexed her, but never as much as today when she voiced her prejudices against Radcliffe. Wanting to say that Radcliffe probably would find her simpering Emeraude a bore, she said nothing but her farewells.

When she was sitting in her carriage, riding to a destination she had selected just in case, Lisabeth told herself that she must have her emotions under control when she arrived at Miss Nolan's house on Soho Square. Mayhap she should have called on Miss Violet Nolan first. The young woman, who lived with her maiden aunt, was a diamond of birth and prettily spoken.

Lisabeth blinked as she entered the Nolan home. Miss Nolan's taste in decor was as brilliant as Mrs. Castleman's was dour. Gilt highlighted the high ceiling and the walls. A wide staircase was embellished with a wrought-iron pattern of vines and roses. Coming down it, Miss Nolan held out her hand to Lisabeth.

Smiling as she greeted Miss Nolan, who had had the misfortune to inherit her father's aquiline nose, Lisabeth said, "Actually I came to ask *you* to tea." She followed Miss Nolan into a brightly decorated sitting room.

"Today?"

"Why not?" She hoped her laugh sounded more sincere to her friend than it did in her ears. "I thought it would be pleasant to chat this afternoon. Lord Radcliffe and I—"

"No!"

Lisabeth regarded Miss Nolan in surprise. After the call on Mrs. Castleman, Lisabeth had not guessed she would receive the same horrified reaction from this young woman who made no secret of seeking a dashing blade to wed.

"Miss Nolan, I think you shall discover that Lord Radcliffe is diverting company."

"Lady Montague, I regret that I shall be unable to visit today."

"Tomorrow, perchance?"

"Tomorrow is my day with my *couturière*. 'Tis an appointment I make a practice never to break." Before Lisabeth could ask another question, Miss Nolan said, "Please do not cause me to be less than polite, Lady Montague. I value your friendship, and I would hate to see it come to an end over a meaningless issue. Whenever you wish, I would be delighted to have tea with you and your mother-in-law."

Lisabeth nodded. "I understand."

"Do you?" Miss Nolan gripped Lisabeth's hands. "My dear Lady Montague, having that man at your house has created so much poker-talk. Think of what a disaster it would be for the *ton* to learn that you are riding about the city trying to procure a wife for him. I never expected such a social solecism from you."

"He is part of my late husband's family," she explained as she had too many times. "Helping him find a wife is a duty I cannot shirk."

"Even when it risks your own standing among the *ton*?"

She did not reply with the truth. At this very moment, she would toss aside the shreds of her reputation to protect her heart. Although as another pang struck her, she feared it might be too late.

Twelve

Lisabeth thanked the lass who brought the tea tray, then reached for the pot. A broad hand blocked hers, and she looked at Radcliffe, who was sitting across from her.

"I thought we were waiting for your guests," he said.

"Guests?"

He smiled. "You need not look astounded, Lisabeth. When I spoke to Wilson, who was disconcerted beyond measure by my questions, she allowed that you were calling on friends to ask them to join us for this victory celebration. Could it be that you did not wish to take tea alone with me?"

"You may be able to forget the favor Norton asked of me, but I have not. How can you meet a young woman when you seldom leave the house?"

"So you called on the Castlemans, the Nolans, and the Toblers, as well as other of your friends."

"Yes," she answered, rising color heating her cheeks. "You have excellent spies, Radcliffe."

"Bond has made many friends in your household." He leaned back and crossed his arms over his chest.

"What is that?"

"What is what?"

Lisabeth reached across the table and touched the watch fob dropping from the upper crescent pocket on his waistcoat. "What are you wearing on this?"

"One customarily wears a pocket watch on a watch fob."

"But isn't that a key?"

He looked down and frowned as he tucked the small key into his pocket. "I owe you another duty, *chère cousine*, for making me look my best for tea." Folding his arms again, he added, "And before you ask the question I can see battering your pretty lips, I will be glad to tell you that the key is simply an affectation."

"But why do you wear it?"

Chuckling, he said, "I have my reasons."

"Which are?"

"Shall I say that I hope it will be the key to a very special heart that will open only for me?"

Lisabeth rolled her eyes and laughed. "Save your nothing-sayings for those who might enjoy them."

"And who might that be? One among this cascade of callers you have arranged for today?"

She lowered her eyes. "There will be no callers today."

"No one wishes to join us?" He lifted the teapot and poured with a grace that filled every motion, save his walking. "Lisabeth, it may be time to admit defeat in this mad plan. Miss Gibbs bores me nigh to death, and you obviously have failed to persuade any of your other acquaintances to call. As skilled as you have been as a tutor, I am afraid you have been less successful as a matchmaker."

"I am unwilling to concede that so soon to Norton."

"True, and on that you are wise, for he would become even more unbearable if his assumptions that he is always correct are proven even a single time." Handing her a cup, he smiled. "Mayhap you would allow me to escort you to the musicale at Smythe's this evening. Lady Edwina has been babbling endlessly about how delighted you must be to attend the gathering, but I suspect your opinion is quite the opposite."

"Mr. Smythe tries to be pleasant, but I fear he is wasting his time pursuing me."

"So let me escort you. That would solve both your problem and mine."

Lisabeth paused, her fingers tightening on the cup. It *was* a simple solution to an increasingly complex problem. Not only would Radcliffe be seen by those who might change their minds once they had a chance to discover he was not feeble, but she would have an excuse not to spend the evening with Mr. Smythe.

With a sigh, she said, "That would be a mistake."

"Why?"

"It is understood by the Polite World that we are involved in achieving the same goal. Think how confused people might be if it appears that you are escorting me. Someone might assume . . ."

Radcliffe laughed. *"Chère cousine,* you are such a charming child! You cling to a child's dreams of making the world come to rights simply because you wish it. If I were your brother, there would be nothing amiss with me being your companion. That I am your cousin should be the same."

"If you were *my* cousin. However, you are Frederick's—"

"Cousin's cousin." Radcliffe sipped his tea and reached for a plate that was piled with small cakes. "I continue to be baffled by the fact that our connection is close enough to allow me to enjoy your hospitality, but it remains too distant for me to escort you to a simple fête."

"Immediate family are those who cannot—" Lisabeth hesitated, again startled by how difficult words had become lately when she spoke to Radcliffe. Words had not been hard with any other man. She had used many against Frederick, for they had been her only weapon to protect her broken heart. With carefully chosen phrases, she had been able to cool—or at least postpone—another pronouncement of Mr. Smythe's ardor. Her easy compliments to Lieutenant Ison kept the conversation focused on him.

Yet, with Radcliffe, every word seemed to possess extra meaning.

Her half hope that he would be a gentleman and disregard her hesitation vanished when he asked, "Is marry the word upon which you hesitate? I could ask myself why, but I think you are the only one who knows that answer. You never speak of your marriage, Lisabeth."

"I thought we had agreed to refrain from discussing the past."

"We can refrain from discussing it, but it is a part of us. Even though we shove our pasts away, hoping they will vanish, they follow us with the swift speed of a runaway carriage. Sometimes we can stay ahead of the past, sometimes not."

"You are talking nonsense."

A hint of a smile tipped one corner of his lips. "I suspect you know I am not. But, if you do not want to acknowledge that truth, mayhap you do not wish to say the word marry because something in our present bothers you about it. Can it be that you do not wish to be reminded of your failure to complete the task given to you by Cousin Norton?"

"I can do no more than teach you what you need to know to find a bride," she retorted, finding words a refuge once more. "Pleasant manners and stylish dress can be my only contributions to your sport of wooing. The rest I must leave in your hands."

"How odd that you put it that way!" He stretched across the table and folded her fingers between his larger hands.

The sweet warmth flooded her anew. For once, his smile did not possess its calculating coolness. Instead it was genuine, bringing a guilelessness to his face that she could not have imagined.

"Why do you tense whenever I offer you friendship, Lisabeth?" he whispered. "I seek to learn more of my cousin who has taught me so much."

"You should remember your earliest lessons. A lady is the judge of what is proper, and I fear you are overstepping yourself."

"If no one else wishes to be my friend, can I believe that you are?"

Lisabeth laughed. "Bravo, Radcliffe! Such a show of humility should win you admirers among the weak-hearted."

"And the weak-minded," he added, but he did not release her hands. "Neither of which describes my cousin Lisabeth. You are a constant trial to me."

"As you are to me. Mayhap we should not try to assert any control over each other. That might augur easier times."

Radcliffe shook his head. "I do not care a rush about ease. I cannot imagine a time when you are not threatening to fly off the hooks because of something I have said." Lifting her hands, he stroked them lightly. "So soft you are."

"Radcliffe, I think—"

His voice dropped to that husky murmur that crept along her skin like a sweet caress. "Do not think. You think too much about what is right and what is wrong by Society's standards and never give thought to what is right and what is wrong for Lisabeth Montague."

He bent and pressed his lips to her hand. The heat that had simmered beneath his touch burst through her, sweeping away her breath.

"Am I intruding?" came a soft voice from the doorway. "Father told me that I would be welcome to call today."

Looking over her shoulder, Lisabeth saw Adelaide Tobler. Although Mr. Tobler had apologized that his daughter could not take tea at Lady Montague's house today, the petite brunette must have persuaded him to change his mind. Lisabeth wondered how, for Miss Tobler seldom expressed any opinions.

Radcliffe released Lisabeth's fingers as he pushed himself to his feet. "Do come in. Thank you for the lesson, Lisabeth. I shall know what to do when introduced to the dowagers this evening."

Lisabeth stood. She avoided looking at Radcliffe as she greeted Miss Tobler and introduced her to Radcliffe. Only when Miss Tobler was seated and balancing a cup and saucer gracefully did Lisabeth dare a glance at him.

As she had expected—dreaded, might be closer to the truth she tried to ignore—he was appraising Miss Tobler without comment, but with a smile. Lisabeth knew she should be elated, for she had guessed that Radcliffe would find Miss Tobler charming. Instead, she suffered from an unnamed malady that churned through her stomach and weighed heavily in her throat.

Lisabeth took a deep breath and nodded toward Radcliffe. He must have understood her silent injunction, because he engaged Miss Tobler in aimless conversation that, while not putting the young woman at ease, began to draw her out of her shyness.

"Yes, Lady Montague is my sponsor," he said with a laugh that was answered by Miss Tobler's bashful smile. "I shall trust you to tell me, as well, if I do something out of hand. The lessons that you have obviously learned with such success are not easy for an old soldier."

"But, my lord, you are not old." Miss Tobler blushed and lowered her eyes.

"I fear I may give you more than a decade, Miss Tobler." He smiled. "Now Lisabeth is frowning at me, for I am being ramshackle to discuss such a sensitive issue as a lady's age. And she is quite right. Shall we speak instead of—?"

Lisabeth did not learn what Radcliffe wished to speak of, for her butler entered the sitting room. "Lieutenant Ison, my lady," he said emotionlessly.

"Do show him in," she urged. She flashed a smile at Miss Tobler. "We shall be quite a party this afternoon."

"So we shall," said Radcliffe.

At his abruptly taut tone, Lisabeth saw he was wearing a savage scowl. Did he believe Lieutenant Ison would be a rival for Miss Tobler's attentions? Impossible, unless Radcliffe was taken with Miss Tobler so quickly. Again that sense of malaise ached in her.

She made certain no one else guessed her disquiet as she welcomed Lieutenant Ison and introduced him to Miss Tobler. He bowed over her hand, then Lisabeth's, before pulling a chair close to the table and Lisabeth's chair.

"I pray you will forgive this outlandish intrusion," Lieutenant Ison said when he held a cup on his knee. Unlike Radcliffe, who wore informal breeches and riding boots, the lieutenant was dressed in prime twig. "I was summoned down from London again until yesterday. Upon my return, I heard of the near catastrophe with your carriage. Although I was assured you were unhurt, my lady, I could not bear not to ascertain that for myself."

Radcliffe muttered, "You should be able to determine that by now, as much as you are gawking at her."

"What is that, my lord?" asked Lieutenant Ison. "Did the cacophony of the cannon affect your hearing? I believe you are mumbling."

"I said it was fortunate Lisabeth was uninjured."

"But you were, my lord!" Miss Tobler put her fingers to her lips, looking as startled as the others at her outburst.

Radcliffe smiled. "You are kind to take an interest in my well-being, Miss Tobler. I can assure you that both Lisabeth and I are fine."

When Miss Tobler flushed, Lisabeth hurried to ask, "Lieutenant Ison, were you being garrisoned?"

While the lieutenant spoke on and on of his duties, Lisabeth did not intrude. She was glad when he had to excuse himself to look in on his uncle, but she assured him that he would see them at Mr. Smythe's that evening. He bowed over her hand again before departing.

Miss Tobler said, "I should leave also. I thank you for inviting me, Lady Montague."

"It was my pleasure."

"Lady Montague and I would be delighted to have you join us this evening at Mr. Smythe's musicale," Radcliffe said, standing when Miss Tobler did.

Miss Tobler whispered, "I am honored by your invitation, my lord. I shall look forward to this evening."

When Lisabeth had seen Miss Tobler to the door and come back to the sitting room, she discovered Radcliffe pacing, his walking stick beating a tattoo on the floor and his mouth set in the straight line she had seen when he was pressing himself to the very limit of the pain he could endure. Recalling Mrs. Castleman's aspersions of him as a cripple, she wished Lady Edwina's friend could see his battle with his weak leg.

"Lisabeth, I failed to hear you return," Radcliffe said as he folded his hands on the high back of a chair.

"I came to learn your impressions of Miss Tobler."

"A little mouse," he said with a laugh. "Almost every word must be enticed from her."

"Yet she jumps quickly to your defense."

"Mayhap she believes I am in need of it when I had to fight my way to my feet."

"I think, rather, that she is in awe of you."

"Me?"

Lisabeth smiled as she placed the cups on the tray. Sitting in her chair by the window, she looked at her beloved garden. "Do not assume a guise of amazement, Radcliffe. You put the girl quite out of countenance with your attentions, and I believe you enjoyed every moment of it."

"Since I have been about you, Lisabeth, I have forgotten how easy it is to disconcert the mild-hearted." He chose a chair opposite hers. "She is, however, everything you suggested. Pretty, with a brain in her head, and, if she could overcome that intolerable meekness, congenial."

"I thought you would find her fetching." When she was sure that she was in control of her expression, she turned to him. He must not guess that each word she spoke burned like acid on her tongue. For the first time, she might have a chance to do as she vowed. She must not make a bumble-bath of it simply because her heart protested with every beat. "You were very gracious to ask her to join us this evening."

"A compliment of the first order! My sole regret is that by escorting Miss Tobler, I leave you to your two dashing admirers. Unless, of course, Ison beseeched you to attend the musicale with him."

"I do not comprehend your distaste for Lieutenant Ison."

"*Chère cousine,* how can you, who have been married and widowed, know so little of what lies in the heart of a man who looks at you as Ison does?"

"I see nothing amiss with how he looks at me." She shuddered with distaste. "He does not stare like Mr. Smythe."

Radcliffe grimaced as he leaned back. "Ah, the inimitable Mr. Smythe. I swear he is about to present his suit at any moment. If you accept, Lisabeth, I shall remove myself from beneath your roof before the next hour grows old."

"You make it quite tempting to consider Mr. Smythe's proposal."

"Proposal?" came an excited voice. "Have you made a match for yourself, Lisabeth dear?"

Lisabeth rose as Lady Edwina came into the room. As always, her mother-in-law was dressed in a vivid shade of green that made her skin appear as pale as a corpse's.

"No, I have not accepted any proposal. It would be quite impossible when nobody has offered one." She shot a withering scowl at Radcliffe, who was grinning with delight at managing to include Lady Edwina in the conversation. "It was nothing but more of Radcliffe's prattling. You know how *he* enjoys mapping out my future. I swear he does not think I have a thought of my own in my head."

"Fudge!" Radcliffe returned with a laugh. "I merely wish to see you settled before I buckle myself to a bride."

"I am quite settled. If you may recall, this is my house. You are the petitioner within it, not me."

"Now, now," said Lady Edwina, chuckling, "there is no need for such demure hits. Lisabeth, was that the Toblers' carriage I saw departing as I came down the stairs?"

Taking a deep breath to submerge her irritation, Lisabeth said, "Miss Tobler joined us for tea. Lieutenant Ison called as well."

"What a charming foursome we made!" Radcliffe's sarcasm filled every word.

"Radcliffe," Lisabeth retorted, the heat returning to her voice, "simply because our guests have left is no reason for you to fall back on your bangster ways."

"Lisabeth!" gasped her mother-in-law. "I would not expect such cant from you."

Radcliffe laughed as Lisabeth flushed. " 'Tis as I thought. You are, deep within you, no more accepting of propriety's ways than I, cousin. You know, Lady Edwina is quite correct. Such language is not befitting a lady who is accepted among the Pink of the *Ton.* "

"You need not box my ears to hide your own shortcomings, Radcliffe! If you will excuse me, I shall see if Wilson has my things ready for this evening. Good afternoon."

When Lisabeth had left the room along with her damaged dignity, Radcliffe continued to chuckle. He recalled the softness of Lisabeth's hands and marveled again at how slight they seemed. Such fervor she restrained in that slender body!

"My lord, do sit down, so I may say what I wish without craning my neck," ordered Lady Edwina as she lowered herself to the settee. When he sat across from her, she continued, "Lisabeth is correct. You enjoy bullocking her, but you must be fathoming that she is not one to listen to such nonsense."

"I think only of bringing laughter to her."

"Laughter?"

He looked at the empty doorway. "I have come to believe that Lisabeth was without laughter in her life for too long. Do you share that belief, my lady?"

"If you think to pump me for information about Lisabeth, you are mistaken."

"No, that was not my intention, although it may have appeared thusly. I was expressing my concern for her."

"Concern? Is that all you feel for her? I doubt that. Do not be hoaxing me, young man! I have seen how you take advantage of every opportunity to be close to her, even when I am here. I do not want to think about what you might try when I am not."

"Lisabeth would permit no untoward behavior."

"Of the quality of her behavior, I am certain. Of yours, I am not, but I shall remind you that bamblusterating me will not be easy. I was cutting my wisdoms before you were out of swaddling."

"Lady Edwina, you shock me with your language."

She shook her finger at him and laughed. "I have heard you say worse, and I daresay, if you remain here, you shall hear worse from me. I have no need for a mere sprig to tell me what I can or cannot say. What I do wish from you, my lord, is honesty."

"Something I endeavor always to offer you."

"Me, mayhap, but are you as honest with Lisabeth? She has worked hard to find you a wife as you requested."

"As our mutual cousin requested," Radcliffe corrected with a smile.

"Bah! Do not split hairs with me. You, my lord, are not a man to allow others to dictate your life. If you had not been fascinated with the idea of obtaining a wife, you would not have hesitated to ignore that churl Norton."

Radcliffe offered her the plate of cakes. When she selected one, he took the last for himself. With a reflective bite, he said, "I see I must disabuse my misapprehensions, Lady Montague. I thought you and Norton were in each other's pockets."

"Norton was my stepson Frederick's compatriot, not mine. I find his habits distasteful and his want of polish even more repellent."

"Norton or Frederick?"

Lady Edwina stood. "My lord, that is not a question you should ask."

Gaining his feet, he said, "Then, allow me to apologize. I did not intend to impugn your memory of your stepson which appears to be far fonder than Lisabeth's."

Lady Edwina's face became an even sadder shade of gray. Lowering herself stiffly back to the settee, she nodded. "You are right, my lord. Norton and Frederick were very much alike, which might explain why he and my stepson were such tie-mates." She clasped her hands in her lap and stared at them. "The finest thing Frederick ever did was marry Lisabeth, so I might have her to comfort me when he died. She is a true treasure, quite past price, as I knew from the moment we first spoke. I was so impressed I wasted no time introducing her to Frederick." Her forehead threaded as her voice fell into a near whisper. "Mayhap I thought then too much of myself and not enough of Lisabeth, for I know, as well, even though she has never uttered a word of complaint, that her days with Frederick were not filled with bliss."

"She is not one to complain." He wanted to reassure Lady Edwina. Lisabeth adored her mother-in-law, so she could not fault Lady Edwina for bringing Frederick Montague into her life.

Before he could decide on the right words to say, Lady Edwina replied, "That may be the most truthful thing you have ever said. She bears her tribulations with the silence of a martyr." She sighed. "Gentle heart that she is, she believes she must consider everyone else's happiness before her own. She refuses to tell that odious Mr. Smythe to take himself far from her because she fears hurting his feelings."

Radcliffe smiled. "Despite her angelic appearance, Lisabeth is no saint."

"Did I say she was? And I cannot argue with the truth that you put so well, my lord. Lisabeth has forgotten how to be happy." She lifted a teacup and took a sip, regarding him with a sudden smile over the rim. "Or I should have said that she *had* forgotten how to be happy."

"Are you suggesting that my arrival has brought back your daughter-in-law's happiness? Instead, I would suggest that I have imposed misery upon her. Mayhap she has come to equate the two as one."

"Again you may be more correct than you suspect, my lord. That is why I must ask you, as Norton did of Lisabeth, a favor. Actually two favors. While she helps you find a marchioness, do nothing to prevent her from finding a husband who will make her happy. I do not believe that man to be Lieutenant Ison, although he professes a true affection for her."

"Ison would be the worst choice for Lisabeth."

"As I share your opinion, although I own a curiosity as to how you formed it, I ask that you do what you might to find another man for her. With Mr. Smythe's fête, you are becoming a true part of the Season. Certainly you will have the chance to sound out a gentleman of good birth and good character—"

"And swimming in lard?"

"Money is not an issue. My late husband's estate was vast enough so even Frederick's fast life could not deplete it. I am more concerned with finding a man who will make her happy."

Radcliffe poured himself a second cup of tea, but disdained her offer of cream. "I shall endeavor to do as you request. What is the second favor you wish to ask?"

"That you focus your search for a wife for you and a husband for Lisabeth beyond the walls of this house." Regarding him steadily, she continued, "I can tell you that there is no man within these walls to whom I would sanction her marriage."

"You wound me, my lady. I thought, with your many compliments, that you considered me a potential match for your daughter-in-law."

When Lady Edwina laughed, Radcliffe smiled. He had suspected that she had put aside her abhorrence for him. He should have known better. What had been Lisabeth's first lesson about the *ton*? Presentation was all-important. Lady Edwina had created an image of friendship between them, but it was as unsubstantial as a theatre set.

"Do you agree to these requests, my lord?" she asked.

He did not hesitate, for there was only one answer he could give. "To see Lisabeth as happy as she wishes me to be, I shall do as you ask."

Thirteen

The closed carriage slowed in front of the home of Mr. Cyril Smythe on the east side of Fitzroy Square off Tottenham Court Road. The rowhouses, which had been built a quarter of a century before, had simple facades. Although only two sides of the square were complete, Mr. Smythe regaled his friends, on every possible occasion, with his expectations of how the Square eventually would be grander than any in Mayfair.

Bond jumped to the ground. Carefully he schooled his face in tranquillity. He hoped to be able to maintain it, but doubted if that would be possible. This outing had begun poorly, and he dreaded that was a sign of events to come during the evening.

He had come into Lord Radcliffe's bedchamber to find the marquess pacing. His delight in the marquess's easier steps had disappeared when he realized Lord Radcliffe was not practicing walking, but furious. The marquess would give him no hint why. Bond did note him glancing frequently at the dressing room and the door within that led to Lady Lisabeth's rooms. It was not astonishing that the lady had sent him flying up into the boughs, because she was one of the few people who was not deterred by Lord Radcliffe's sometimes odd sense of humor.

Lord Radcliffe's smile had returned when he greeted Miss Tobler, confirming Bond's suspicions that Lady Lisabeth was the focus of his dismay. Bond wondered if Lord Radcliffe was beginning to discover what Bond had believed since shortly after their arrival. The marquess was looking too far afield for the perfect wife.

Yet Lord Radcliffe's attentions seemed aimed solely at Miss Tobler. Bond wondered why the marquess did not dismiss her as no more than a lass.

All in all, it was completely baffling, although everyone seemed to be acting as if everything was as it should be. Lady Edwina had been exultant as they prepared to drive south to Hanover Street and the Tobler home before turning north to Fitzroy Square. Lady Lisabeth had greeted Miss Tobler prettily.

Yet Bond knew, with a sense that had been honed during the war, that something was wrong. Was his lordship's laugh too hearty? Or could it be that Lady Lisabeth never looked at Lord Radcliffe? It must be more than Miss Tobler's bashful ways, for the unease had started before the carriage left Cavendish Square.

Whatever it was, Bond wished he could halt it before disaster swept away the polite smiles. He did not like this feeling of being unprepared to protect himself and his major, who was stepping from the carriage and turning to hand the women from it.

Lisabeth noticed the uneasiness on Bond's face, but did nothing to alleviate it. Anything she said could be misconstrued. It would be better if she concentrated on the task Norton had given her.

She scrutinized Adelaide Tobler while Radcliffe helped Lady Edwina. The young woman was comely, with a self-effacing manner that bespoke her excellent upbringing. Against her dress of unblemished white, Miss Tobler's ebony hair was the perfect foil. Pearls had been strung through the shining strands to match the necklace about the long column of her throat. Miss Tobler's appearance was perfect for what might be only the first of many occasions when she was seen on Lord Radcliffe's arm.

When Radcliffe handed the younger woman out, Miss Tobler said in her melodic voice, "Thank you, Lord Radcliffe."

Lisabeth tried not to grimace, but she was sure Miss Tobler had said nothing other than *yes, no,* and *thank you, Lord Radcliffe* since she had entered the carriage. With a sigh, Lisabeth told herself she was the only one exasperated with Miss Tobler's attractive modesty. Certainly Radcliffe seemed impressed with the young woman.

Radcliffe turned back to the carriage. "Are you joining us, Lisabeth?"

"Am I—?" She laughed softly to cover her agitation. "Forgive me, for I fear I was daydreaming."

" 'Tis evening," he teased as he took her hand.

Even through her evening gloves, she could sense the warmth of his fingers. It spread upward, like midday sunshine, along her arm. Her smile wavered, but she rearranged it on her taut lips. Now was not the time to reveal how bewildered Radcliffe's touch made her.

"Thank you," she whispered.

"My pleasure." Radcliffe winked at her brazenly before offering his arm to Miss Tobler.

Lisabeth glanced at Bond and again saw disquiet on the valet's normally gregarious face. She was surprised, for she would have guessed Radcliffe's man would be delighted to view such a lass on the marquess's arm. As she should be. Mayhap Bond had his own reasons for not being pleased with this match. She did, but she must disregard them as she had tried throughout the evening.

Giving her bonnet and cloak to a servant, Lisabeth climbed the stairs with the others to the music room. She had to own that Mr. Smythe had an extraordinary ability to judge how the whims of Society would dictate fashion.

His home reflected each turn of style at the very moment it burst upon the *ton*.

When her host bustled over, Lisabeth found it difficult to smile. Only the fact that she had accepted Mr. Smythe's invitation weeks ago had prevented her from bowing out with an unpersuasive excuse.

"My dear Lady Montague!" Mr. Smythe scooped up her hand and attempted to kiss it. When she withdrew it and snapped her fan open to keep a barrier between them, he continued, "Did you come alone? I could have sent my carriage for you."

"Lady Edwina spoke to you upon our arrival moments ago."

"I fear I am blind to anyone else when I am in your glorious company."

"Mr. Smythe, please remember yourself. Lady Edwina and I came with Lord Radcliffe and Miss Tobler."

"Miss Tobler?" His eyes widened as he turned and chuckled under his breath. "What a unique match—the ramshackle marquess and a child who is barely fired off! However do you conceive these amusing matches, Lady Montague? First that prattle-box Miss Gibbs, now Miss Tobler, who, I daresay, has said no more than a dozen words in her eighteen years!"

Lisabeth looked past him and saw that Radcliffe and Miss Tobler had been pounced upon by Miss Gibbs, who was chattering nonstop. Delia Gibbs had accepted her dismissal with equanimity. Or mayhap, she considered Adelaide Tobler nothing more than a *à suivie* flirtation enjoyed by the Marquess of Radcliffe.

"Do you think he will invite both of them to sit with him during the performance?" crowed Mr. Smythe.

"Do restrain yourself," Lisabeth chided. " 'Tis rag-mannered to be gabble-grinding like this. I do not enjoy gossip, especially when it is aimed at my friends."

"Do you consider Lord Radcliffe a friend as well as family?"

"Miss Tobler and Miss Gibbs are my friends, although I have had the pleasure of speaking with Miss Tobler on a few occasions. She was a sweet child, and she has not lost that sweetness now that she is out of the schoolroom."

"I collect that Lord Radcliffe does not view her as a child still."

Lisabeth was about to reprimand Mr. Smythe again, when she realized another man had spoken. Turning, she met Lieutenant Ison's smile.

"How lovely you look tonight, Lady Montague," he said, bowing over her hand. When he seemed loath to release it, she drew her fingers away. His smile did not waver. "Good evening, Smythe. I believe someone is trying to get your attention."

Although Mr. Smythe hesitated, he could not ignore the dowager waving toward him. He excused himself and scurried away like the round hedgehog he resembled.

"Disagreeably grim chap, don't you think?" Lieutenant Ison asked.

"I have counted Mr. Smythe among my friends," Lisabeth said, wondering why she was having to repeat herself. "I prefer not to hear my friends stigmatized."

"Forgive me. I forget how many people you generously consider your friends." His smile tilted his mustache higher. "But how could anyone *not* be your friend when you are so engaging?"

Rather than answering his impertinent question, she said, "I hear the music about to start."

"Then, allow me to escort you to your seat . . . unless you have another escort this evening."

Lisabeth wanted to sigh. Staying home this evening would have been the best course, but wasn't this what she had been waiting for through her year of hypocritical mourning? To be among the *ton,* to partake of their conversations, to enjoy the affinity of her bosom-bows. Now those plans seemed tepid and flavorless, and the image of remaining home enticed her. No, 'twas not just that image that enchanted her, but the idea of being *en famille* with Radcliffe.

"My lady?"

She smiled at Lieutenant Ison, who was showing more patience than Radcliffe ever would. "I told Lady Edwina that I would join her, but I am sure she would be as delighted as I with your company."

Delighted was not the word to describe Lady Edwina's reaction. She tersely commanded Lieutenant Ison to sit next to her with Lisabeth on her far side. During the performance, Lisabeth was aware of her mother-in-law's dissatisfaction. Now, what was wrong? Lady Edwina had been pleasant to Lieutenant Ison each time they had met before.

As soon as the musical program was complete and the orchestra paused before beginning the music for dancing, her mother-in-law whisked her away to talk to Lady Prospera Fry. Lady Edwina wanted to determine if Prospera's situation was as grim as rumor suggested. Lisabeth found herself listening to a long recital of Prospera's woes.

Looking about the room with disdain, the tall brunette said, "I did my duty once by marrying. Why should I legshackle myself again? Surely you understand, Lisabeth."

"I have given no thought of marrying again, but—" she hastened to add when she realized her mother-in-law was listening, "I am so recently out of mourning."

Prospera sipped her wine. "I wish for an extraordinary man as my husband." Her eyes narrowed as she smiled. "I find your cousin most fascinating."

"Do you?" Hearing Lady Edwina's muffled chuckle, Lisabeth suspected her response had been too sharp. "I shall convey that to him."

"Do," she urged. "Soon he will tire of lasses just out of

the schoolroom." She sighed, then smiled when Mr. Hinkle approached. Asking them to excuse her, she linked arms with the short man and walked away, prattling about the games they would enjoy at the whist table. Lady Edwina followed, freeing Lisabeth to speak with whom she wished.

She had no chance because Lieutenant Ison hurried to her side, warning that he had been watching her closely.

"My lady, at last."

"You sound," replied a deeper voice, "like the villain in a badly written play."

Lisabeth wanted to cheer when she turned to smile at Radcliffe. Her smile wavered when she noted that Miss Tobler had her hand on his arm.

"Good evening, my lord."

"Ison, I saw you lurking nearby," Radcliffe replied. "I had thought you might have left Town already to ride about on the useless tasks that your superiors give you to keep you far from their company."

"My present duties are something I cannot speak of."

"Odd, for you spouted endlessly about them this afternoon."

"Not my *present* duties. You should understand, being as you once deigned to play at soldiering."

"Gentlemen," Lisabeth hurried to say when Radcliffe scowled, "there is no need for cross words. If you deem it necessary to be at outs with each other, I implore you to allow me and Miss Tobler to excuse ourselves. We have no interest in your breezes."

"Forgive me, Lady Montague." Lieutenant Ison shot a venomous glare at Radcliffe.

"Yes, we stand corrected." Radcliffe's voice was less sincere. "Let us indulge in the pretty talk my cousin assures me is *de rigueur* for these social occasions. So you have been to the country, Ison? Mayhap for the hunt?"

"You speak of the pursuits of a titled gentleman, my lord, and I did not have the good fortune to be born heir to a title." To Lisabeth, he added, "Do forgive me, for I must bid you *adieu,* Lady Montague."

"You are leaving so soon?" she asked, hoping she sounded sincerely regretful rather than relieved.

"*I* have work that cannot wait."

"Your duties must take precedence, Lieutenant."

He aimed a superior smile at Radcliffe. Taking Lisabeth's hand, he lifted it to his lips. His mustache pricked her skin as he kissed her hand. "You are a jewel. I shall call as soon as I can."

As he walked away, Lisabeth heard Radcliffe laugh. She saw dismay on Miss Tobler's face, but said, "Radcliffe, I trust you have a reason for putting him to an interrogation."

"The good lieutenant has clearly set his cap on you, despite your mother-in-law's expectations that you can make a better match. It behooves me, as your cousin, to be sure he is a man of rare integrity."

"I do not need *you* matchmaking for me."

"As you wish," he agreed so quickly that Lisabeth gasped. He lifted her hand, bowed over it in a parody of Lieutenant Ison's perfect manners, then walked away with Miss Tobler.

Lisabeth lingered by the door. How dare Radcliffe put her out of curl this evening! The whole situation was ridiculous. She wanted neither man dangling after her.

When her pudgy host rushed toward her, she discovered her mistake. She should have made herself inconspicuous, so she could have avoided Mr. Smythe, but it was too late.

"A very pleasant program," Lisabeth said as he demanded her opinion of the music. "You created a successful evening of entertainment."

"I think you are the one to be congratulated on a triumph. Miss Tobler has scarcely left Lord Radcliffe's side. I never doubted that you would find the marquess a wife as you promised. Now that you have completed that task, you may put your mind to other things."

"The task, as you deem it, is far from complete. I promised I would help Radcliffe find a wife. At the moment, he has found nothing more than a girl who does not bore him."

"Or who is not repelled by him."

"Mr. Smythe!"

He tried to apologize, but Lisabeth ignored him as she went to where Lady Edwina was in the midst of a conversation with Mrs. Castleman. Lisabeth noted that Mrs. Castleman seemed unduly interested in Radcliffe and Miss Tobler. Mrs. Castleman mused endlessly, wondering if Radcliffe and Miss Tobler would dance when the orchestra began to play again. Mayhap the matron was having second thoughts about her refusal to allow Emeraude to call.

Lisabeth had no second thoughts about Mr. Smythe. She would not suffer his company again. In the time that Radcliffe had been her guest, she had been able to avoid the rotund man, and she wanted no part of Mr. Smythe's malicious poker-talk.

"Lady Montague, may I speak with you a moment?"

Her smile returned when she met the bright eyes of a man who was not much taller than she was. His nearly bald pate bore wisps of black hair which dropped over his high collar. Although not a member of the frippery set, Mr. Tobler was a congenial man. She had enjoyed conversation with him and, for that reason, had thought of his daughter as a potential match for Radcliffe.

"I always have a moment for you, Mr. Tobler." When he handed her a glass of ratafia, she added, "Thank you. Your discernment into my needs is exemplary."

"I pray you will prove to be as discerning."

Lisabeth laughed. "It takes no amount of intuition to guess that you wish to speak of Lord Radcliffe. Allow me to introduce you to him."

"That was what I hoped." He offered his arm, and she put her fingers on it. While they walked through the crowded room, he spoke of the latest book of poetry he had purchased. "None of our poets is as gifted as Byron, I fear. Now that he has left England in disgrace, I pray he will find inspiration still blossoming within him."

"I hope his next poem is better than the last few."

Mr. Tobler said, "I did not know that you were a devotee of poetry. Pray do not think me bold when I suggest that you and the members of your household are welcome to join Adelaide and me any Monday evening. That night we read and discuss poetry."

"What a charming invitation! I shall suggest it to Lady Edwina and Lord Radcliffe."

Lisabeth was not surprised to find Radcliffe and Miss Tobler again caught in conversation with the irrepressible Miss Gibbs. Radcliffe made no effort to hide his pleasure at the interruption. Miss Gibbs drifted away to find someone else to listen to her harmless prattle.

"Mr. Tobler," Lisabeth said, as if there had been no conversation between them beforehand, "it is my pleasure to introduce Tristan Radcliffe."

The shorter man dipped his head toward Radcliffe. "I am honored, my lord. It is most decent of you to ask Adelaide to join you and Lady Montague this evening. When I feared I would be unable to attend, my dear daughter was heartbroken until she came home with the tidings of your invitation."

"I would have been remiss not to ease Miss Tobler's heart pain, sir," said Radcliffe with his warmest smile. Lisabeth noticed how effective it was. Both Mr. Tobler and his daughter beamed in response.

"So you would. I guessed that, my lord, after hearing of your generous nature."

Lisabeth clasped her hands behind her as she listened to the balding man gush. A single glance at Radcliffe warned her that he was amused by Mr. Tobler's compliments. His kindness toward a very nervous Mr. Tobler suggested he might be feeling the beginnings of affection for Miss Tobler, who clearly was delighted by his attention.

Again Lisabeth's smile faltered, but she pushed her lips upward. So close she was to fulfilling the promise that had been forced on her. She should not be distressed now.

Her attention was brought back to the conversation when Radcliffe spoke her name. "It is my hope that Lisabeth and I will enjoy a long friendship with your daughter."

Miss Tobler blushed at the intimation that she would be a welcome caller at Cavendish Square. When Mr. Tobler reminded his daughter that she must speak with Mrs. Castleman, she whispered her request for them to excuse her.

Radcliffe continued to smile as he watched the young woman disappear into the crowd. Lisabeth had never seen him so pleased with himself. That made her happy . . . and miserable.

Radcliffe tapped the arm of a passing servant with the top of his walking stick. When the man paused, shocked, Radcliffe took a glass of wine from the servant's tray. The man gave him a peculiar glance as he continued on his way.

With a smile, Radcliffe touched his glass to the one Lisabeth held. "To a most successful evening. Not only have I managed to remain on my feet, but I recalled my lessons so not to embarrass either you or Miss Tobler."

"I would say you have achieved more, for you have made an undeniable conquest of Mr. Tobler."

"He seemed anxious to impress me, Lisabeth." Taking a sip, he grimaced. "Smythe must be a pinchpenny to serve such poor vintage."

"You impressed Mr. Tobler."

He laughed and put the glass on a table. "You need not try to charm me with flummery. My title fascinates Tobler.

He is exceedingly anxious to gain it for his daughter. An exemplary father."

Radcliffe frowned when Lisabeth did not respond to his teasing. Looking into her face, he saw the pain she tried to hide with increasingly less success. No longer could her smile masquerade her anguish from him.

"Dance with me?" he asked.

"Can you?"

"As well as some of the heavy-footed chaps out there. Will you dance with me?"

She shook her head. "Tonight is for you and Miss Tobler."

"Miss Tobler is busy accepting congratulations for her apparent conquest of the Marquess of Radcliffe, so stand up with me, Lisabeth." He held out his hand. "Or do you hope to be rid of me so quickly?"

"You must know that I look forward to success on this matter," she said, but her gaze refused to meet his.

"Lisabeth . . . ?"

"Do not ask the impossible."

"I ask only a dance." When he held out his hand, Lisabeth knew she should give him an excuse—any excuse—not to dance with him. She had warned him earlier that he would be unwise to solicit a dance from anyone but Miss Tobler. That he refused to listen at this critical juncture proved that he intended to bend his will to no one's, most especially not Society's.

Even as she was thinking that, her hand rose to settle on his. Again she was swallowed by the warmth that began where her fingers brushed his palm. It urged her to step closer to him, to discover if this gentle fire burst only from his hands.

Taking her glass, he put it next to his. "Shall we, *chère cousine*?"

"I would prefer not to dance." When his brows lowered in the stormy expression she knew meant trouble, she

added, "Forgive me for being such a block tonight,
but . . ." In a rush, she said, "I am trying to avoid Mr.
Smythe. He is being most disobliging, and, if I dance with
you, he shall insist that I dance with him."

His smile returned. "As you wish, Lisabeth, I will not
twirl you about. Instead, will you sit with me a moment?"

Lisabeth gasped, "Sit? Are you feeling poorly?"

"Only tired. My recovery is far from miraculous, so I
must recall the need for moderation. That is not an easy
task for a man of my temperament."

"So I have noticed."

When he chose chairs in a far corner, she guessed he
did not want their conversation to be observed. He must
be learning more about the *élite* than she had guessed.

"I hope that Miss Tobler is not being influenced by her
father's wishes," Lisabeth answered when Radcliffe asked
of her thoughts.

"As you were when Frederick asked you to marry him?"

"How did you know?"

"Norton was not completely close-mouthed in telling
me about you."

She looked out at the dancers. Once she had been hap-
piest among them, swirling to country tunes and laughing
when the pattern was broken and elated when a set was
completed without a misstep. "I should have guessed he
would be glad to fill your head with his opinions of me."

"By now, you should realize that I prefer to make my
own conclusions." His finger turned her face toward him.
"I have heard enough from Norton and Lady Edwina to
know that your marriage to Frederick Montague was not
a love match. Why did you marry him?"

"My father was ill," she said softly. "He feared I would
be all alone, and, when Frederick asked him for my hand,
Father agreed readily."

"And you could not disobey?"

"Not when he longed to see me wed before he died."

She closed her eyes. "He lasted only a week after the wedding."

"Lisabeth, you are a constant amazement."

She stared up into his enigmatic eyes. "Why?"

"I see the strong-willed woman you are, and I see the gentleness you hide so deeply within you. The two parts of you battle endlessly, but your kind heart wins too often. It has convinced you to help me, and it persuaded you to marry a man you could not love."

"Radcliffe, I prefer not to speak of that."

"Odd, for it would be good for you to voice the thoughts that have been stripping the joy from your face." Radcliffe kept his voice low so his words would reach no farther than Lisabeth's ears. "It may be none of my bread-and-butter, but I would be pleased if you could consider me a good enough friend that you are not afraid of being honest with me."

"I do."

"Words which your mother-in-law would delight in hearing you speak again."

"I have no plans to."

"So you will let the past continue to shadow your life."

"The past is over."

"Yet you harbor this pain which you refuse to share." He smiled sadly. "The agony of battle is best put behind one by finding another enemy to defeat or, mayhap, even another dragon to slay."

Watching as she ran her finger along the fourth finger of her left hand, which was unadorned beneath her gloves, he was not surprised when she said, "This is one battle I shall not engage again. I know Lady Edwina has begged your assistance in finding me another husband, Radcliffe, but I entreat you not to."

"You wish to find your own husband?" He rested his hands on the top of his walking stick. "I agree that my assistance is something you have scant need of. A quick glance about the room assures me that Smythe is not the only one eager for your smiles. Even Tobler appeared to be thinking of other than his daughter's marital future. Mayhap he was thinking of his own as well."

"Leave off! I wish to hear no more of this."

Before he could respond, she rose and crossed the room to where her mother-in-law was a bright beacon among the pale gowns. He leaned back in the chair and reflectively rubbed his aching knee. Reaching into his upper pocket, he lifted out the key that Bond had stolen. Her words presented another aspect of this puzzle he had yet to solve, but solve it he would.

Fourteen

Lisabeth's breath caught as she descended the stairs to see Radcliffe emerging from the sitting room. Although his white breeches and navy cutaway coat with an embroidered waistcoat and perfectly tied cravat were in high kick, his teasing grin gave him a raffish appearance that no fop would wear. When he held his hand up to assist her down the final trio of steps, she forced a smile as she had too frequently.

How many more nights was she going to serve as watchdog for Radcliffe and his abashed Miss Tobler? How long before the two of them made public what was being whispered in corners? During the past fortnight, there had been few evenings when their curious threesome had not been seen about Town. They attended parties together and sat at the theatre together and went for rides together in the Park. She suspected Radcliffe was more serious about Miss Tobler than he had ever been about Miss Gibbs.

Yet, if that was so . . . why had there been no announcement? Radcliffe showed no sign of tiring of evenings with the many friends he had made amid the *ton*. Always Miss Tobler stood mute by his side, listening and watching.

Lisabeth understood none of it. But then, she had never understood anything about Radcliffe, so she wondered why she assumed she might guess when he planned to propose to Adelaide Tobler.

"Have I kept you waiting?" she asked when Radcliffe edged back as she reached the lowest riser.

"If I may be so brazen as to say so, the wait was worth every bit of impatience. You are, without question, going to be the most beautiful woman this evening," Radcliffe said with a smile which appeared more genuine than hers.

"Save your *bon mots* for Miss Tobler."

He laughed as he lifted the lace dripping from the sleeves of her white gown that was accented by a pale blue train dropping from the back of the high bodice. Running his finger along the curve of the stiff collar rising nearly to her golden hair that was piled in a crown of curls, he mused, "I have plenty of pretty flummery for her, you can be sure."

"You are always determined to be a vulgar cove, my dear marquess."

"Do you wish to engage in a dagger-drawing tonight, my dear viscountess?" he returned in the same light tone. "I fear you would find that I shall match you parry for parry."

"No doubt, but I have no interest in doing myself harm in anyone's eyes by being seen in a brangle with you." She looked past him. "Here comes Bond. I would guess by his rush that he has your carriage waiting."

Radcliffe shifted his walking stick to his left hand as he held out his other arm to her. "Allow me, *chère cousine.*"

"You are beyond kindness." She smiled, astounded anew. The battle of words that he instigated with her on every possible occasion always tore her out of her dismals.

"I shall endeavor to keep your high regard through the evening."

"A noble quest."

He laughed as he led her toward the door. "One, I am certain, you shall reprimand me for soundly if I fail. You have become much the taskmaster of late, Lisabeth. Nothing I do seems to gain your favor."

"You are wrong."

"Am I?" Pausing before the open door and ignoring Doherty, who was waiting to close it behind them, he asked with abrupt sobriety, "Why, then, do you never sparkle as you once did? Now you are as dreary as when I first arrived. You skulk about the house as if you fear I might speak to you."

"Radcliffe, you are imagining things," she answered. If the rest of the evening went like this, it was sure to be among the worst in her life. She hated being false, but she dared not be honest. How could she be happy when she was helping him marry another woman? How could she tell him of her despair when she had not changed her plans never to remarry?

"Am I?" he asked.

"Without question." She did not look at him as she went with undue haste down the stairs and nodded her thanks to the footman who was holding the door of the open carriage. She must maintain this coolness, or, she feared, she would collapse into tears. So close she was to completing her task, but she did not savor the exultation she should.

All she felt was wretched . . . and alone.

The ballroom of the Castleman home was as dark as the rest of the house. As Lisabeth scanned the crowded room, smiling at acquaintances, she was cheered that she had managed to keep the conversation on the way to Miss Tobler's home from focusing on the questions Radcliffe had posed in the foyer. Miss Tobler's company had prevented the subject from being reintroduced, although she had seen frustration etched into Radcliffe's face.

"Yes, it is lovely," she murmured absently to Miss Tobler, who was exclaiming about the ceiling friezes.

"I never imagined I would be invited to so many won-

derful gatherings during my first Season. You and Lord
Radcliffe have been so kind to include me."

Lisabeth looked at Miss Tobler. Dressed in a gown of
the palest pink which flattered her fresh beauty, Adelaide
Tobler was alight with excitement. Glad to be frank for
the first time since she had left her house, Lisabeth said,
"It has been a joy to have you with us." That was not a
lie, for Lisabeth enjoyed the young woman's company.
"Here comes Radcliffe. As I hear the orchestra completing
its preparations, I suspect he wants to ask you to dance."

"Dance? Should he?"

"You should let him worry of such things, although you
are a dear to be concerned. I—" She hushed herself when
Radcliffe came within earshot. He would not like being
the object of their gossip. As weak as her barriers to him
had become, she was not sure what might ensue if he fired
heated words at her. Surrendering in tears would bring
more questions she did not want to answer.

"Miss Tobler," Radcliffe said as he bowed over her fingers with a smoothness that belied the hours he still spent
working to strengthen himself, "would you consider me
past decency if I asked you to stand up with me? I hear
the beginning of the set, and I would enjoy your company
during it, if Lisabeth will excuse us."

Lisabeth's eyes were caught by Radcliffe's, but she was
unsure what emotions sparkled within them. "Of course,"
she said. "Go and enjoy yourselves."

As he led Miss Tobler to the dance floor, Radcliffe
glanced back at Lisabeth. She had no idea what his smile
of satisfaction signified. Without a doubt, he must be
pleased to be able to manage the intricate turns of a qua-
drille. So, too, must he be quite gratified that Miss Tobler
continued to welcome his attentions.

She hoped he would continue to be gracious to Miss
Tobler. His words, which were often swathed in sarcasm
when he spoke to Lisabeth, might undo Miss Tobler. But,

she recalled with surprise, he never said anything untoward to Miss Tobler. Radcliffe treated her with a tenderness Lisabeth would not have guessed he could show when he first came to her home.

"How proud you must be, Lady Montague!" gushed Mrs. Castleman as Radcliffe and Miss Tobler took their places amid the other dancers. "Your generosity in opening your house to that young man is to be admired."

"As I am sure you recall," Lisabeth said tightly, "his cousin is my late husband's cousin, so that makes us family. I know you remember us discussing this before."

Mrs. Castleman had the decency to flinch, but said, "I wish for you to know that when Lord Radcliffe becomes overwhelmed with ennui with that chit who seldom says more than two words in a row, my dear Emeraude would be delighted to invite you and him for tea."

"How kind of Emeraude to think of us now that she has seen that the marquess is no longer a cripple! Mayhap she wishes to lessen his burden while she effortlessly spends his inheritance. Think how much easier it would be for him to walk if he was no longer so plump in the pocket."

"Lady Montague!"

Lisabeth knew she should apologize for her outrageous words, but she walked away to leave Mrs. Castleman sputtering in furious astonishment. Bleak laughter twisted through Lisabeth as she heard Radcliffe's voice within her memory. So often he had taunted her, telling her that she, too, chafed at the constraints of Society, although she refused to own to that. She had pooh-poohed his suggestion, but she had proven him right with her coarse words to Mrs. Castleman.

Yet she would retract not a single one. The truth needed to be spoken, for she did not want Radcliffe involved with Emeraude Castleman and her scheming mama. She laughed. Why was she worried about protecting Radcliffe? He was as sly as a lion.

Selecting a glass of Malaga, Lisabeth sipped it while she tried to soothe her agitation. When Lady Edwina heard of her exchange with Mrs. Castleman, which Mrs. Castleman would make sure she did at the earliest opportunity, Lisabeth would be rung a regular peal.

"Good evening, my lady."

At the greeting in a deep voice, Lisabeth looked away from the whirl of the dancers to discover Lieutenant Ison standing beside her. She smiled, for he looked dashingly handsome in his dark coat that accented his tawny hair. "Lieutenant Ison, you are in and out of Town so often, I daresay, I never know when I might see you."

He bowed over her hand. "Can it be possible that you're alone? It is a sad statement on the wits of the *élite* that its most lovely woman is alone."

Lisabeth's smile wavered, and she battled to keep it in place, for she did not want to chance another exchange of fiery words as the last time Radcliffe and the lieutenant had met. "I am here with Lord Radcliffe and—"

"Miss Tobler." His voice dropped to a whisper. "Is it true that they are soon to announce their intentions?"

"You would need to ask Lord Radcliffe or Miss Tobler that, Lieutenant. I do not share in their confidences."

"No? I would have thought as Lord Radcliffe's sponsor, you would be very involved in their *affaire*. Mayhap they intend to make an announcement at the end of this dance."

Waving her fan, Lisabeth hoped it would prevent him from seeing her dismay. Why did he endlessly have to use that tone that suggested he was eager to denounce Radcliffe? "Lieutenant Ison, I came here this evening to talk with friends and mayhap to laugh at a few sallies. What reasons the others chose to attend is something I cannot speak to. If you will excuse me . . ."

"Lady Montague," he said, stepping in front of her to block what she had hoped would be the pattern-card of

an angry exit. His mustache fluttered. "Forgive my impertinence in quizzing you. As always, you are correct. 'Tis a
foolish heart that urges me to speak so when I wish only
to ask you to dance with me."

"Dance?"

"Why not? We never have danced. I could understand
your reluctance when you were in mourning, but you have
set that aside. Do dance with me."

Lisabeth had never wanted less to dance, but she had
no reason to excuse herself. Tonight Mr. Smythe was not
in attendance, so she need not worry about him insisting
that she dance with him as well. She doubted if her smile
had ever been more artificial than when she put her hand
on the lieutenant's arm.

He led her to where the dancers were reforming for the
next set. Surprised that the orchestra was continuing to
play country reels instead of waltzes, she wondered if it
was because Emeraude Castleman was unbelievably awk-
ward. It was another unworthy thought that was revealing
she had the manners of a rough diamond tonight.

"Good evening, my lord, Miss Tobler."

At Lieutenant Ison's terse words, Lisabeth was wrenched
from her thoughts. He had led her to a spot not far from
Radcliffe and Miss Tobler. Curious about where Radcliffe
had put his walking stick during the dancing, she saw the
triumphant smile Lieutenant Ison flashed Radcliffe.

"Ison, it is kind of you to bring Lisabeth out to dance,"
said Radcliffe in a genial tone that clearly shocked Lieutenant Ison, for his mouth gaped. "She has been more concerned about my enjoyment at these routs than her own.
'Tis time Lisabeth thinks of herself."

She was spared from having to answer either his words
or the challenging twinkle in his dark eyes by the start of
the music. Turning from Radcliffe, she curtsied to Lieutenant Ison. The music enticed her into its spell while they
spun to its bright tempo. When she laughed softly, she saw

his amazement. How could she have forgotten how much she loved dancing? Dash it! She found it vexing that Radcliffe had been right again. She could not let her past continue to dim the happiness she might enjoy now.

She followed the pattern of the dance to whirl with Mr. Green, a robust, young man with sweaty hands. She had not danced since before her betrothal. Frederick had considered dancing a waste of time.

Back she went to Lieutenant Ison. Even when his hand slipped along her waist, she did not think of anything but her joy. She danced in the other direction to another partner.

She gasped when Radcliffe took her hands in his. The familiar—frighteningly familiar—warmth erupted through her as he smiled at her. Although his steps were not as smooth as Lieutenant Ison's, she noticed only the fires burning in his ebony eyes. She reminded herself hastily that the fires were not for her, but for Miss Tobler, who was winning his heart.

As he had won Lisabeth's.

She wanted to refute the thought that careened through her brain. It was impossible. When had she been so all about in the head as to fall in love with this humdurgeon of a marquess who reveled in his rag-mannered ways?

As Radcliffe bowed and stepped away, turning to Miss Tobler again, Lisabeth's hands were seized by Lieutenant Ison. She was jerked back into the dance, her legs wooden as her mind tried to comprehend her insanity.

Radcliffe did not love her, although he had told her that he considered himself her friend. *Friend!* It seemed nigh onto an insult when her heart yearned for more. Surreptitiously glancing to where he was spinning Miss Tobler in his strong arms, she fought tears as she thought of Radcliffe leaving her house forever. How empty her life would become again!

Lieutenant Ison spoke as the music ceased, but Lisabeth

shook her head. She did not want to dance again. She did not want to chatter brightly. She wanted only to crawl away and nurse her newly shattered heart.

"Lady Montague," said the distressed lieutenant, "if I have said or done something to discompose you, I pray that you will give me the dashed sharp trimming I so rightly deserve."

"Forgive me," she said, gathering her ragged composure together enough to smile. "I fear I was woolgathering. You have been the epitome of kindness."

He led her from the dance floor. "Then, will you allow me to take you into dinner later?"

Lisabeth wanted to demur, saying that Radcliffe would escort her. She was an air-dreamer! He was making no pains to hide his growing attachment to another woman. "Yes, Lieutenant Ison, and it is another sign of your kindness that you asked me."

"Having won the favor of your company, may I be so bold as to ask another question? May I take you for a walk in the garden?"

"Yes," she answered as lowly as she had before. Leaving the ballroom, which seemed too crowded when she was forced to watch Radcliffe with Miss Tobler on his arm, seemed an uncommonly grand idea.

Moonlight pelted the path, stripping color from everything. The garden was smaller than the one Lisabeth tended with such care. Mrs. Castleman had managed to obtain many unique plants, but Lisabeth had no interest in them tonight. She could think only of the scene she had left behind. Radcliffe's smile refused to be banished from her mind. Radcliffe's smile that was not for her.

"You seem distant this evening, my lady," murmured the lieutenant.

She looked at Lieutenant Ison and saw how the light danced off his pale hair. He was a handsome man. She had seen the admiring looks the ladies aimed in his direction, and she was certain he had as well. Lieutenant Ison seemed to exult in such attention, unlike Radcliffe.

Radcliffe! She wanted him out of her thoughts!

"Forgive me once again," Lisabeth said. "The hush of the garden does take one away. It seems wrong to dash it with talk."

"But we must, for I wish to speak to you of a matter that does not need to be heard by the ears of a dozen prattle-boxes."

She sighed, wondering what Radcliffe had said to Lieutenant Ison this time to try to stir the coals. Had they exchanged words during the dance when her heart had deafened her to anything but its delight and its misery? She sat on a bench at the edge of the garden path and nodded when he asked permission to join her.

He grasped her hands between his.

She gasped, "Lieutenant Ison, you are overstepping yourself."

"Indulge me."

"I should say not!" She tried to pull her fingers away, but his hold tightened. Unforgotten sensations of panic threatened to strangle her, and she struggled to say, "Lieutenant Ison, I swear I shall scream if you do not release me."

"I shall relinquish your soft hands when you listen to my petition."

"I wish to hear no more of the petty bickering between you and Lord Radcliffe."

"I do not wish to speak of Lord Radcliffe, my lady, but of you and me." His voice deepened. "I wish to speak of you becoming my wife."

"Your wife?" This time when she tugged, he released her hands. They trembled, and she clasped them in her lap. "You overmaster me with your proposal which shows that the affection you feel for me is stronger than I had guessed."

He put his broad hands on her shoulders, leaning her toward him. Lisabeth stiffened, and he drew back again. Entreaty filled his voice. "My dear Lady Montague, make me happier than any mere mortal should aspire to being by telling me that you look upon my supplication with favor."

"I cannot—"

"Of course, you cannot tell me now." He bent toward her, but she turned her face away so his lips brushed her cheek. His voice was laced with despair. "Tell me you shall think about my petition, my sweet Lady Montague. Think of it when you lie in your bed tonight, knowing that I am dreaming of the moment when you shall be mine."

"I shall think of this." Rising, she said, "Excuse me."

He stood, calling after her, but she rushed into the house and away from this complication she had not envisioned. She did not want to pierce his heart with her cold refusal when she understood too well the pain of an unrequited love.

Lisabeth was grateful Lieutenant Ison was captured by Miss Gibbs and imprisoned in one of her unending conversations. That allowed Lisabeth to avoid his company as she waited for the evening to end. Each hour seemed a lifetime long. Declining other offers to dance, she ignored the inquisitive glances at her peculiar behavior.

When Radcliffe approached her, she considered turning away. That was foolish, for she must deal with both him and the state of her heart.

"You seem to be having a wonderful time this evening," Lisabeth said, once again glad the trite covered her true emotions.

"If dancing myself into exhaustion equates with having a wonderful time, then that is what I am doing."

"Where is Miss Tobler? 'Tis nearly time to go in to dinner."

"Miss Tobler regrets that she promised Mr. Green, more than a month ago, that he could take her into dinner tonight. Can I believe you remain without an escort, Lisabeth?"

"You think me so lacking in suitors that I would have to go into dinner alone?"

"I thought you might prefer my company to Ison's." When she flinched, he frowned. "Is that nod-cock bothering you? *Chère cousine*, why don't you send him from your company? Smythe is no longer dangling after you, prompting me to be curious about what you said to him at his musicale. Why not do the same to Ison? A few of the needle-sharp words you fire at me would soon have him wounded beyond recovery."

"I save them for you." Her eyes widened when she realized that she had spoken out of turn.

"So, if I must endure the sharpest edge of your tongue, do let me offer you my arm and company at dinner."

"If you hope that escorting me will still the conversation about you and Miss Tobler—"

"I fear nothing shall accomplish that." His eyes narrowed. "You are avoiding giving me an answer, *chère cousine*. I am growing curious enough to demand why you resist going into dinner with me."

"Because she has already consented to be my dinner partner," said Lieutenant Ison coldly, coming to stand beside her.

"Is that so?" Radcliffe did not raise his voice, a warning that he was furious. "My *chère cousine*, you must stop allowing your pitying heart to rule your head in the company of this carpet knight."

Lieutenant Ison bristled. "Lady Montague, I can understand why you have become sorely bored with this man's cavalier behavior. Why do you allow him to bully you into silence? Do you wish me to defend your honor?"

"She is quite capable of defending herself." Radcliffe folded his arms across his chest and scowled at the hand Lieutenant Ison had on her arm. "Or can it be that you have no wish to, Lisabeth? If you wish to be taken in by this sad excuse for a soldier, I shall not stand in your way."

"Enough, Radcliffe!" she said. "I fail to understand why you try to put Lieutenant Ison and me in a stew every time we have the occasion to speak."

"Lieutenant Ison and *you*?" he spat back as if it was an obscenity. Clenching his walking stick, he nodded. "I see that I am as wanted here as a lame horse at a race. I bid you both a good and pleasant evening."

"Radcliffe!"

He turned toward her, his lips smooth with fury, his eyes without the twinkle she had grown to love. "Yes, cousin?"

Looking from Lieutenant Ison's smile to Radcliffe's anger, she bit her lip to keep from asking why he called her for the first time only cousin and not *chère cousine*. Rather, she said, "From what I understand, Miss Gibbs needs a dinner partner."

"Thank you. I trust *you* will understand as well I am being honest when I assure you that I shall enjoy her gabblegrinding more this evening than your company, cousin." He turned on his heel and walked away, taking her heart and leaving her with grief.

Fifteen

Lisabeth wandered along the upper corridor. Pausing by a window, she pulled back the drapes to peer into the foggy day. The gloom beyond the panes settled on her as she saw Radcliffe entering his carriage. Bond climbed in after him, and the horses were whipped up. She watched until the vehicle vanished around the corner and, she suspected, south toward the Tobler residence.

"My lady, come away before you catch your death from the dampness!"

Wilson's scolds were something Lisabeth did not want to listen to when her spirits were so tangled. She went into her room. Sitting on the nearest chair, she watched as her abigail stored clean clothes in the cupboard next to her dressing room.

"I took the liberty of having your pink gown pressed, my lady," continued Wilson as she placed the dress on the bed. "I was sure you would want it this evening."

"This evening?" Lisabeth frowned. "I have no plans for this evening."

Wilson paused, her round face long with dismay. "I may have been wrong to assume that when his lordship said . . ."

"Said what?"

"That he wished to complete his errands so he might

rest before an entertaining night tonight that might well go past dawn."

Wrapping her arms around herself, Lisabeth said, "Thank you, Wilson."

"Of course, my lady. If—"

"Thank you, Wilson," she repeated.

Only when the door had closed behind her abigail did Lisabeth sigh and let her stiff stance vanish. Radcliffe planned a late night . . . without her. No longer would the Marquess of Radcliffe, Miss Tobler, and Lady Montague be seen together. The curious trio would be dissolved to allow the *ton's* attention to focus on Radcliffe and his young lady.

How long before Radcliffe came to her with the tidings that Miss Tobler had accepted his offer of marriage? She should tell him the truth that she had fallen in love with his impossible ways, but how he would laugh! And well he should! She had insisted over and over that she would never remarry, and, if the truth be told, she still did not want to marry again. So she should let Radcliffe marry Miss Tobler and be happy. She would remain his *chère cousine.*

"But I am not his cousin," she whispered as she went to the bed to look at the pink gown. She recalled when she last had worn the elegant dress. It had been the night before Frederick had left in a pelter to go to the country. He had died in a riding accident at a friend's house, too drunk to be able to see that his horse could not take the fence.

Norton had been on Cavendish Square the evening before Frederick departed for the final time, and the two men had been well into their cups. Although Lisabeth had taken no part in the conversation—in retrospect, she wondered if Frederick would have allowed her to speak even if she had been interested—her husband had insisted that she be present. The night had been long until she had been able to sneak away while they slept off their brandy.

Dropping to the bed, she tried to push aside the memories of what followed when Frederick had stormed into their room and shook her awake. His vile words as he had accused her of trying to make him look like a fool before his cousin had led to worse. Because, for the first time since their marriage, she had refused to capitulate to his cruel words that were meant to torment her.

She had tried to love him. She had tried to please him. She had tried to make his friends welcome in their home, but everything she did had displeased him. She was too quiet. She was too flirtatious. She was a hideous shrew who thought only of getting her hands on his father's money.

No, she would never be able to get that night out of her mind. She could not forget the way he had treated her and the things he had accused her of, but, most of all, she could not forget what she had said as he walked out, leaving her battered and shuddering.

"I hope you go and never come back!" The words rang through her head now as they had that night when she could barely hear the door slam over the pain reverberating across her head. Then she had made the vow she had never thought she would come to regret, "If I can escape this marriage alive, I swear I shall never marry again."

She stood and looked at the dressing room that had been the boundary between that perdition and the life she had rebuilt for herself. No longer could she lie to herself. As horrid as that night had been, it had not been as terrible as last night at Mrs. Castleman's ball.

With a strangled sob, Lisabeth picked up the pink dress. She buried her face in the bodice and sobbed as she had not by Frederick's grave.

Lisabeth listened while Mrs. Outhwaite supervised the new maid, who was removing the tea tray from the sitting room. As soon as the lass was out of earshot, Lisabeth said, "Do allow her time to adjust to our strange household."

"You are too kind," the housekeeper said with a smile. "I have been trying to keep the under stairs from prattling too much. No doubt, when his lordship marries and is gone, things will become much more normal."

"No doubt." Why did everyone seem compelled to comment endlessly on Radcliffe's intentions? She chided herself for her anger that should not be directed at her household. After all, they knew that he had come to Town specifically to find a wife. "Has Lady Edwina returned from her calls?"

"I can ask Doherty, my lady."

"No need." Lisabeth wandered to the window and looked out to discover the fog had lifted, and the garden was awash with color. With her low spirits, she had not noticed the sunshine. How swiftly the Season was passing! She had not had a moment to enjoy her garden since Radcliffe's arrival. If what everyone including herself suspected was true, he soon would be gone with his child-bride, and Lady Frederick Montague would be left with her well-ordered life and pretty garden . . . and heartache.

"Is there anything else, my lady?"

"Not now," she said without turning. Pretending not to be distressed was easier when she did not have to meet the eyes of those who knew her too well.

As the sound of Mrs. Outhwaite's footsteps drifted away, Lisabeth went to a small table, which she used as a writing table. Taking a moment to compose her thoughts, she began the letter that she had delayed writing for too long.

Norton,
    You shall be more than pleased with your cousin's progress. He has gone a fair way to making a complete recovery. Not only can he walk, but he has taken to driving and dancing. I daresay your cousin has become quite the

hit of the Season. His rare wit has enraptured the hearts
of two young women, both of excellent families. Either
would make a charming and capable marchioness. Delia
Gibbs and Adelaide Tobler have been seen in his com-
pany, but it has become clear he prefers the latter. I would
not be surprised if an announcement is forthcoming.

Lisabeth started to add more, but paused and reread
what she had written. When the letters blurred, she raked
herself down for being a ninnyhammer. No one in the
house had anticipated that she would find two women
eager to marry him.

But she was not surprised. Radcliffe was a handsome
man. The fact that he was full of juice and highly titled
would have made him desirable in certain quarters, such
as Prospera Fry's greedy heart, even if he had been confined to his chair.

She dipped her pen and continued.

I shall inform you of his plans as I learn of them.
Whatever happens, I assure you that your cousin should
consider his Season a success. I know you will be pleased
with his accomplishments.
I remain,

                                   Your devoted cousin

Before Lisabeth could sign her name, she heard the as-
sertive sound of uneven footsteps. Her heart thudded
against her breast. She quickly said, "Good afternoon,
Radcliffe." She hoped her voice masked the pounding of
her heart. "I did not realize that you had returned."

"Just." He crossed the room. "I see you are busy."

"Just finished. If you would like—"

"Finished with what?"

"Merely a note to Norton."

"To Norton?" He snatched the sheet from the table.

She gasped a warning that the ink might not be dry, but he ignored her. His frown was fierce. "I had no idea you were reporting on me to him, Lisabeth."

"Norton asked that I keep him informed of your progress."

"Clearly you took that to mean more than my physical progress." He tapped his fingers against the page.

Keeping her chin high as she met his eyes without flinching, Lisabeth said, "If you wish me to discontinue my correspondence, you may suggest that to me *and* to Norton."

He smiled and tossed the page on the table. "Write what you wish to whom you wish. As you have told me so often, your life is your own. I only wish to remind you that my life is *mine.*"

"Odd that you should say such a thing when you seem eager to interfere with mine."

"You must be referring to my last conversation with that goosecap Ison. As you should recall as well, I left you to make your own mistakes, cousin."

Lisabeth stood. "Good afternoon, Radcliffe."

Walking into the garden, she gave him no chance to answer. She feared she might let him vex her into speaking the truth.

"Are you letting my words put your nose quite out of joint, Lisabeth?"

Whirling, she saw he had followed her. "I find it unconscionable that you believe I appreciate being scolded. My private epistles are not your concern."

"They are when the topic of your correspondence is me."

"As it has been since your arrival."

"You have been writing to that chucklehead since—?" He cursed, then laughed. "Come, cousin, I cannot believe that I can raise your color with coarse words after all this time."

She sat on the cast-iron bench and said nothing as he

lowered himself cautiously beside her. His tentative motion warned that his leg was bothering him. She hushed her sympathy. To allow herself to have compassion for him could open her heart to spilling out other emotions.

"I fail to understand what you find so distressing," Lisabeth said, "for I put nothing in that letter but the truth. Norton has great concern for you. He was so insistent that your recovery be quickened."

"You quickened my recovery, Lisabeth."

"Nonsense!" she answered, although she could not halt a burst of pleasure at his heartfelt words. "I did no more than offer you a challenge, which you accepted. First, you relearned to walk. Then you set out to find a bride. You have succeeded at the first and soon will at the second."

"You are correct, as usual, Lisabeth." He gave her an ironic smile. "My hand has been forced by the unceasing attentions of Prospera Fry."

"Prospera is desperate to find a husband to satisfy her father."

"I wish to entangle myself with neither the lady nor her father, so I have decided to hazard a proposal to Miss Tobler this evening."

She heard her voice from a great distance, for a strange buzzing, as if a swarm of honeybees filled her head, distorted her words. "Congratulations, Radcliffe. Or mayhap, I should offer congratulations to both of us, for I have played a part, however minor, in bringing about this happy circumstance."

"You played more than a minor part in this. However, nothing is decided until Miss Tobler agrees to my suit. I thought I might impose upon you this evening to entertain us." He folded his hands on top of his walking stick. "It shall be a surprise for Miss Tobler." With a laugh, he looked up at the windows above. "I let your abigail think I had plans for this evening that would take us far from the house. I would prefer this celebration to be only with the ones I care for most. That includes you, Lisabeth."

"Of course you are welcome to invite Miss Tobler and her father here." Her voice still sounded faint. "I have urged you to consider this your home. I assume you will be staying while the arrangements for the wedding are being made."

"I had hoped to, if that is agreeable with you." He laughed again. "You are assuming that Miss Tobler will look upon my suit with favor."

"She will be delighted." Gazing across the garden, she mused, "Miss Tobler seems quite taken with you, as does her father."

He leaned forward until her gaze was caught by his. "Trust my *chère cousine* to see the truth. I fear Tobler is more expressive of his appreciation of my attention to Miss Tobler than she is."

"Every father is grateful to see his daughter settled."

"You sound like the professorial Lady Montague I first met." Putting his hand on her arm, he said, "I would rather hear you tell me you are pleased that you have succeeded in finding a winsome bride for this old soldier."

"Of course I am pleased," Lisabeth answered, forcing the words past the heavy lump in her throat. Smiling was easier than she had expected. She had learned well how to wear this counterfeit smile. "Miss Tobler is uncommonly charming. She shall make you a wonderful marchioness."

"Will I be assuming too much if I assure her, upon her acceptance of my petition, that you would assist with planning the events surrounding our nuptials?"

Lisabeth blinked, struggling to hold on to her pose of poise. How could he think that she would be interested in helping with preparations for his marriage to another woman? *Because,* accused the thought that would not be silenced, *you have broken your vow to be honest with him.* "If Miss Tobler wants my help, I shall gladly offer it."

"Will you?"

Rising, she pretended to admire the flowers to avoid Radcliffe's gaze. "Do you wish me to make it a vow?"

"Like the one Norton commanded from you?"

"I pray that I shall be as successful at doing as I agreed for you and Miss Tobler as I have been for Norton."

"Yes, you have done admirably."

Lisabeth recoiled from the sarcasm in his voice. "You make our accomplishment sound like a sin."

"Quite the contrary. I admire your achievement when you had so little to work with."

"You underestimate yourself." Her smile seemed so brittle she feared it would break. "I failed to tell you that Mrs. Castleman was anxious to let me know her beloved Emeraude would be exceedingly desirous of your attentions if you find yourself overcome with ennui with Miss Tobler."

Radcliffe laughed tersely. "I did not realize my worth had increased so."

"Often a woman finds out too late that she wants what another has." Lisabeth flushed as she turned away again, hoping he would not guess how those words echoed the agony within her.

"I have no interest in Miss Castleman or in Prospera or any of the young lasses who have been looking at me with calf eyes. For years, I have prided myself on setting my mind on one course and seeing it through. No skirts flipped in my direction will alter my determination to win myself a bride who will be all I could hope for in a marchioness."

Lisabeth whispered, "I wish you every happiness as you seek your heart's desire, Radcliffe."

"Pray look at me, *chère cousine*, while I ask you a favor beyond any I have asked of anyone."

"What is it?"

He took her hands in his. "Promise me that you will be

by my side tonight when I ask Miss Tobler to be my wife. You were here at the beginning of this courtship. Say you will be with me through to its end."

"You wish me to be present when you ask Miss Tobler to marry you?" she choked.

Radcliffe laughed at her astonishment. "I was unafraid of facing the guns of that mad Corsican, but I quiver at the thought of asking that young miss to become my wife." Standing, he leaned on his walking stick. "Be my ally, Lisabeth. I have been able to depend on you since I arrived in London. Will you desert me at the very time when I need you so much?"

"If marrying Miss Tobler will make you happy, Radcliffe," she whispered as she gazed into the endless depths of his ebony eyes, "I shall do all I can to—"

His hand settled on her arm. As she looked from it to his face where a teasing smile was tilting his lips, she took a step backward. He moved closer to keep the distance between them the same.

"I know you will help me," he said softly, "for you have never denied me your assistance, even when you believed what I was doing was wrong."

"I was honest when I said Miss Tobler would make an excellent marchioness."

His voice remained hushed. "If you thought otherwise, I daresay you would have refrained from inviting her to your home. Just be with me tonight when I am embarking on this new life."

"I said I would," she said in a tight voice. Tears burned in her throat, but she refused to let them reach her eyes. Radcliffe was happy with Miss Tobler. She should be happy for him. "If you will excuse me, Radcliffe, I must—"

Unable to devise a lie, Lisabeth walked to the house. She was unsure how much longer she could contain her tears. Weeping would be jobbernowl. That she had learned in her room, for her anguish had not been lessened, and she had been left with a dress stained with salt.

She faltered when she saw Bond standing in the doorway to the sitting room. She should have known he would be here, for he was seldom far from Radcliffe. When he stepped aside, nodding to her, she wished that she could ask him to help her talk sense into Radcliffe's head. That was impossible when Radcliffe was, for once, doing something everyone would consider sensible.

"Are you planning to stamp away like this and leave me alone tonight?" Radcliffe called to her back.

"Alone tonight . . . ?" She swallowed her shock at his provocative question, then reminded herself he was thinking only of seeking Miss Tobler's hand. "Radcliffe," she added when he continued to regard her with the hint of a smile, "I wonder why you feel it necessary to demand a promise from me."

"Because I am a first-rate rogue, *chère cousine*. A man with decent manners would believe a lady."

"You do not believe——?"

"I believe you wish to help me." Sitting on the settee, he drew her beside him. "Tell me, Lisabeth, how best to ask this sweet baggage to be my wife."

"What do you mean?"

He laughed and twirled his walking stick between his hands. "Share with me, *chère cousine*, your insight into the mind of a young maiden who dreams of a dashing swain wooing her heart into his possession. Have you no suggestions of what I might do and say to win her devotion?"

"I have often thought," she said softly, "that it would be a delight to be asked to be wed in the midst of a waltz."

Radcliffe shook his head. "Impossible! That foppish dance does not lend itself to romance."

"No?"

Resting his arm along the back of the settee, he faced her. As she had been so many times, she was caught by his eyes, but she saw the unmistakable glint of mirth. "What could be more unromantic than me lurching a lovely lass about the floor?"

"But the waltz is *de rigueur,* Radcliffe."

"Then, teach me."

"Here?"

"Why not?" He stood and held out his hand as he leaned his walking stick against the settee.

"My lord, if I may intrude—"

"You may not, Bond," he retorted with an impatience that Lisabeth had never heard when he spoke to his valet. "You may retire now."

"Yes—yes, my lord," Bond said, startled.

Radcliffe held out his hand in front of Lisabeth's face. It was not a request, but an order that she dance. Slowly she raised her fingers to put them in his.

His fingers were strong as they closed around hers, and the warmth of his hand brushing her waist was without a tremble. The invalid had vanished to be replaced by this dynamic man who regarded her without compromise.

"Radcliffe," she whispered, "do you know the steps?"

"Yes. Do you?"

"I know the gentleman leads."

"Then, lead you I shall."

Her breath caught in her throat as he spun her with only a hint of unsteadiness. Her skirts grazed the furniture, but he guided her through the maze of mahogany and satin. There was no music, but none was necessary as she followed a rhythm that came from within. Her legs melted with the bewitching tingle that began at the point where his fingers touched hers and his palm grazed her waist. As she had so often, she did not meet his eyes. She feared that her joy would be unmasked.

"You dance beautifully, Lisabeth," he murmured.

The brush of his breath against her hair was beguiling. She wished she could gauge the tremor in her voice before she spoke. To let Radcliffe discover her true thoughts would be caper-witted.

"Lisabeth?"

Her gaze rose before she could stop it. His hand tightened around her fingers as he slowed. When he continued to hold her, she whispered, "I think you have proven yourself in error."

"About what?"

Although she was tempted to proclaim what was in her rebellious heart, Lisabeth fell back on the habit of half truth. "You dance well. Miss Tobler will be pleased when she discovers how well you can turn her about the floor." She stepped back. "You should consider presenting your suit while you dance."

His hand on her waist kept her from moving away. A gentle pressure brought her to face him. She knew she should flee. She knew that being in his arms when he spoke of proposing to another woman was insane. She knew that, but let him bring her the half step closer until a single deep breath would brush her against him. There was no danger of that when her breath ran shallow and fast while her fingertips ached to touch the rugged planes of his face.

"Stay a moment, Lisabeth, and allow me to lean on you."

A rush of tears threatened to flood her eyes. What she had considered his eager attention had been nothing but weakness. "You have pushed yourself too hard."

"No, *you* have pushed me too hard, Lisabeth."

"You should sit and rest."

"I should." A whisper of laughter lightened his words as his hand slipped upward along her back, bringing her against his firm body.

She should have pulled away, but he might fall if she made a sudden motion. To own the truth, she wanted this stolen moment in his arms.

"You no longer surprise me, Radcliffe," she whispered, wondering how long she could hold her breath so she did not brush against his rock hard chest. "I was sure you could dance when you have mastered far more challenging tasks."

"Such as convincing you that I am not simply an obligation you assumed when your generous heart could not tell our mutual cousin that he asked too much of you?"

"I never meant to intimate that I consider you a burden."

"But I have been."

"Yes, you have been a burden. Quite an insufferable one at times, if you wish me to be honest."

"I wish you to be honest always, *chère cousine.*"

His thumb beneath her chin tilted her gaze to meet the fiery heat of his. When his fingertip traced a languid path along her cheek, she closed her eyes, savoring his touch, knowing it was wrong, but unable to deny herself this sweet delight.

"As I wish to be honest with you," he continued while his finger caressed her lips. "And what I wish to be honest about is how lovely you are. Your cheeks are tinted the color of the roses in your garden." He lightly kissed her right cheek. When she gasped and would have pulled away, his hand curved along her nape, keeping her against him. "They have a lovely flavor, but I long to taste, if honest you wish me to be, your soft lips."

"Radcliffe, don't be foolish!"

"Have no doubts that this may be the wisest thing I have ever done."

He teased her mouth with a questing kiss, gentle and surprisingly hesitant, as if he expected her to jerk away. Mayhap, for once, he had not guessed what she was thinking, because he would have known that she wanted to be within his embrace.

When he raised his mouth from hers, he smiled. "Is

that pleasure I see on your face, my sweet cousin, or can it be nothing more than astonishment that I am so brazen?"

"Radcliffe—"

"No, do not tell me. Let me determine the truth myself."

He captured her mouth and pulled her against him until she could sense his heartbeat echoing her own. Caressing her, he urged her to soften in his arms. Her hands slipped along his arms, rediscovering their strong sinews. At his nape, her fingers combed upward through his hair. When his mouth tasted her cheeks before etching liquid fire along her neck, her breath matched the eager tempo of his kisses.

Slowly he drew away and whispered, "Lisabeth, sweet Lisabeth, so long I have wished to hold you like this."

She stiffened as his words recalled Lieutenant Ison's when he had asked for her hand. How could she have allowed Radcliffe to make her go queer in the attic? She did not want to marry Lieutenant Ison, and she did not want to marry Radcliffe. Nor did he wish to do more than dally with her, for he had spoken just moments ago of presenting his petition to Miss Tobler.

He was no better than Frederick to kiss her when he intended to ask Miss Tobler to marry him. And she was no better than the harlot that Frederick had accused her of being.

Radcliffe caught her hand before she could flee.

"Let me go," she whispered, too ashamed to speak louder or to look at him. She could hear him telling her how Norton had spoken of her. Had Radcliffe kissed her only to prove to himself that she was as horrid as Frederick had led his cousin to believe?

"Lisabeth, stay a moment."

"No, that would be unwise."

"Unwise?" He spun her to face him. The hard lines had

returned to his face. "Is that all this kiss was to you? A mistake? Don't be false with me, for I sampled the truth on your lips."

Again she stepped away. "Desist, Radcliffe. If you wish the truth, it is that I do not want you kissing me."

"You continue to be false, Lisabeth!"

"You think *that* because I refuse to laud the splendid war hero as so many other women have."

When his face became gray beneath his warm tan, she wanted to retract the words. She had not wanted to hurt him. Or had she, for she had aimed her words at his most vulnerable spot? "Radcliffe—"

"Say no more, my lady." He turned, grasped his walking stick, and strode toward the door. "I will impose my company upon you no longer this afternoon. If someone should inquire of me, you may inform them that I am at Tobler's house where I shall be asking Miss Tobler to be my wife. I bid you good afternoon, Lady Montague."

"Radcliffe," she began again, but he went down the stairs without looking back. Rushing to the top of the steps, she heard the door crash closed behind him. She was left to stare at it and wonder if he would return, and what she would do if he did.

Sixteen

Radcliffe sat in the chair at the foot of his bed, his elbow on the arm, his chin on his fist. Blast it! This was all wrong. He had thought his announcement of his plan to marry Miss Tobler would make Lisabeth happy. Instead, she was miserable. He should have heeded Norton's second thoughts and remained in the country.

No sound came through the dressing room tonight. That confirmed his deepest fear. The weeping had been Lisabeth's, for he knew, even without seeing the light coming beneath the door, that she was as unable to find sleep as he was. How could she? For once, she had been unable to conceal her true feelings from him. When she had trembled in his arms, it had not been from outrage at his outrageous kiss, but from the passion that had woven the melodies of their hearts into one.

He slammed his fist into the arm of the chair, ignoring the pain springing up his arm. She had been unable to hide her despair and disgust from him either.

"Sir," said Bond, addressing him as he did when they were alone, "it has been a long day."

"Longer than you can know, Bond."

"If you need something—"

His laugh as he looked again at the dressing room was cold. "What I need cannot be mine." Shoving himself to his feet, he said, "And it appears that it never will be."

"It is not like you to give up so easily."

"This is not the battlefield, Bond! What would you have me do that will not make more of a jumble of this?"

Bond gave him no answer. Radcliffe did not expect him to, for he feared there was none.

Lady Edwina lowered the *Morning Post* to the breakfast table and smiled at Lisabeth. "Congratulations, my dear. It appears you have succeeded. Tobler would not be having his fête next week listed if he were not about to announce his daughter's betrothal."

Lisabeth kept her chin high. Not once during the night had she piped her eyes, and she would not now. "I am sure he is delighted with the turn of events. Radcliffe intended to present his suit to Miss Tobler last night. It appears that he has met with success."

Lady Edwina lifted the newspaper again. "I know I told you that I thought the task was a burden beyond what you should shoulder, but, once you assumed it, I had no apprehensions about you achieving your goal." Her nose wrinkled in distaste. "I suppose we must ask Norton Radcliffe to stay with us during the wedding. How I abhor that odious man! I never did understand what Frederick saw in his cousin."

Instead of tarnishing Frederick in his stepmother's eyes, Lisabeth said, "I began a letter to inform Norton that an announcement might be forthcoming. I shall rewrite it." She swallowed the anguish aching in her heart. "Unless you prefer me to offer an excuse, I must invite him."

"I trust you to do what you deem best." Glancing at the paper, she mused, "Ah, here is an item of note! Miss Castleman has been seen keeping company with Mr. Green the past few evenings. And this is of interest."

"What is it?"

" 'Lady Frederick Montague has been seen on the arm of Lieutenant Hamlin Ison. Lieutenant Ison is the son of—' "

Rising, Lisabeth put her napkin on the table. "I have no interest in listening to rumors about my friends."

"And about you?"

"Rumors!" she returned. "If you will excuse me, I shall go and pen a missive to Norton."

When Lisabeth paused in the doorway, disturbed that she had spoken so vehemently, she looked back to discover Lady Edwina immersed in the newspaper. She smiled, wishing her life had remained so well-ordered. Then she turned away. Why did she want that? Her life would be that way again when Radcliffe left to take his bride to Cliffs' End. Well-ordered and boring.

The door to the street opened, letting in the fresh breath of morning. She paused at a warm laugh. Telling herself she must have her garret empty to linger, she stared at Radcliffe's smile as he handed his hat to Doherty.

The amusement faded from Radcliffe's voice when he saw her. He crossed the foyer and rested one arm on the banister, inches from her fingers. "Not a single word of felicitations, Lisabeth?"

"I am happy to see you settled as Norton requested." She knew he did not believe her, for his eyes narrowed.

"Adelaide urges you to call soon, so that she might speak to you about the wedding."

How easily he spoke his beloved's name, but did he love Miss Tobler? If he did, how could he have kissed Lisabeth with such fire? "I am honored Adelaide is asking me to help her."

"As you helped me?"

"Yes." She did not wait for him to say more. She hurried up the stairs with inappropriate speed.

Going into her room, Lisabeth locked the door. She did not want to be disturbed, not even by Wilson. Muttonhead that she was, she had tried to convince herself last night that Radcliffe would not ask Miss Tobler to wed. Now she must watch the man she loved marry another woman.

The grandest room in the Tobler house looked more elegant than Lisabeth had ever seen it. Choke-full, it was thick with smoke and conversation and the aroma of wine. She did not see Lieutenant Ison, and, for that, she was relieved. Since Mrs. Castleman's fête, he had called several times, but she had fortunately been busy with Adelaide. She was not ready to confront him and break his heart.

"Lady Montague?"

She turned to see Adelaide's pale face. The young woman had been so nervous for the past week that Lisabeth had urged the Toblers' housekeeper to have feathers ready to be burnt to revive Adelaide from a swoon.

"I must speak with you," Adelaide continued in the same agitated tone.

Lisabeth smiled. "Of course. What—?"

"Oh, there you are, my dear." Mr. Tobler smiled as he came forward. "How lovely you look, Lady Montague," he said politely, then continued, "Adelaide, do come and chat with the duchess. Her Grace has expressed her eagerness to meet Lord Radcliffe's future wife. You will excuse us, Lady Montague?"

"Of course," Lisabeth said to his back.

"In quite a dither, isn't he?"

Lisabeth smiled at Prospera Fry's wry question. "I thought you were returning to your father's house."

Prospera smoothed her pale blue gown and gave an indifferent shrug. "I had hoped to dissuade Lord Radcliffe from buckling himself to Adelaide Tobler, but I fear it is too late."

"It is too late." Realizing how sorrowful her words sounded, Lisabeth smiled again. "Prospera, there must be another man you can wed to satisfy your father's demands. Have you considered Mr. Hinkle?"

"To own the truth, he is more in debt than I." She sighed again. "I was jobbernowl to pin my hopes on Lord Radcliffe. Lisabeth, you are the most fortunate woman I know. You have kept your heart free."

Although Lisabeth wanted to tell her how untrue her words were, she said nothing as Prospera went to offer her congratulations to Adelaide. The young woman would have no suspicions that she spoke to an unsuccessful rival for Lord Radcliffe's affections.

Another unsuccessful rival, she corrected herself.

Lisabeth tried to let the music and the conversation soothe her, but her gaze continued to wander to where Radcliffe stood beside Adelaide. He never had looked so handsome as when he wore his best evening dress. His white waistcoat glittered in the candlelight almost as brilliantly as his ebony hair and eyes.

Feeling smothered, Lisabeth wandered into the foyer. She had entered it a dozen times in the past week, but each time she had been sure this hour would never come. It had, and she must keep her tears unshed as she raised her glass in a toast to Radcliffe and Adelaide.

"Lisabeth!"

At the strident voice, she turned. Her eyes widened as she saw Norton Radcliffe. His pinched face appeared to have been left out too long in the sun. He was tall, but his shoulders stooped. When he had not replied to her letter, she had assumed that he would not attend the betrothal party.

Holding out her hand, Lisabeth said, "Norton, what a pleasure! You must let me present you to Adelaide Tobler."

"Did you select her?" he asked, ignoring her hand.

"Yes." She lowered her hand, knowing that he intended to be his normal irascible self. "Her cousin married the

Earl of Dybrook the same month Frederick and I wed. 'Tis a fine family."

"What made Tristan choose the chit?"

"Adelaide Tobler is no chit, Norton."

He grumbled something, but she did not ask him to speak louder, for she suspected his phrases were unsuitable for the ears of Mr. Tobler's guests. Lisabeth asked him about his journey, then wished she had refrained as he gave her every detail, including suffering from carriage-sickness.

"Pray do not continue," she said, with a shudder, "for I fear your tale shall make me as ill. Be glad, Norton, you are here. Let us find Lady Edwina. I know she will be as happy as I to see you."

"That old tough?" He grimaced. "She abhors me and has the decency not to be hypocritical about it."

Wishing he had remained in the country, she said, "Look, there is Radcliffe." Her heart halted in mid-beat when she saw Radcliffe and Adelaide waltzing in perfect harmony with the music and each other.

"Is that the woman he plans to marry?" Norton's amazement seemed more honest than his complaints. "Good God, did he steal her from the schoolroom?"

"This is Adelaide's first Season." Lisabeth saw his face drawn down in a frown. "Why are you dismayed? I thought this is what you wished."

"Did you?" Norton folded his hands behind his back. "I find it senseless to discuss anything with you, for you have nothing in your brain but thoughts of arrant mischief."

"I fear you mistake me for another."

"You do not need to try to disabuse me from what I have seen with my own two good eyes and from what your late, obviously unlamented husband told me."

Lisabeth's chin rose. "What Frederick told you I shall

not respond to, but you cannot name a single time when I was involved in what you term arrant mischief."

"Need I remind you of what you have written me of rides with the marquess?"

She regarded him with bafflement. "You need only ask Lady Edwina to soothe your thoughts about any improprieties. We never rode without a chaperon."

"Even to Vauxhall Gardens?" He laughed when she gasped. "You need not ask me how I know, Lisabeth, for you know as I do that your behavior was, as I understand it is too often, shameless. What would your suitor Ison think?"

Lisabeth fought to keep her voice serene. "Good evening, Mr. Radcliffe. I trust you can find someone else to listen to your spurious comments."

She walked away. Blinking back tears, for a wet-goose had no place at the party, she wondered if this was how it all must end. Radcliffe wedding another woman and her own reputation in ruins.

Leaving the joyous laughter behind her, Lisabeth walked into the small garden behind the house. It needed trimming, but she was pleased with its ragged shadows. How she wished Radcliffe would seek her out and tease her sorrow away as he had so often!

She sat in a shadowed arbor, but Norton Radcliffe's cruel words followed her. She would not—*could not*—invite him to stay at Cavendish Square. When he had chided her for hypocrisy, he had been correct, but she would be dishonest no more.

Hearing a light whistle, Lisabeth peered around the vine-covered arbor. Was it Radcliffe? Those silly expectations bolted when another man stepped from the shadows. She pulled back, but Lieutenant Ison saw her.

He bowed over her hand, then kissed it eagerly as he sat beside her. "Forgive me for being late and leaving you alone for so long," he said with a smile. "My duties kept me from your side."

"You need not apologize. Instead I should, for I have left you standing in my foyer this week while I was busy with Miss Tobler."

"Will she return the favor when the time comes for our wedding?" he asked with a boyish smile.

"Lieutenant Ison—"

"Please call me Hamlin."

She closed her eyes. Hurting him as she had been hurt was what she had hoped to avoid, but she must be honest with him. He deserved as much. "No, it would be inappropriate, for I cannot wed you."

"Impossible!"

Lisabeth looked at the moonlight sparkling on the path. "I regret that I cannot offer you the affection you wish."

"Because you wish to offer it to Lord Radcliffe?"

She feigned surprise to keep him from guessing how accurate he was. "You astound me, sir."

"Do I?" His face tightened. "I own that I never expected you to believe his aspersions against me."

"Lord Radcliffe has—"

"Filled your head with tales of his heroics," he said, so furious he forgot his manners. "Did he regale you with how he was wounded while single-handedly saving a company of men from falling prey to Boney's troops?"

"Did he?"

"That is what the reports said when they crossed my superior's desk."

Lisabeth faltered as she wondered why she never had asked how Radcliffe had been wounded. "But you do not believe the reports?"

"I question them."

"Why? Because you suspect Radcliffe penned them?" She gave him no time to answer. "How is that possible when he was near death when he arrived back home on English soil?"

Lieutenant Ison set himself on his feet, his mustache not hiding his pursed lips. "My lady, I question their validity."

"Then, you must believe that Radcliffe exaggerated his exploits for whomever wrote the report."

He hesitated. "I believe that the report was written from information gathered from the men under his command."

Lisabeth snapped her fan open and stood. "I find your accusations, which are so unfounded that you find them uncomfortable to speak, to be of the worst taste, Lieutenant. Although I have no knowledge of Radcliffe's time with the army, I can assure you that he holds truth paramount."

"As you do?"

"Of course."

"Then, why are you not honest about the fact that you look with opposition upon my suit because you are in love with Lord Radcliffe?"

"I was honest when I said that I do not have a *tendre* for you. I am sorry."

"But you love Lord Radcliffe?" he persisted.

She looked over her shoulder at him. "That, sir, is not a topic I wish to discuss with you."

"You have a knock in the cradle to love a man about to marry another!"

Raising her chin, she said, "Lieutenant Ison, you are overwrought. I think you would be wise to leave until you are more yourself."

Again he took her hand and bowed over it, but without an eager kiss. Turning on his heel, he walked away. She was tempted to call after him, telling him that she understood his broken heart, but that would cause more trouble. Lieutenant Ison was the gentleman she had urged Radcliffe to be—the epitome of the Pink of the *Ton*, but she could not love him.

She looked at the seat in the arbor, certain there was no haven for her anywhere. Reaching the foyer, she glanced at the front door. If she told Lady Edwina she was leaving, her mother-in-law might be placated with the promise of a later explanation. Yet, if she withdrew, her absence would stir the coals of conversation. She was Radcliffe's sponsor. For this final night, her place was beside him as he proclaimed that he would have another woman at his side for the rest of his days.

Taking a deep breath, she reached for a glass of champagne. She must be sure that no one guessed the state of her heart tonight, for, if she loved Radcliffe, she should wish him happiness. And he expected to find that with Adelaide.

Lisabeth's thoughts were jarred when a hand settled on her arm. "Adelaide!" she gasped. "I own you are the last person I expected to see in the foyer. Why aren't you enjoying your party?"

The young woman shivered. "I have been seeking you everywhere! Where have you been?"

Lisabeth's smile faded at the younger woman's distress. "Are you about to announce your betrothal? Is that why you came to find me? So I would not miss it?" Lisabeth knew she was prattling like Miss Gibbs, but could not halt herself. "What a dear you are to think of others on this important night! If—"

Adelaide caught Lisabeth's hands in hers. "I must speak with you. Now! No one else will heed me."

Lisabeth realized Adelaide's disquiet did not come from shyness. Something was amiss. "Where may we find a quiet spot?"

"My bedchamber?"

She shook her head, a gentle smile tilting her lips. In so many ways, Adelaide Tobler remained a child. "You are the hostess tonight. It would be unheard-of for you to sneak away to the upper floors."

"We can go into my father's book room." Uneasily she glanced at the crowded drawing room. "It is private, and we can leave the door ajar, so that anyone who may wish to find me will be able to."

The chamber was dusky with the light from a single lamp. The furniture was worn, but Lisabeth sensed this room contained the heart of the Tobler house. So easily she could imagine Adelaide and her father here as they read or wrote or talked of the events of their lives. She wondered why she and Radcliffe had never been invited into this room before.

Adelaide moaned, "Oh, Lady Montague, I cannot begin to tell you how despondent I am!"

"Despondent? Adelaide, what is wrong?"

Adelaide drew Lisabeth to sit with her on the settee. "Can you stop the announcement from being made tonight?"

"Why do you wish to postpone it?"

"I do not wish to postpone it. I want to halt it. Lord Radcliffe frightens me."

"Frightens you?" She laughed. This was no more than a nervous bride-to-be. She prayed her laughter covered her unsettled feelings, for her heart had jumped like a fleeing stag when she heard Adelaide's words. With a silent sigh, she reminded herself that she had promised to do all she could to help Radcliffe win a bride. That promise still bound her. "Lord Radcliffe is a gentleman."

"He does seem to be trying to like me. He pats my hand and calls me dear child. Is that the way a suitor should act?"

"He is older than you," said Lisabeth, although each banal word tasted repulsive. "Mayhap he wishes not to overmaster you with more than a chaste kiss."

Adelaide wrung her hands in her white silk gown. "He has not kissed me, not even on the cheek, for his manners have been those of a brother."

"Then, what frightens you?"

"Being married to him frightens me." She hid her face in her hands. "I have never wished to marry him. Father wants me to be a marchioness, for once not caring that I shall certainly be miserable as no one has ever been."

Lisabeth stiffened. To see Adelaide Tobler forced into a marriage that would make her as unhappy as Lisabeth had been when she wed Frederick Montague was appalling. During the week since he had stormed out of the house to ask for Adelaide's hand, Radcliffe had not been the happy man he should have been upon obtaining his heart's desire, but she was unsure if he would agree to put an end to the betrothal. Breaking a betrothal on the night of its proclamation was sure to send rumors vibrating throughout the Polite World.

"Have you spoken to Radcliffe of this?" Lisabeth asked quietly.

Tears glistened in her dark eyes. "How could I speak to him when he has been here so seldom?" She must have noted Lisabeth's astonishment, for she said with unusual petulance, "Even on his single call here this week, he and Father sat and talked and ignored me."

Lisabeth tried to sort out her bafflement. Radcliffe had left Cavendish Square every evening, and she had guessed he was calling upon the Toblers.

"Do not ignore my pleas for help, my lady." Again Adelaide caught Lisabeth's hands in hers. Trembling, she said, "Whether he has a *tendre* for me or not, I long to marry Lord Jacot."

"Jacot?" she repeated, surprised, for she had not seen the burly viscount during the month Radcliffe had been squiring Adelaide.

Adelaide's smile grew soft. "I have loved him since he was in short pants, and he possesses affection for me. His mother's poor health has kept him in the country, but he . . ." She lowered her eyes, then reached within her bodice to pull out a crumpled page. "Please read this."

"I have no wish to intrude by reading a private missive."

"Please, my lady. Read it so you might understand."

The dispatch proved that Adelaide's devotion for Lord Jacot was returned twofold. When Lisabeth read how he pined for his beloved and loving Adelaide, she sighed and refolded the page. "It seems this betrothal should be halted at once."

"How can I do that when everyone here tonight expects—Oh!" she moaned as she hid her face again.

Lisabeth was tempted to tell the young woman to stop weeping. Adelaide was sure to succumb to vapors if Lisabeth said anything so straightforward. Sighing, she tried to imagine a way to unravel the complicated tangle of hearts.

"Adelaide, Norton Radcliffe arrived a short time ago. He also is Lord Radcliffe's cousin and a closer relative than I." She hesitated, then knew she could not inflict Frederick's cousin on this young woman. "I shall speak with him."

Adelaide's eyes brightened. "No, Lady Montague, you have been too kind already. I shall approach Mr. Radcliffe, for the problem is mine."

"And if he is unwilling to intercede on your behalf?"

"I pray he is most willing." She rose and looked toward the hall. "He must be, my lady, for marrying Lord Radcliffe shall make both his lordship and me unhappy for the rest of our days." Her large eyes filled with more tears as she whispered, "And you do not want that, do you?"

Lisabeth was sure she was being more honest than she had been in years when she said, "No, I do not want that."

Seventeen

Radcliffe tried to spare his feet from Miss Castleman's as they danced. Unlike Lisabeth, who was graceful, Miss Castleman waltzed with the heavy steps of a weary soldier marching into battle. He almost chuckled, for the unworthy thought would gain him a scold and a reluctant smile from Lisabeth.

Dash it! He should not be thinking of her, not tonight when he was about to embark on a life with another woman. Although, he had to own, calling Miss Tobler a woman was a stretch of the word, for she was very much the naïve, charming child he once had accused Lisabeth of being.

Looking over Miss Castleman's head, he frowned when he could not see Lisabeth among the dancers or in conversation with the dowagers. Curiosity teased him, but his only reward was Miss Castleman stepping on his toes . . . again.

He was grateful when the music ended. Escorting her back to her mother, he was glad when he saw his host motioning to him. He bowed his head and said, "Thank you for the delightful dance, Miss Castleman."

"My lord—" began her mother.

"I beg you to excuse me." He had never been so grateful for an interruption.

Tobler hurried toward him with surprising haste. In his

wake, the guests turned to stare, then smile as they noted his destination. Radcliffe attempted a smile, too, but it was difficult when he had come, during the past week, to understand the trepidation of a man about to hang at Tyburn.

"The time is nigh for the betrothal announcement, my lord." Mr. Tobler glanced around, then cleared his throat. "I thought Adelaide would be by your side."

Radcliffe realized the man was as nervous as the bride-to-be, who had been more subdued than usual tonight. He had failed to win a single smile from Miss Tobler, for she had become as withdrawn as Lisabeth. Dash it! Why was Lisabeth littering his mind *now*? He had done as everyone wished, but had succeeded at making no one happy, including himself.

"I earlier saw Adelaide speaking with Lisabeth in the foyer. They were walking toward your book-room."

"My book-room?" Tobler's eyes nearly bulged from his head.

Radcliffe allowed his laugh to sound condescending. "No doubt, the ladies are tending to last-minute arrangements. I trust we would be wise to let them do so."

When Tobler agreed, albeit with reluctance, Radcliffe wandered about the room, listening to curious questions, and answering none of them. He frowned when he heard a familiar voice. Seeing his cousin on the far side of the room, Radcliffe wondered what Lisabeth had penned to Norton that had convinced him to leave his country nest for Town. He looked in the other direction, wanting to avoid Norton. With his first honest smile of the night, he walked to where Lisabeth was standing near a marble hearth. He admired the light blue ribbons along her simple bodice. The color matched her mercurial eyes.

"I did not expect you would be hiding, Lisabeth," he said softly.

"I wanted a quiet moment to think."

"Fiddle! You are not supposed to think at a party. You are supposed to have fun."

She laughed. "Who told you that?"

"My dearest teacher."

Lisabeth lowered her eyes, not wanting Radcliffe to discover how his teasing words stirred that luscious fire inside her. Noting how his hands clenched and unclenched at his sides, she knew he was not as nonchalant as he sounded. She followed his gaze toward where his cousin stood, debating something loudly. Was it only Norton Radcliffe's presence here that unsettled Radcliffe? Or—and her heart gave a joyous beat—was he as unsure as Adelaide about this match? No, she could not comfort herself with falsehoods. Nobody could force Radcliffe into an unwanted marriage. He had chosen this course himself.

To keep him from guessing her thoughts, she asked, "Can't you believe that I enjoy the quiet?"

"As you enjoy dancing in the quiet? Or could it be that you might enjoy dancing with music as much?"

Color rose along her cheeks. "I have had no chance to determine that tonight, Radcliffe, for no one has asked me."

"Not even the unparalleled Lieutenant Ison?"

"No," she said, adding no more.

"Then, you should stand up with me, *chère cousine.*"

Lisabeth shook her head. "Dancing does not fit with my state of mind."

"Nor with mine."

At the soft huskiness in his voice, she saw the strong emotions he made no attempt to hide. Warmth glowed within his eyes' dusky depths as his gaze caressed her tenderly. The answering heat bubbled in her heart, but she turned away before he could thoroughly enchant her with a mere look. Too late, she knew, for she wanted to wrap that magic around her along with his arms.

His fingertip brought her face back toward him. A hint

of a smile warmed his straight lips. "You are troubled, Lisabeth. I thought you would be filled with joy at your success in bringing out this old rake."

"You are no loose screw."

Laughing, he said, "I was not always as you see me now. Once I was quite the dashing blade, renowned for his rackety ways."

"You are quite dashing now . . . I mean—"

"I thank you for your generous compliment, but I know what I am." His voice softened. "What I am right now is willing to own that I was wrong."

"Wrong?" she asked with a sudden smile. Mayhap Radcliffe was as anxious to be done with the betrothal as Adelaide. And then. . . . She did not want to think of the future or the past, just of this moment when they might have been the only two in the room or in the world.

"I find I am most eager to waltz with you again."

"No, Radcliffe." Silencing her sorrow at turning aside her dreams, she said, "Rather I would speak with you."

His smile returned, but without its gentle edge. "Of what? Pray do not fill my ears anew with what I must or must not do during the pronouncement of my proposal to Miss Tobler."

"I wish to speak to you of where you have been this past week when you were not at Cavendish Square and not here."

"I should have known better than to allow you two to intrigue against me. Did Miss Tobler ask you why I had not been calling on her?" The music continued, uninterrupted for more than a minute before he added, "I, too, needed quiet to think, so I went to the Park."

"At night?"

"I have little fear for brigands or for my standing in the *ton*. Do you think I could have had a moment to myself if I came here and was surrounded by the preparations for this rout?"

"So you went to be alone?"

"To think."

"Of what?" She flushed at her forthright question.

"*Chère cousine,* a man about to embark upon marriage has many matters to consider." He held out his hand, but froze as he looked past her.

Lisabeth turned. Framed by the arch of the door leading to the foyer, Adelaide was in conversation with Norton Radcliffe. Lisabeth bit her lip as she saw Radcliffe's jaw tighten. She put her hand on his arm as he started to walk away.

He faced her. "Yes?"

Although she wanted to recoil from his frigid tone, she said, "Radcliffe, I must speak with you."

"No, you must excuse me." Drawing away, he bowed toward her. He went toward the door, leaving her staring after him. She hoped he would take care to find out why Adelaide was speaking with his cousin. Otherwise, he might cause more trouble.

Radcliffe paused in the doorway, saying nothing. Miss Tobler's soft voice faltered. Astonished by the trepidation in her eyes, he stepped forward.

Norton turned. Again, Radcliffe was surprised, but now because he was able to meet his cousin's eyes evenly. He had not stood in Norton's presence since his return from the war, for, instead of goading Radcliffe to try ever harder as Lisabeth had, Norton had been satisfied to let him molder away in a chair and suffer from the doctoring of that quack who had done more to hinder his recovery than help.

As Norton lifted his half-emptied champagne glass in a silent greeting, Radcliffe soothed his exasperation. He could not blame his cousin when he had let his own discouragement steal his determination to walk again.

Radcliffe kept his voice hushed, for he had no wish to dismay Miss Tobler further. "Has my cousin said something to disturb you?"

She looked beseechingly to Norton.

He took a sip. " 'Tis not I who disturbs this young woman. Miss Tobler has appealed to me as your nearest relative to find a way to dissolve her betrothal to a man who repulses her."

"I do not find the marquess repulsive!" gasped Adelaide. Looking at him, she whispered, "My lord, I would not have accepted your offer if that was the truth."

Radcliffe restrained his increasing irritation. He should have guessed that Norton would stir the coals as soon as possible. "Miss Tobler knows that I hold her in the highest regard." Taking Miss Tobler's hand in his, he noticed how it trembled in tempo with her lower lip. "If you wish, Miss Tobler, I will release you from the betrothal promise you made me."

"Thank you, my lord," she said. Two tears edged along her pale cheeks.

He handed her a handkerchief. "I shall speak to your father if you wish."

Miss Tobler hesitated, then stood on tiptoe and kissed his cheek. He clasped his hands behind his back as he watched her flee up the stairs, no doubt to pipe her eyes in the privacy of her room. He sighed. By not breaking Miss Tobler's heart, he was sure to have hurt Lisabeth's precious reputation among the *ton*. The poker-talk was sure to be of Lady Montague's mistaken matchmaking. Dash it! Why did this have to be so blasted complicated?

"What a nincompoop that chit is!" Norton's raspy voice trespassed on his thoughts. "She should have known that *she* did nothing to cause your change of heart."

"I would prefer that you would not speak so of Miss Tobler."

Norton emptied his glass and put it on a table. "Shall we speak of another woman whose name has been connected with yours, then?"

"Prospera Fry or Miss Gibbs?"

He sniffed. "You have teased many hearts, cousin, but I speak of a woman who has no heart."

"And who might that be?"

"Your hostess during your tenure in Town."

"I assume you mean Lisabeth, although your description of her is hardly accurate. Have you spoken with her?" He knew the answer. A conversation with his choleric cousin would be enough to steal the light from her lovely eyes.

"I have had that so-called pleasure." Norton eyed him up and down. "I see she convinced you to get out of that chair. Not that I'm surprised, for one sight of her would be enough to get a rise even out of a nearly dead man."

"Like me?"

"You wound me, Tristan. I thought Lisabeth had taught you to speak as nicely as a lord." Laughing coldly, he added, "As she clearly failed at that, I am led to wonder what other lessons my late cousin's wife gave you."

"I would prefer that you did not speak of Lisabeth so." Radcliffe folded his arms over his waistcoat. "Why do you disparage her when she has done exactly as you asked?"

"Yes, she has done *exactly* as I asked, hasn't she?"

"But you expected her to fail." Comprehension struck him as viciously as the ball had his leg. "You had hoped that I would be humiliated and crawl back to the country to die of ennui. Then who would have the title of the Marquess of Radcliffe? Not you, for it would rightfully go to my eldest sister's young son."

Norton's lips tightened in a frown. "Are you intimating that I am undeserving of it?" Not giving Radcliffe a chance to answer, he snapped, "You were ever the grand lord. You and Frederick! The marquess and the viscount . . . and Norton, who could offer no title grand to his heir."

"Was it your jealousy that goaded Frederick to recklessness, so he would try to take a hedge when he was wrapped up in warm flannel? Was it your jealousy that made you play the patriot and urge me to do a young man's duty, as you called it, and buy a commission that would take me into death's maw?"

"Your accusations prove you are cockle-brained," Norton returned, but his face was becoming a sickish gray. "After all, I was the one who took you in after your unfortunate injury."

"True, but you took control of my estate as well as your own while the doctor you chose kept me half out of my wits with his powders. Will I find that there has been a correct accounting of each estate?"

"Upon your return? Does that mean you tire of Town?" His eyes narrowed. "Or mayhap you intend to lend your *affaire* countenance by marrying my cousin's widow." Norton swayed as he glanced toward the crowded room, warning Radcliffe that his cousin was cup-shot. "Frederick often complained of how she flipped her skirts at any man with a bit of life within him. He told me how he had been a beef-head to marry a harlot who had disguised herself as a lady. It appears that she has given you back your manhood with her light-skirted ways."

Radcliffe struggled to keep his voice even. "I shall be gentleman enough to allow you to withdraw those words. You may insult me as you wish, but not Lisabeth. If you cannot recognize that she is a diamond of birth, then offer her respect for her attempts to bring your hypocritical wishes to fulfillment."

"And what do you owe her for the pleasure she has given you?" He smiled with satisfaction. "No doubt, I am not the only one asking that."

Radcliffe's hand tightened on his walking stick. His cousin was altogethery. Getting Norton out of the Toblers' house before his insults were overheard was paramount. "Let us speak of this elsewhere."

"No!" He shook off the hand Radcliffe had put on his arm. "You have embarrassed our family with your antics with that harlot. You give me no choice. I ask you to name your friend to meet me for grass before breakfast."

"A duel? Are you mad?"

Norton gave another drunken laugh, louder than before. "Mayhap you are not willing to risk more than some flimsy words in her defense."

"You are mauled! Put aside the wine and listen to sense."

"So you will not defend Lisabeth's name?" His voice rose on every word.

Radcliffe noted the curious glances in their direction. Dash it! Norton's bombastic voice was going to cause a scene. An end must be put to this immediately. If he could give his cousin a chance to clear his head, Norton might be willing to apologize; then all could be forgiven.

"Very well," he said. "I shall, of course, bring Bond."

Norton's smile faltered; then he squared his shoulders, proving he had more courage than Radcliffe had expected. "I should have known that you would be willing to defend the lost honor of your convenient. You were ever the fool. Very well, in an hour, we shall meet in the Park—"

"At dawn." That should allow Norton time to find his more sober wits.

"In an hour," he insisted. "The challenge is mine. I shall choose the hour of our meeting."

Hoping an hour would be enough to cool Norton's overheated head, Radcliffe nodded. "An hour it shall be. Give the details of the place to my man."

Norton flinched when Radcliffe smiled. Good! Mayhap Norton was already seeing the absurdity of this. Although Norton had sent him to Town to learn his lessons, Radcliffe intended to give his cousin one before dawn.

"I shall, and—"

"For now, I suggest you remove yourself."

"This is not Cliffs' End. You may not order me out."

"If you wish, I can have Tobler's servants toss you onto the street, but I suspect you would prefer to retain whatever of your reputation you think is worth salvaging." He turned, not caring to watch his cousin leave.

Radcliffe glanced into the room where Lisabeth had been caught in a conversation with Mrs. Castleman and her daughter. One more bit of fortune for him. He wanted to soothe her, but he must deal with another problem first. How had he allowed his life to become such a jumble?

He walked about the room, ignoring the curiosity about the delay with the announcement. The deuce! Where was Tobler? Mayhap he had had an inkling of the truth and had gone to be with his daughter.

"Radcliffe?"

He forgot his vexation as he looked into Lisabeth's face, which revealed her disquiet. "Forgive me, *chère cousine,* but I must speak with Tobler about a matter of some consequence."

"Of course," she said softly, but sorrow continued to dim her eyes.

Curving his hand along her soft cheek, he smiled sadly. Too late, he understood that her sorrow was for him and Miss Tobler. "I trust you knew of the impending dissolution of my betrothal before I."

"Adelaide sought me out. She professes an enduring affection for Lord Jacot."

"That pup?"

Lisabeth laughed, but asked, "Who can know what the eyes of love see? To Adelaide, Lord Jacot is her dashing swain."

"You are much the romantic, Lisabeth."

"Mr. Tobler may be distressed." She hesitated, then added, "But he must see it is wrong to force his daughter into marriage."

"As you were."

She nodded, and he sighed. He was about to add to her

pain, for she would be horrified when she learned of his determination to teach that stupe Norton a lesson.

His fingers lingered along her cheek as he murmured, "I think we should take our leave as soon as I am done speaking with Tobler. Will that be acceptable with you?"

"Yes." She glanced toward where Lieutenant Ison was deep in conversation with Miss Castleman. "There is nothing to keep me here tonight."

Questions taunted him, but he silenced them as he crossed the room. His path toward Tobler was blocked by a determined Mrs. Castleman and a smiling Lady Edwina.

"My lord," Mrs. Castleman gushed, "I cannot wait to tell that we all are agog at how prettily you and Emeraude danced together. So sadly, Lady Montague did not have the pleasure of seeing you."

Lady Edwina wafted her fan with its green feathers in front of her face. "If I may add my mite, do ask Emeraude to stand up with you again, so I may view this charming tableau."

Radcliffe resisted saying his prayers backward, for cursing would help nothing. Nor did he succumb to the temptation to comment that Mrs. Castleman's compliment was something a cripple, as she had deemed him heartlessly, could not have anticipated. He had seen the result of bitterness in his cousin, and in himself, and he would be its victim no more.

"I believe Emeraude is busy with Lieutenant Ison," he replied.

"Ison?" Mrs. Castleman gasped as she excused herself. Lady Edwina chuckled.

Radcliffe was startled, then realized Lisabeth's mother-in-law was enjoying her friend's hubble-bubble over making the perfect match for her daughter. Although he, under other circumstances, would have shared her laughter, he excused himself also. He did not want to talk with Mrs. Castleman or Lady Edwina. Only Tobler. He slipped through the press of guests to where Tobler wore a strained expression on his kindly face.

Being forthright was the only choice. "Tobler, your charming daughter has been kind enough to let me know the state of her heart. It does not center on me."

"Adelaide said nothing of this to me," he said, clearly shaken. When Radcliffe took a glass of wine from a passing servant, Tobler sipped it gratefully. "Forgive me, my lord. This is most unlike Adelaide."

"Surely she saw how happy you were, Tobler. A dutiful daughter, she wanted nothing to cause you unhappiness. Under the circumstances, I ask your leave to retire."

"Yes, yes." Tobler sighed. "I thank you for your interest in my daughter, my lord."

"From what Lady Montague tells me, and it appears your daughter and she have become confidantes, your daughter is much more taken with Lord Jacot. Mayhap they are more of a mind."

Tobler's eyes began to twinkle again. "I had despaired of the lad ever speaking his heart to Adelaide."

"It appears that your time of despair is past. Good evening, Tobler."

"Good evening, my lord." He hesitated, then, offering his hand, said, "Best of fortune go with you."

As Tobler rushed away to seek his daughter, Radcliffe muttered, "I may need it more than you know."

Eighteen

Only the wheels of Radcliffe's carriage clattering against the cobbles broke the foggy silence. Lisabeth had not imagined this evening would end with Radcliffe breaking off his betrothal. What would happen now? Would he continue his search for a wife or would he return to Cliffs' End?

As if he were privy to her thoughts, he said as he gazed out the window of the carriage, "I miss seeing the stars here in Town."

"Fog obscures them most nights."

"They were always so clear at Cliffs' End."

"Were they?" She spoke in barely more than a whisper, unsure why he spoke of this now.

"I remember often sneaking away from my sleeping governess to stand on the very edge of the cliffs and watch the stars sparkling above in the sky while the sea glistened beneath them. When the wind groaned along the cliffs, I would imagine it was the call of the invaders whose slaughter gave my family its name." He laughed with irony. "No one ever explained if my family descended from the Anglo-Saxon defenders or the Viking invaders."

"Mayhap it has been forgotten during the ensuing centuries of civilization."

"Civilization?" Again he laughed. "Do you truly believe we are more civilized than those warrior hordes?"

She could not silence her anxiety any longer. "Radcliffe, what is wrong?"

He turned to face her, but she could not read his expression in the shadowed carriage. "It went better than I had hoped with Tobler. He was, as ever, the gentleman you strive for me to be."

"Then, why do you act as if a devil sits on your shoulder?"

"I fear I have made a shocking mull of the situation with Norton."

Lisabeth locked her fingers together. "Radcliffe, do not let his high fidgets tonight upset you. You must be pleasant when he calls at Cavendish Square."

"Calls? I thought you had invited him to enjoy your gracious hospitality."

"Lady Edwina does not like him."

"I always considered your mother-in-law a lady of rare taste." He laughed with an odd intensity. "If you wish the truth, Lisabeth, my cousin is a gabble-monger when he has seen the bottom of a bottle. His gabble is irritating at best, but tonight he was insufferable, a condition you would no doubt suggest I am due after being so insufferable to you."

"I would wish Norton Radcliffe on no one."

She was not sure if he had heard her attempt to buoy his spirits, for he continued, "We exchanged heated words when I grew tired of his pitiful whining that he was denied a title by his unfortunate birth."

"I would admire you for one thing, Radcliffe, if nothing else. You must have had more strength of will than you realized to live under the roof of that ramshackle boor. His behavior is beneath reproach."

"What did he say to you?"

She smiled sadly. "Nothing he has not before."

"That son of a sow!" He hit his palm with his fist. "Blast

him. He is going to deserve everything that happens to-night."

"Tonight? What is going to happen tonight?"

"Within the hour, Norton and I shall face each other in a duel."

"A duel?" She surely had imbibed as much champagne as Norton, for her head spun like a child's toy. "Tell me you are jesting."

"I wish I could soothe you by saying yes." He slid his arm along the back of the seat. When his fingers brushed her shoulder, he whispered, "Do not shiver so, for I trust Norton shall find his senses when the wine stops bubbling through his brain."

"But he has no sense!"

"At last, we have found something upon which we both agree wholeheartedly." His voice took on the low huskiness that sent renewed quivers through her. Not of fear, but of yearning for him to draw her within the arc of his arm and hold her to his chest and the steady beat of his heart which she did not want stopped. "My dear Lisabeth, my foolishness has dragged you from the party and your attentive Ison."

"Lieutenant Ison shall be attentive to me no more."

"You told him that you would not marry him?"

"How——?" Wishing she could see his face more clearly, she asked, "Mayhap I should say *who* told you of his offer?"

He lifted her hand and stroked it. "*Chère cousine,* your mother-in-law was eager to regale me with your accomplishment. Although she told me, on more than one occasion I assure you, that she considers the lieutenant unsuitable, Ison must have sought her approval before offering you his boastful heart."

"If you knew he had asked . . ." She closed her eyes and whispered, "But 'tis meaningless now. Radcliffe, you must halt this silly duel over a woman who is in love with neither of you."

"You thought this was about Miss Tobler?" He laughed, surprising her anew. "My cousin spoke disparagingly of another lady, one he should admire as I do." He took her other hand in his. "I could not allow that."

Lisabeth withdrew her fingers and turned to the window. Fog contorted in the streetlamp's cool light. Lightning flashed, and she flinched as the answering rumble filled the sky. "Why are you upset when you have intimated that he spoke to you of me in the past?"

"I did not know you in the past."

"So you believed—"

"I have told you that I shall make my own opinions, not heed the words of another. Now I know I owe you more than I can ever repay, and I shall not have Norton sullying your name."

Lisabeth faced him. "If you believe you owe me a duty, repay me by withdrawing your challenge."

"I cannot. He challenged me."

"He challenged you? But I thought you said that this was about what he said."

"It is."

"I do not understand."

"All you need do now is wish me luck, *chère cousine*. We meet within the hour. Norton wants no chance of the fog dispersing so our affair of dubious honor can be witnessed."

"Let him wait out alone in the storm. The rain might sober his mind and cool his temper."

"I fear neither he nor his temper will be readily sobered."

"Then, why do you consider hazarding your life again? And for nothing!"

"But honor."

"Your honor is secure. Lieutenant Ison told me that you are a hero."

He shook his head. "I was a fool. I dared to believe I was invincible. I have been paying the price of that since."

"But you saved your men's lives."

"Yes, but 'twas my orders that placed them in danger to begin with." He sighed. "Just as it is my intrusion in your life that has brought us to this muddle. So, for honor's sake, I must meet Norton."

She wanted to shake him, to force some sense into his head, to throw herself in his arms and beg him not to risk his life when she wanted him to be a part of hers. All she could do was say, "Honor means little if you are put to bed with a shovel. Is that what you aspire to? A hero's grave?"

"That shall not await me. There is no honor in being bested by a noodle." With his hand against the side of her face, he tilted her lips toward his. "Trust me, Lisabeth."

She turned, so she did not have to see his anguish when she avoided the kiss she wanted as much as he did. How could she be satisfied with a single kiss? She wanted so much more, but she dared not give in to her longings. Her vow—her skimble-skamble vow—never to give her heart again was in tatters about her. She had been so sure of her determination not to trust any man, and Radcliffe had given her every reason to be wary of him. His sharp words, his arrogant demands, his impatience—in all of these ways, he resembled his cousins. But she could not ignore his gentle touch and his concern for those about him and the way his sharp words were softened by his teasing smile.

He said nothing as the carriage slowed in front of her door. When the footman jumped from the boot, Radcliffe motioned for him to hand her out. She stepped to the damp walkway and looked back. "Radcliffe—"

"Wish me luck, *chère cousine.*"

She gasped and ran toward the street as he gave the

command to whip up the horses. The carriage was gone before she could countermand Radcliffe's order.

Behind her, the door to the house opened. Doherty held up a lantern to light her way home. So many nights, she had been a part of this same scene, but never had her heart ached so.

Doherty peered past her into the night. "My lady, are you alone?"

"Radcliffe is involving himself in a fool's task," she answered bitterly. "How can he fulfill his want-witted cousin's dreams without losing his own?"

"My lady?"

She pulled off her gloves and threw them onto the table. "What good is a title if it brings only heartbreak? Why would anyone gamble on something that has no price?"

"My lady, I—"

Fisting her hands by her sides, she whispered, "What good is a title if it brings only sorrow? Father thought he could die without regret as long as I had a titled husband, for he believed that was the route to insured comfort. Mr. Tobler was ready to sacrifice his daughter in the same unknowing attempt to guarantee her happiness. Norton is willing to die to assuage his envy at having a title no grander than the one of his birth. Only Adelaide has had the good sense to see the truth." She turned to see a red-faced Doherty staring at her in amazement. "Doherty . . ."

"My lady, if you need nothing else, I shall retire."

She guessed her cheeks were as flushed as his. It was not proper that she should speak so to her butler. Astonishment spread through her as she realized that although he had served her during her years in this house, she had no idea what his first name might be or what he did on his rare days away from his post.

"Doherty, forgive me. I should not be burdening you with my concerns."

"If you wish me to remain, my lady . . ."

"No." She gathered up her gloves and frowned as something fell to the floor. A calling card. Before Doherty could dart forward and retrieve it, she picked it up. She read the name engraved on it in fanciful letters and smiled. "Wait, Doherty."

"My lady?"

She tried to keep excitement from creeping into her voice. This idea was audacious, and if it failed, she risked her reputation. But, if it succeeded, she might save Radcliffe's life. "Have the phaeton brought for me. I believe I may yet prove to all of us what Miss Tobler so clearly knows."

Fog clung close to the banks of the Serpentine as Radcliffe crossed the damp grass. Behind him, the carriage waited. Its lights could not pierce far into the mist. Overhead, thunder grew louder as it chased the lightning, but he paid it no mind.

He glanced at Bond, grateful that the man was with him during yet another battle. Seeing motion near a clump of trees that was lit dimly by a pair of lanterns, he said, "This way, Bond."

"Yes, my lord."

"My lord?" he asked with a laugh.

Bond's frown did not ease. "*Major* Radcliffe would not be so willing to chance throwing his life away for nothing."

"I would not call Lisabeth's honor nothing."

"She does not want you to fight this duel. If she knew it was about her—"

"Bond, remind me one of these days to give you a direct order to cease your eavesdropping."

He had expected Bond to smile at his jesting, but Bond said only, "Yes, my lord."

Dash it! The whole world was turning inside out in the midst of this bumble-bath. He had thought that Bond, of all about him, would understand what he intended to do and why.

Tersely he greeted his cousin by where the lanterns sat in the grass. The addle cove! Had Norton given no thought to the idea that a simple move might topple them and set Hyde Park on fire? No, Norton thought only of slaying his cousin to ease his jealousy.

Radcliffe did not recognize the pudgy man whom Norton had brought as his second and paid no attention when the man was introduced. "Let us get this underway, Norton."

"You recall the ways of civilization enough to know the rules of this?" asked Norton as he slipped off his coat.

"I know them well," returned Radcliffe. "However, I suspect there is something more civilized about warfare than this charade."

Norton bristled as he tossed his coat to his man. "If you would choose to reconsider, you may."

"I do not intend to allow you to continue spouting your spurious insults about Lisabeth."

Again Norton's face grew wan, but he said, "You are the one taken-in by her coy ways. Do you think she will be any more faithful to you than to Frederick?"

Radcliffe shrugged off his coat without replying. The longer Norton continued prattling, the greater was the chance that the wine would ooze out of his brain.

"So you think," Norton taunted, "that she will cease her flirting because of you? Frederick offered her everything when she had nothing, and she played him for the cuckold. Oh, she boldly denied the truth when he confronted her, but she refused to change even when he tried to teach her a lesson or two by . . ." He swallowed and looked away.

"When he what?"

"It is of no import."

Grasping two handfuls of his cousin's waistcoat, Radcliffe growled, "Tell me, Norton, or I swear you will be unable to heft a weapon in this duel."

Norton's man stepped forward, but Bond seized his arm, pulling him back.

"You ill-mannered cur!" Norton cried. "Release me!"

"Tell me!" He tightened his grip, pulling Norton's nose within an inch of his own. "Tell me now."

"All right. All right." When Radcliffe loosened his hold slightly, Norton raised his chin in defiance. "Why shouldn't you know? Mayhap you will see that I am trying to do you a favor by telling you the truth you deny."

"Spit it out!"

"All right. Frederick told me how his wife embarrassed him endlessly. Either she refused to speak to any of his friends, or she was dallying about them like a cheap coquette."

"So you said."

"He tried to break her of her bad habits."

Sickness ate at Radcliffe, choking his voice as he whispered, "Break her of her bad habits how?"

"I told you. Talking to her and—" He swallowed hard again. "And when that did not work, he resorted to harsher means."

"He struck her?" When Norton nodded, Radcliffe shoved him away with a curse. He looked at Bond and saw the shock on his man's face. Bond must be recalling, as he was, how Lisabeth had cowered in consummate terror when Radcliffe had raised his arm to put it around her shoulders. No wonder she wept in the night as she fought nightmares. They were not bad dreams, but horrible memories. Rounding on his cousin again, he demanded, "If you knew of this, how could you allow this to continue?"

" 'Twas none of my bread-and-butter."

Radcliffe winced at the phrase he had used too often to

distance Lisabeth when she was distressed as he delved too closely into her past.

"Besides," Norton continued, "you have no idea how horrible Frederick's temper was. I did not want it aimed at me."

"So you acted like a coward and left her to suffer?"

"If she had wanted to air her troubles, she has many bosom-bows. Mayhap she did not because she knew his accusations were true."

Presentation is everything, my lord. Her words echoed in his head with heinous mockery. Lisabeth would have kept silent to protect Lady Edwina from being scorned by the Polite World.

"So you believe Montague was not wrong?" Radcliffe asked.

"About how he treated his wife? Yes." Norton frowned. "Do not paint me with his crimes. Even provoked as he was provoked, I would not resolve the matter that way. A gentleman—"

"Seems an oddly undefinable thing." He clasped his hands behind him. "But you believed his accusations?"

"Yes." Norton's scowl deepened. "Enough prattle! Did you bring the weapons?"

"Yes, although I was unsure if Ison's butler would allow me to *borrow* them." Radcliffe chuckled as he recalled the expression on the butler's face when they paused at Ison's address after Bond had suggested a unique source for the weapons for this duel.

"Very well. We shall start back-to-back, take ten paces on the count your man may give—I assume he can manage to count to ten—turn, and let fly the pop."

"Guns at ten paces?" Radcliffe laughed, but his lips tightened at the insult to Bond. "You give me sparse credit for imagination." He smiled as Bond came forward with a long case. "Open it, Norton."

Norton's hands trembled as he reached for the latch on

the rosewood box. It opened with a reluctant creak. Radcliffe was not surprised, for he doubted if Ison ever allowed himself an opportunity to have the case opened.

"Sabers?" choked Norton as he stared at the two blades resting on lush velvet.

Radcliffe lifted out one foil and balanced the brass hilt in his hand. As he had expected, Ison's sabers were of the first quality. "I think you shall find these toasting-irons a trifle more deadly than the ones you usually use, cousin."

Norton snatched the other sword from the box and slashed the fog, making the blade whistle. "I have beaten you often, and I shall do so tonight."

"You are correct that you have defeated me, but that was many years ago when I was a child."

Norton raised his tilter. "Now you are as lame as Cripplegate. *En garde.*"

"Stop!"

Radcliffe halted at the order, but wisely kept his sword up in front of him. Turning his head, he saw Lisabeth stepping out of the fog. She drew her pelisse tighter as she walked toward them.

"I beg your indulgence to listen before you continue with this idiocy," she said in an even voice.

"You have nothing that we wish to hear, Lady Montague." Norton smiled. "Instead you shall watch as I put this sword in your paramour's beef."

Her voice remained calm. "If you will not heed me, will you listen to another?"

Radcliffe saw amazement on his cousin's face as two more women stepped from the concealing fog. Lady Edwina put her arm around her daughter-in-law's shoulders as the taller woman continued toward them.

Norton lowered his sword and gasped, "Prospera?"

She smiled. "Norton, when Lisabeth came to me with the tale of your misery, my heart was so moved that I had to fly to your side and chide you for failing to speak to me at the Toblers'. Mayhap you did not know that now that I am out of mourning, my father has ordered that I find a husband and a family."

"How is the earl?" Norton asked, a smile growing across his face.

"Anxious to bounce his grandson on his knee." She held out her hand.

Laughter almost shamed Radcliffe, but he silenced it as his bombastic cousin scurried to the tall woman's side. As Norton bent over her hand, pressing it to his lips, Radcliffe saw Prospera's satisfied smile. Not even a blind buzzard could fail to understand the simplicity of Lisabeth's scheme.

A woman in need of a husband with plump pockets and a man who desired, above all else, a respected title for his line. Together they could gain what they each wanted.

Giving his sword to Bond, Radcliffe offered Prospera a good evening before turning to Norton. "If you wish to retract your slanderous words about Lisabeth, we can withdraw, so you may renew your friendship with Prospera."

"You said something untoward about my dear Lisabeth?" asked Prospera before Norton could answer. "How ignoble of you!" She laughed. "Speak your apology, Norton, and I shall let you drive me back to the Toblers' party. They were setting up the tables when Lisabeth came for me. We shall spend the evening playing cards and talking of times past."

"And times to come," he said with an eagerness that threatened to release Radcliffe's amusement once more. "I own that I should have refrained from speaking of Lisabeth while in my cups." He handed the saber to Radcliffe before offering his arm with unexpected grace to Prospera.

"Very prettily said," Prospera murmured.

"As pretty as a lord," Radcliffe could not resist adding under his breath.

Prospera flashed Radcliffe a smile as they walked away.

He laughed. It would certainly not be a marriage made in heaven, but he guessed they would be well-suited. Passing the sword to Bond, he glanced up as the sky lit again with the storm.

"Bond, take Lady Edwina to the carriage posthaste."

"Yes, sir." He grinned. "May I say well done?"

" 'Tis not yet done." He walked to where Lisabeth was standing alone, oddly silent, as Bond herded Lady Edwina back across the grass.

When he saw how Lisabeth shivered, he urged, "Let us go, *chère cousine*. I know you abhor storms. You should have sought shelter as soon as you saw the duel would not be fought. It—"

She threw her arms around his shoulders, and her mouth covered his, snatching his breath away. More powerful than the storm overhead, his craving for her overwhelmed him. She leaned against him, and he put his arms around her silken form. He tasted her lips with barely restrained passion. When she pressed closer, her lips softening, he probed within, wanting each of her quivers to come from his touch. She trembled and combed her fingers up through his hair.

Releasing her before he could no longer resist the temptation to unleash his desire for her right here, he whispered, "Lisabeth, is that how a lady acts?"

"It is when she is about to ask a gentleman to marry her."

"Marry you? I thought you never intended to remarry."

"I thought so, too. After my marriage to Frederick—"

He put his finger to her lips. "I know about that." Stepping back, he reached into the watch pocket on his waistcoat. He unlatched the fob from his pocket watch and slid the key off the gold chain. "Before I give you my answer, here."

Lisabeth took the key. Her eyes widened when she realized it was one she had seen often in her rooms, for it had been set in her dressing room door. "Where did you get this?"

"Bond, in a mistaken attempt to make me see what I already should have known, purloined it." He cupped her elbows and brought her back to him. As she gazed up into his shadowed eyes, he whispered, "We were anxious when we heard weeping in your rooms."

"So it truly was you?"

"Me?"

"Who came and stood by my bed, so I could escape the nightmares."

"Lisabeth, I would never invade your private rooms in the middle of the night." He gave her a rakish grin. "Although you must know that I have been sorely tempted by that single door between your rooms and mine."

"But . . ." She leaned her head against his shoulder. "It must have been only a dream that eased my despair."

"I would do whatever I can to lighten your grief."

"Mayhap it was your concern I was sensing."

"Or my heart." He lifted her hand and pressed it over the center of his chest. "Our hearts know more than our minds will acknowledge. Mine knew I love you, Lisabeth."

"And I love you."

"But you would have let me marry Miss Tobler?"

She nodded. "I wanted you to be happy, and I was unsure if you loved me, too, until we danced together."

"Then you believed it was too late to speak the truth." He lifted her fingers to his lips. Her heart sang so ardently when his mouth brushed her hand that she had to struggle to discern his words. "When I learned that Ison had offered for you, I knew that you would never think of your future until mine was settled, so I tried to help you reach your goal."

"At the cost of your own happiness?"

He ran a fingertip along her cheek as the first fitful

drops of rain fell. "How could I be happy with anyone but you, my dearest Lisabeth? You cared for me when I was the least lovable, for you saw neither the hobbling man nor the marquess who was swimming in lard. You saw Tristan Radcliffe, and still you liked him. Liked him? I dared to believe you had come to love him. To love me." Framing her face with his hands, he whispered, "Let us both take a vow here before we take our vows before a minister. We will always be honest with each other."

"And to perdition with Society?"

He kissed the tip of her nose. "Now you are beginning to understand, Lisabeth, *ma chère.*"

"Not your dear cousin any longer?"

"Just my dear wife-to-be." As she lifted her face for his kiss, she heard applause behind her. She turned to see Lady Edwina clapping wildly.

" 'Tis time you two owned to the truth."

"The truth, Lady Edwina?" Radcliffe asked. "If you wish the truth, I would have guessed you to be furious. Didn't you say you did not want me to marry Lisabeth?"

Lady Edwina's green gown swished as she came toward them with a grinning Bond holding her umbrella over her head. Her aged eyes twinkled merrily as she handed another to Radcliffe. "You think you two are the only ones with a bit of sly wit about you, don't you? If I had hinted from your arrival, my lord, that I was sure you would be the proper husband for Lisabeth, both of you would have given me a score of reasons why I was a goose."

"So you pretended to be anxious to separate us?" Radcliffe asked, opening the umbrella over his and Lisabeth's heads.

"Both of you are stubborn. I needed only to tell you one thing to have you do the opposite." Lady Edwina smiled with satisfaction. "I urged Lisabeth to ask you to remove yourself when I suspected she might do so. I asked you, my lord, to find her another man, sure the request would make you open your eyes to the woman in love with you."

Radcliffe laughed. "I doff my cap to you, Lady Edwina. Your plot was worthy of that dirty Corsican himself."

Kissing Lisabeth's cheek, Lady Edwina said, "I thought you would guess my scheme before this."

"How could we have known of your double-dealing?" asked Lisabeth.

"Because I have my own reasons for wanting you to wed Lord Radcliffe—Tristan, if I may be so familiar. Lisabeth, your soon-to-be husband is the first I have met in years who gives me a true challenge at the card table." Lady Edwina chuckled with anticipation. "As soon as you marry, we shall journey to Cliffs' End where we can play cards every night."

Radcliffe laughed and drew Lisabeth into his arms. As his lips descended toward hers, he whispered, "Not *every* night."

AUTHOR'S NOTE

Lord Radcliffe's Season was a story I've been wanting to tell for a long time—the story of a man and a woman who must depend on each other to find healing for their wounded hearts. I hope you have enjoyed it. My next Zebra Regency will be *An Unexpected Husband,* which is scheduled to be on sale in January, 2000. It tells the story of a woman who is very happy in her life until she meets a handsome, mysterious man who may threaten everything she treasures—mayhap even England itself.

I enjoy hearing from my readers. You can contact me by E-mail at:

jaferg@erols.com

or by mail at:

Jo Ann Ferguson
VFRW
PO Box 350
Wayne, PA 19087-0350

Happy reading!

BOOK YOUR PLACE ON OUR WEBSITE AND MAKE THE READING CONNECTION!

We've created a customized website just for our very special readers, where you can get the inside scoop on everything that's going on with Zebra, Pinnacle and Kensington books.

When you come online, you'll have the exciting opportunity to:

- View covers of upcoming books
- Read sample chapters
- Learn about our future publishing schedule (listed by publication month *and author*)
- Find out when your favorite authors will be visiting a city near you
- Search for and order backlist books from our online catalog
- Check out author bios and background information
- Send e-mail to your favorite authors
- Meet the Kensington staff online
- Join us in weekly chats with authors, readers and other guests
- Get writing guidelines
- AND MUCH MORE!

**Visit our website at
http://www.zebrabooks.com**

More Zebra Regency Romances

Put a Little Romance in Your Life With
Fern Michaels

__Dear Emily	0-8217-5676-1	$6.99US/$8.50CAN
__Sara's Song	0-8217-5856-X	$6.99US/$8.50CAN
__Wish List	0-8217-5228-6	$6.99US/$7.99CAN
__Vegas Rich	0-8217-5594-3	$6.99US/$8.50CAN
__Vegas Heat	0-8217-5758-X	$6.99US/$8.50CAN
__Vegas Sunrise	1-55817-5983-3	$6.99US/$8.50CAN
__Whitefire	0-8217-5638-9	$6.99US/$8.50CAN

Celebrate Romance With Two of Today's Hottest Authors

Meagan McKinney

__The Fortune Hunter	$6.50US/$8.00CAN	0-8217-6037-?
__Gentle from the Night	$5.99US/$7.50CAN	0-8217-5803-?
__A Man to Slay Dragons	$5.99US/$6.99CAN	0-8217-5345-?
__My Wicked Enchantress	$5.99US/$7.50CAN	0-8217-5661-?
__No Choice but Surrender	$5.99US/$7.50CAN	0-8217-5859-?

Meryl Sawyer

__Half Moon Bay	$6.50US/$8.00CAN	0-8217-6144-7
__The Hideaway	$5.99US/$7.50CAN	0-8217-5780-6
__Tempting Fate	$6.50US/$8.00CAN	0-8217-5858-6
__Unforgettable	$6.50US/$8.00CAN	0-8217-5564-1
